A
PLUPURRFECT
PREDICAMENT

Thirty-seven days out, Fuzzy Britches, the family flatcat, had eight golden little kittens. Each was exactly like its parent, but only a couple of inches across when flat and marble-sized when contracted.

Everyone, including Captain Stone, thought they were cute. Everyone enjoyed petting them, stroking them with a gentle forefinger and listening to the tiny purr. Everyone enjoyed feeding them and they seemed to be hungry all the time.

Sixty-four days later the kittens had kittens—and the population bomb had been ignited.

In a spaceship of limited capacities, with no port in sight, the Stones were in for trouble . . .

The Rolling Stones

Robert A. Heinlein

A Del Rey Book

BALLANTINE BOOKS • NEW YORK

For LUCKY and DOC and BARBARA

RLI: $\dfrac{\text{VL: 7 \& up}}{\text{IL: 7 \& up}}$

A Del Rey Book
Published by Ballantine Books

Copyright © 1952 by Robert A. Heinlein

All rights reserved. Published in the United States by Ballantine Books, a division of Random House, Inc., New York, and simultaneously in Canada by Random House of Canada Limited, Toronto.

A condensed version of this book was published in *Boy's Life* under the title *Tramp Space Ship*.

ISBN 0-345-30332-6

This edition published by arrangement with
Charles Scribner's Sons

Manufactured in the United States of America

First Ballantine Books Edition: June 1977
Sixth Printing: July 1983

Cover art by Darrell K. Sweet

CONTENTS

I THE UNHEAVENLY TWINS

THE TWO BROTHERS stood looking the old wreck over. "Junk," decided Castor.

"Not junk," objected Pollux. "A jalopy—granted. A heap any way you look at it. A clunker possibly. But not junk."

"You're an optimist, Junior." Both boys were fifteen; Castor was twenty minutes older than his brother.

"I'm a believer, Grandpa—and you had better be, too. Let me point out that we don't have money enough for anything better. Scared to gun it?"

Castor stared up the side of the ship. "Not at all—because that thing will never again rise high enough to crash. We want a ship that will take us out to the Asteroids—right? This superannuated pogo stick wouldn't even take us to Earth."

"It will when I get through hopping it up—with your thumb-fingered help. Let's look through it and see what it needs."

Castor glanced at the sky. "It's getting late." He looked not at the Sun making long shadows on the lunar plain, but at Earth, reading the time from the sunrise line now moving across the Pacific.

"Look, Grandpa, are we buying a ship or are we getting to supper on time?"

Castor shrugged. "As you say, Junior." He lowered his antenna, then started swarming up the rope ladder left there for the accommodation of prospective customers. He used his hands only and despite his cumbersome vacuum suit his movements were easy and graceful. Pollux swarmed after him.

Castor cheered up a bit when they reached the control room. The ship had not been stripped for salvage as completely as had many of the ships on the lot. True, the ballistic computer was missing but the rest of the astrogational instruments were in place and the controls to the power room seemed to be complete. The space-battered old hulk was not a wreck, but merely obsolete. A hasty look at the power room seemed to confirm this.

Ten minutes later Castor, still mindful of supper, herded Pollux down the ladder. When Castor reached the ground Pollux said, "Well?"

"Let me do the talking."

The sales office of the lot was a bubble dome nearly a mile away; they moved toward it with the easy, fast lope of old Moon hands. The office airlock was marked by a huge sign:

DEALER DAN
THE SPACESHIP MAN
CRAFT OF ALL TYPES * SCRAP METAL *** SPARE PARTS**
FUELING & SERVICE
(*AEC License No.* 739024)

They cycled through the lock and unclamped each other's helmets. The outer office was crossed by a railing; back of it sat a girl receptionist. She was watching a newscast while buffing her nails. She spoke without taking her eyes off the TV tank: "We're not buying anything, boys—not hiring anybody."

Castor said, "You sell spaceships?"

She looked up. "Not often enough."

"Then tell your boss we want to see him."

Her eyebrows went up. "Whom do you think you are kidding, sonny boy? Mr. Ekizian is a busy man."

Pollux said to Castor, "Let's go over to the Hungarian, Cas. These people don't mean business."

"Maybe you're right."

The girl looked from one to the other, shrugged, and flipped a switch. "Mr. Ekizian—there are a couple of Boy Scouts out here who say they want to buy a spaceship. Do you want to bother with them?"

A deep voice responded, "And why not? We got ships to sell."

Shortly a bald-headed, portly man, dressed in a cigar and a wrinkled moonsuit, came out of the inner office and rested his hands on the rail. He looked them over shrewdly but his voice was jovial. "You wanted to see me?"

"You're the owner?" asked Castor.

"Dealer Dan Ekizian, the man himself. What's on your mind, boys? Time is money."

"Your secretary told you," Castor said ungraciously. "Spaceships."

Dealer Dan took his cigar out of his mouth and examined it. "Really? What would you boys want with a spaceship?"

Pollux muttered something; Castor said, "Do you usually do business out here?" He glanced at the girl.

Ekizian followed his glance. "My mistake. Come inside." He opened the gate for them, led them into his office, and seated them. He ceremoniously offered them cigars; the boys refused politely. "Now out with it, kids. Let's not joke."

Castor repeated, "Spaceships."

He pursed his lips. "A luxury liner, maybe? I haven't got one on the field at the moment but I can always broker a deal."

Pollux stood up. "He's making fun of us, Cas. Let's go see the Hungarian."

"Wait a moment, Pol. Mr. Ekizian, you've got a heap out there on the south side of the field, a class VII, model '93 Detroiter. What's your scrap metal price on her and what does she mass?"

The dealer looked surprised. "That sweet little job? Why, I couldn't afford to let that go as scrap. And anyhow, even at scrap that would come to a lot of money. If it is metal you boys want, I got it. Just tell me how much and what sort."

"We were talking about that Detroiter."

"I don't believe I've met you boys before?"

"Sorry, sir. I'm Castor Stone. This is my brother Pollux."

"Glad to meet you, Mr. Stone. Stone . . . Stone? Any relation to— The 'Unheavenly Twins'—that's it."

"Smile when you say that," said Pollux.

"Shut up, Pol. We're the Stone twins."

"The frostproof rebreather valve, you invented it, didn't you?"

"That's right."

"Say, I got one in my own suit. A good gimmick—you boys are quite the mechanics." He looked them over again. "Maybe you were really serious about a ship."

"Of course we were."

"Hmm . . . you're not looking for scrap; you want something to get around it. I've got just the job for you, a General Motors Jumpbug, practically new. It's been out on one grubstake job to a couple of thorium prospectors and I had to reclaim it. The hold ain't even radioactive."

"Not interested."

"Better look at it. Automatic landing and three hops takes you right around the equator. Just the thing for a couple of live, active boys."

"About that Detroiter—what's your scrap price?"

Ekizian looked hurt. "That's a deepspace vessel, son —it's no use to you, as a ship. And I can't let it go for scrap; that's a clean job. It was a family yacht—never been pushed over six g, never had an emergency landing. It's got hundreds of millions of miles still in it. I couldn't let you scrap that ship, even if you were to pay me the factory price. It would be a shame. I love ships. Now take this Jumpbug . . ."

"You can't sell that Detroiter as anything but scrap," Castor answered. "It's been sitting there two years that I know of. If you had hoped to sell her as a ship you wouldn't have salvaged the computer. She's pitted, her tubes are no good, and an overhaul would cost more than she's worth. Now what's her scrap price?"

Dealer Dan rocked back and forth in his chair; he seemed to be suffering. "Scrap that ship? Just fuel her up and she's ready to go—Venus, Mars, even the Jovian satellites."

"What's your cash price?"

"Cash?"

"Cash."

Ekizian hesitated, then mentioned a price. Castor stood up and said, "You were right, Pollux. Let's go see the Hungarian."

The dealer looked pained. "If I were to write it off for my own use, I couldn't cut that price—not in fairness to my partners."

"Come on, Pol."

"Look, boys, I can't let you go over to the Hungarian's. He'll cheat you."

Pollux looked savage. "Maybe he'll do it politely."

"Shut *up*, Pol!" Castor went on, "Sorry, Mr. Ekizian, my brother isn't housebroken. But we can't do business." He stood up.

"Wait a minute. That's a good valve you boys thought

up. I use it; I feel I owe you something." He named another and lower sum.

"Sorry. We can't afford it." He started to follow Pollux out.

"Wait!" Ekizian mentioned a third price. "Cash," he added.

"Of course. And you pay the sales tax?"

"Well . . . for a cash deal, yes."

"Good."

"Sit down, gentlemen. I'll call in my girl and we'll stat the papers."

"No hurry," answered Castor. "We've still got to see what the Hungarian has on his lot—and the government salvage lot, too."

"Huh? That price doesn't stand unless you deal right now. Dealer Dan, they call me. I got no time to waste dickering twice."

"Nor have we. See you tomorrow. If it hasn't sold, we can take up where we left off."

"If you expect me to hold that price, I'll have to have a nominal option payment."

"Oh, no, I wouldn't expect you to pass up a sale for us. If you can sell it by tomorrow, we wouldn't think of standing in your way. Come on, Pol."

Ekizian shrugged. "Been nice meeting you, boys."

"Thank you, sir."

As they closed the lock behind them and waited for it to cycle, Pollux said, "You should have paid him an option."

His brother looked at him. "You're retarded, Junior."

On leaving Dealer Dan's office the boys headed for the spaceport, intending to catch the passenger tube back to the city, fifty miles west of the port. They had less than thirty minutes if they were to get home for supper on time—unimportant in itself but Castor disliked starting a family debate on the defensive over a side issue. He kept hurrying Pollux along.

Their route took them through the grounds of General Synthetics Corporation, square miles of giant cracking plants, sun screens, condensers, fractionating columns, all sorts of huge machinery to take advantage of the burning heat, the bitter cold, and the endless vacuum for industrial chemical engineering purposes—a Dantesque jungle of unlikely shapes. The boys paid no attention to it; they were used to it. They hurried down the company road in the flying leaps the Moon's low gravity permitted, making twenty miles an hour. Half way to the port they were overtaken by a company tractor; Pollux flagged it down.

As he ground to a stop, the driver spoke to them via his cab radio: "What do you want?"

"Are you meeting the Terra shuttle?"

"Subject to the whims of fate—yes."

"It's Jefferson," said Pollux. "Hey, Jeff—it's Cas and Pol. Drop us at the tube station, will you?"

"Climb on the rack. 'Mind the volcano—come up the usual way.' " As they did so he went on, "What brings you two carrot-topped accident-prones to this far reach of culture?"

Castor hesitated and glanced at Pollux. They had known Jefferson James for some time, having bowled against him in the city league. He was an old Moon hand but not a native, having come to Luna before they were born to gather color for a novel. The novel was still unfinished.

Pollux nodded. Castor said, "Jeff, can you keep a secret?"

"Certainly—but permit me to point out that these radios are not directional. See your attorney before admitting any criminal act or intention."

Castor looked around; aside from two tractor trucks

in the distance no one seemed to be in line-of-sight. "We're going into business."

"When were you out of it?"

"This is a new line—interplanetary trade. We're going to buy our own ship and run it ourselves."

The driver whistled. "Remind me to sell Four-Planet Export short. When does this blitz take place?"

"We're shopping for a ship now. Know of a good buy?"

"I'll alert my spies." He shut up, being busy thereafter with the heavier traffic near the spaceport. Presently he said, "Here's your stop." As the boys climbed down from the rack of the truck he added, "If you need a crewman, keep me in mind."

"Okay, Jeff. And thanks for the lift."

Despite the lift they were late. A squad of marine M.P.s heading into the city on duty pre-empted the first tube car; by the time the next arrived the ship from Earth had grounded and its passengers took priority. Thereafter they got tangled with the changing shift from the synthetics plant. It was well past suppertime when they arrived at their family's apartment a half mile down inside Luna City.

Mr. Stone looked up as they came in. "Well! the star boarders," he announced. He was sitting with a small recorder in his lap, a throat mike clipped to his neck.

"Dad, it was unavoidable," Castor began. "We—"

"It always is," his father cut in. "Never mind the details. Your dinner is in the cozy. I wanted to send it back, but your mother went soft and didn't let me."

Dr. Stone looked up from the far end of the living room, where she was modeling a head of their older sister, Meade. "Correction," she said. "Your father went soft; I would have let you starve. Meade, quit turning your head."

"Check," announced their four-year-old brother and got up from the floor where he had been playing chess with their grandmother. He ran towards them. "Hey, Cas, Pol—where you been? Did you go to the port? Why didn't you take me? Did you bring me anything?"

Castor swung him up by his heels and held him upside down. "Yes. No. Maybe. And why should we? Here, Pol—catch." He sailed the child through the air; his twin reached out and caught him, still by the heels.

"Check yourself," announced Grandmother, "and mate in three moves. Shouldn't let your social life distract you from your game, Lowell."

The youngster looked back at the board from his upside down position. "Wrong, Hazel. Now I let you take my queen, then— *Blammie!*"

His grandmother looked again at the board. "Huh? Wait a minute—suppose I refuse your queen, then— Why, the little scamp! He's trapped me again."

Meade said, "Shouldn't let him beat you so often, Hazel. It's not good for him."

"Meade, for the ninth time, quit turning your head!"

"Sorry, Mother. Let's take a rest."

Grandmother snorted. "You don't think I let him beat me on purpose, do you? You play him; I am giving up the game for good."

Meade answered just as her mother spoke; at the same time Pollux chucked the boy back at Castor. "You take him. I want to eat." The child squealed. Mr. Stone shouted, "QUIET!"

"And stay quiet," he went on, while unfastening the throat mike. "How is a man to make a living in all this racket? This episode has to be done over completely, sent to New York tomorrow, shot, canned, distributed, and on the channels by the end of the week. It's not possible."

"Then don't do it," Dr. Stone answered serenely. "Or work in your room—it's soundproof."

Mr. Stone turned to his wife. "My dear, I've explained a thousand times that I can't work in there by myself. I get no stimulation. I fall asleep."

Castor said, "How's it going, Dad? Rough?"

"Well, now that you ask me, the villains are way ahead and I don't see a chance for our heroes."

"I thought of a gimmick while Pol and I were out. You have this young kid you introduced into the story slide into the control room while everybody is asleep. They don't suspect him, see?—he's too young so they haven't put him in irons. Once in the control room—" Castor stopped and looked crestfallen. "No, it won't do; he's too young to handle the ship. He wouldn't know how."

"Why do you say that?" his father objected. "All I have to do is to plant that he has had a chance to . . . let me see—" He stopped; his face went blank. "No," he said presently.

"No good, huh?"

"Eh? What? It smells—but I think I can use it. Stevenson did something like it in *Treasure Island*—and I think he got it from Homer. Let's see; if we—" He again went into his trance.

Pollux had opened the warming cupboard. Castor dropped his baby brother on the floor and accepted a dinner pack from his twin. He opened it. "Meat pie again," he stated bleakly and sniffed it. "Synthetic, too."

"Say that over again and louder," his sister urged him. "I've been trying for weeks to get Mother to subscribe to another restaurant."

"Don't talk, Meade," Dr. Stone answered. "I'm modelling your mouth."

Grandmother Stone snorted. "You youngsters have it too easy. When I came to the Moon there was a time when we had nothing but soya beans and coffee powder for three months."

Meade answered, "Hazel, the last time you told us about that it was two months and it was tea instead of coffee."

"Young lady, who's telling this lie? You, or me?" Hazel stood up and came over to her twin grandsons. "What were you two doing on Dan Ekizian's lot?"

Castor looked at Pollux, who looked back. Castor said cautiously, "Who told you that we were there?"

"Don't try to kid your grandmother. When you have been on—"

The entire family joined her in chorus: " '—on the Moon as long as I have!' "

Hazel sniffed. "Sometimes I wonder why I married!"

Her son said, "Don't try to answer that question," then continued to his sons, "Well, what *were* you doing there?"

Castor consulted Pollux by eye, then answered, "Well, Dad, it's like this—"

His father nodded. "Your best flights of imagination always start that way. Attend carefully, everybody."

"Well, you know that money you are holding for us?"

"What about it?"

"Three per cent isn't very much."

Mr. Stone shook his head vigorously. "I will not invest your royalties in some wildcat stock. Financial genius may have skipped my generation but when I turn that money over to you, it will be intact."

"That's just it. It worries you. You could turn it over to us now and quit worrying about it."

"No. You are too young."

"We weren't too young to earn it."

His mother snickered. "They got you, Roger. Come here and I'll see if I can staunch the blood."

Dr. Stone said serenely, "Don't heckle Roger when he is coping with the twins, Mother. Meade, turn a little to the left."

Mr. Stone answered, "You've got a point there, Cas. But you may still be too young to hang on to it. What is this leading up to?"

Castor signaled with his eyes; Pollux took over. "Dad, we've got a really swell chance to take that money and put it to work. Not a wildcat stock, not a stock at all. We'll have every penny right where we can see it, right where we could cash in on it at any time. And in the meantime we'll be making lots more money."

"Hmmm . . . how?"

"We buy a ship and put it to work."

His father opened his mouth; Castor cut in swiftly, "We can pick up a Detroiter VII cheap and overhaul it ourselves; we won't be out a cent for wages."

Pollux filled in without a break. "You've said yourself, Dad, that we are both born mechanics; we've got the hands for it."

Castor went on, "We'd treat it like a baby because it would be our own."

Pollux: "We've both got both certificates, control and power. We wouldn't need any crew."

Castor: "No overhead—that's the beauty of it."

Pollux: "So we carry trade goods out to the Asteroids and we bring back a load of high-grade. We can't lose."

Castor: "Four hundred per cent, maybe five hundred."

Pollux: "More like six hundred."

Castor: "And no worries for you."

Pollux: "And we'd be out of your hair."

Castor: "Not late for dinner."

Pollux had his mouth open when his father again

yelled, "QUIET!" He went on, "Edith, bring the barrel. This time we use it." Mr. Stone had a theory, often expressed, that boys should be raised in a barrel and fed through the bunghole. The barrel had no physical existence.

Dr. Stone said, "Yes, dear," and went on modeling.

Grandmother Stone said, "Don't waste your money on a Detroiter. They're unstable; the gyro system is no good. Wouldn't have one as a gift. Get a Douglas."

Mr. Stone turned to his mother. "Hazel, if you are going to encourage the boys in this nonsense—"

"Not at all! Not at all! Merely intellectual discussion. Now with a Douglas they could make some money. A Douglas has a very favorable—"

"Hazel!"

His mother broke off, then said thoughtfully, as if to herself, "I know there is free speech on the Moon: I wrote it into the charter myself."

Roger Stone turned back to his sons. "See here, boys—when the Chamber of Commerce decided to include pilot training in their Youth-Welfare program I was all for it. I even favored it when they decided to issue junior licenses to anybody who graduated high in the course. When you two got your jets I was proud as could be. It's a young man's game; they license commercial pilots at eighteen and—"

"And they retire them at thirty," added Castor. "We haven't any time to waste. We'll be too old for the game before you know it."

"Pipe down. I'll do the talking for a bit. If you think I'm going to draw that money out of the bank and let you two young yahoos go gallivanting around the system in a pile of sky junk that will probably blow the first time you go over two g's, you had better try another think. Besides, you're going down to Earth for school next September."

"We've been to Earth," answered Castor.

"And we didn't like it," added Pollux.

"Too dirty."

"Likewise too noisy."

"Groundhogs everywhere," Castor finished.

Mr. Stone brushed it aside. "Two weeks you were there—not time enough to find out what the place is like. You'll love it, once you get used to it. Learn to ride horseback, play baseball, see the ocean."

"A lot of impure water," Castor answered.

"Horses are to eat."

"Take baseball," Castor continued. "It's not practical. How can you figure a one-*g* trajectory and place your hand at the point of contact in the free-flight time between bases? We're not miracle men."

"*I* played it."

"But you grew up in a one-*g* field; you've got a distorted notion of physics. Anyhow, why would we want to learn to play baseball? When we come back, we wouldn't be able to play it here. Why, you might crack your helmet."

Mr. Stone shook his head. "Games aren't the point. Play baseball or not, as suits you. But you should get an education."

"What does Luna City Technical lack that we need? And if so, why? After all, Dad, you were on the Board of Education."

"I was not; I was mayor."

"Which made you a member ex-officio—Hazel told us."

Mr. Stone glanced at his mother; she was looking elsewhere. He went on, "Tech is a good school, of its sort, but we don't pretend to offer everything at Tech. After all, the Moon is still an outpost, a frontier—"

"But you said," Pollux interrupted, "in your retiring speech as mayor, that Luna City was the Athens of the future and the hope of the new age."

"Poetic license. Tech is still not Harvard. Don't you boys want to see the world's great works of art? Don't you want to study the world's great literature?"

"We've read *Ivanhoe*," said Castor.

"And we don't want to read *The Mill on the Floss*," added Pollux.

"We prefer your stuff."

"My stuff? My stuff isn't literature. It's more of an animated comic strip."

"We like it," Castor said firmly.

His father took a deep breath. "Thank you. Which reminds me that I still have a full episode to sweat out tonight, so I will cut this discussion short. In the first place you can't touch the money without my thumbprint—from now on I am going to wear gloves. In the second place both of you are too young for an unlimited license."

"You could get us a waiver for out-system. When we got back we'd probably be old enough for unlimited."

"You're too young!"

Castor said, "Why, Dad, not half an hour ago you accepted a gimmick from me in which you were going to have an eleven-year-old kid driving a ship."

"I'll raise his age!"

"It'll ruin your gimmick."

"Confound it! That's just fiction—and poor fiction at that. It's hokum, dreamed up to sell merchandise." He suddenly looked suspiciously at his son. "Cas, you planted that gimmick on me. Just to give yourself an argument in favor of this hare-brained scheme."

Castor looked pious. "Why, Father, how could you think such a thing?"

"Don't 'Father' me! I can tell a hawk from a handsaw."

"Anybody can," Grandmother Hazel commented. "The Hawk class is a purely commercial type while the

21

Hanshaw runabout is a sport job. Come to think about it, boys, a Hanshaw might be better than a Douglas. I like its fractional controls and—"

"Hazel!" snapped her son. "Quit encouraging the boys. And quit showing off. You're not the only engineer in the family."

"I'm the only good one," she answered smugly.

"Oh, yes? Nobody ever complained about my work."

"Then why did you quit?"

"You know why. Fiddle with finicky figures for months on end—and what have you got? A repair dock. Or a stamping mill. And who cares?"

"So you aren't an engineer. You're merely a man who knows engineering."

"What about yourself? You didn't stick with it."

"No," she admitted, "but my reasons were different. I saw three big, hairy, male men promoted over my head and not one of them could do a partial integration without a pencil. Presently I figured out that the Atomic Energy Commission had a bias on the subject of women no matter what the civil service rules said. So I took a job dealing blackjack. Luna City didn't offer much choice in those days—and I had you to support."

The argument seemed about to die out; Castor judged it was time to mix it up again. "Hazel, do you really think we should get a Hanshaw? I'm not sure we can afford it."

"Well, now, you really need a third crewman for a—"

"Do you want to buy in?"

Mr. Stone interrupted. "Hazel, I will not stand by and let you encourage this. I'm putting my foot down."

"You look silly standing there on one foot. Don't try to bring me up, Roger. At ninety-five my habits are fairly well set."

"Ninety-five indeed! Last week you were eighty-five."

"It's been a hard week. Back to our muttons—why don't *you* buy in with them? You could go along and keep them out of trouble."

"What? Me?" Mr. Stone took a deep breath. "(A) A marine guard couldn't keep these two junior-model Napoleons out of trouble. I know; I've tried. (B) I do not like a Hanshaw; they are fuel hogs. (C) I have to turn out three episodes a week of *The Scourge of the Spaceways*—including one which must be taped tonight, if this family will ever quiet down!"

"Roger," his mother answered, "trouble in this family is like water for fish. And nobody asked you to buy a Hanshaw. As to your third point, give me a blank spool and I'll dictate the next three episodes tonight while I'm brushing my hair." Hazel's hair was still thick and quite red. So far, no one had caught her dyeing it. "It's about time you broke that contract anyway; you've won your bet."

Her son winced. Two years before he had let himself be trapped into a bet that he could write better stuff than was being channeled up from Earth—and had gotten himself caught in a quicksand of fat checks and options. "I can't afford to quit," he said feebly.

"What good is money if you don't have time to spend it? Give me that spool and the box."

"You can't write it."

"Want to bet?"

Her son backed down; no one yet had won a bet with Hazel. "That's beside the point. I'm a family man; I've got Edith and Buster and Meade to think about, too."

Meade turned her head again. "If you're thinking about me, Daddy, I'd *like* to go. Why, I've never been *any place*—except that one trip to Venus and twice to New York."

"Hold still, Meade," Dr. Stone said quietly. She went on to her husband, "You know, Roger, I was thinking just the other day how cramped this apartment is. And we haven't been any place, as Meade says, since we got back from Venus."

Mr. Stone stared. "You too? Edith, this apartment is bigger than any ship compartment; you know that."

"Yes, but a ship seems bigger. In free fall one gets so much more use out of the room."

"My dear, do I understand that you are supporting this junket?"

"Oh, not at all! I was speaking in general terms. But you do sleep better aboard ship. You never snore in free fall."

"I do not snore!"

Dr. Stone did not answer. Hazel snickered. Pollux caught Castor's eye and Castor nodded; the two slipped quietly away to their own room. It was a lot of trouble to get mother involved in a family argument, but worth the effort; nothing important was ever decided until she joined in.

Meade tapped on their door a little later; Castor let her in and looked her over; she was dressed in the height of fashion for the American Old West. "Square dancing again, huh?"

"Eliminations tonight. Look here, Cas, even if Daddy breaks loose from the money you two might be stymied by being underage for an unlimited license—right?"

"We figure on a waiver." They had also discussed blasting off without a waiver, but it did not seem the time to mention it.

"But you might not get it. Just bear in mind that I will be eighteen next week. 'Bye now."

"Good night."

When she had gone Pollux said, "That's silly. She hasn't even taken her limited license."

"No, but she's had astrogation in school and we could coach her."

"Cas, you're crazy. We can't drag her all around the system; girls are a nuisance."

"You've got that wrong, Junior. You mean 'sisters' —girls are okay."

Pollux considered this. "Yeah, I guess you're right."

"I'm always right."

"Oh, so? How about the time you tried to use liquid air to—"

"Let's not be petty!"

Grandmother Hazel stuck her head in next. "Just a quick battle report, boys. Your father is groggy but still fighting gamely."

"Is he going to let us use the money?"

"Doesn't look like it, as of now. Tell me, how much did Ekizian ask you for that Detroiter?"

Castor told her; she whistled. "The gonoph," she said softly. "That unblushing groundhog—I'll have his license lifted."

"Oh, we didn't agree to pay it."

"Don't sign with him at all unless I'm at your elbow. I know where the body is buried."

"Okay. Look, Hazel, you really think a Detroiter VII is unstable?"

She wrinkled her brow. "Its gyros are too light for the ship's moment of inertia. I hate a ship that wobbles. If we could pick up a war-surplus triple-duo gyro system, cheap, you would have something. I'll inquire around."

It was much later when Mr. Stone looked in. "Still awake, boys?"

"Oh, sure, come in."

"About that matter we were discussing tonight—"

Pollux said, "Do we get the money?"

Castor dug him in the ribs but it was too late. Their father said, "I told you that was out. But I wanted to ask you: did you, when you were shopping around today, happen to ask, uh, about any larger ships?"

Castor looked blank. "Why, no, sir. We couldn't afford anything larger—could we, Pol?"

"Gee, no! Why do you ask, Dad?"

"Oh, nothing, nothing at all! Uh, good night."

He left. The twins turned to each other and solemnly shook hands.

II A CASE FOR DRAMATIC LICENSE

AT BREAKFAST THE NEXT MORNING—"morning" by Greenwich time, of course; it was still late afternoon by local
sun time and would be for a couple of days—the Stone
family acted out the episode Hazel had dictated the
night before of Mr. Stone's marathon adventure serial.
Grandma Hazel had stuck the spool of dictation into
the autotyper as soon as she had gotten up; there was
a typed copy for each of them. Even Buster had a
small side to read and Hazel played several parts, crouch-
ing and jumping around and shifting her voice from
rusty bass to soprano.

Everybody got into the act—everybody but Mr. Stone;
he listened with a dour try-to-make-me-laugh expression.

Hazel finished her grand cliff-hanging finale by knock-
ing over her coffee. She plucked the cup out of the
air and had a napkin under the brown flood before
it could reach the floor under the urge of the Moon's
leisurely field. "Well?" she said breathlessly to her son,
while still panting from the Galactic Overlord's fran-
tic attempts to escape a just fate. "How about it? Isn't
that a dilly? Did we scare the dickens out of 'em or
didn't we?"

Roger Stone did not answer; he merely held his
nose. Hazel looked amazed. "You didn't *like* it? Why,
Roger, I do believe you're jealous. To think I would
raise a son with spirit so mean that he would be en-
vious of his own mother!"

Buster spoke up. "*I* liked it. Let's do that part over

27

where I shoot the space pirate." He pointed a finger and made a zizzing noise. "Whee! Blood all over the bulkheads!"

"There's your answer, Roger. Your public. If Buster likes it, you're in."

"I thought it was exciting," Meade put in. "What was wrong with it, Daddy?"

"Yes," agreed Hazel belligerently. "Go ahead. Tell us."

"Very well. In the first place, spaceships do not make hundred-and-eighty-degree turns."

"This one does!"

"In the second place, what in blazes is this 'Galactic Overlord' nonsense? When did he creep in?"

"Oh, that! Son, your show was dying on its feet, so I gave it a transfusion."

"But 'Galactic Overlords'—now, really! It's not only preposterous; it's been used over and over again."

"Is that bad? Next week I'm going to equip *Hamlet* with atomic propulsion and stir it in with *The Comedy of Errors*. I suppose you think Shakespeare will sue me?"

"He will if he can stop spinning." Roger Stone shrugged. "I'll send it in. There's no time left to do another one and the contract doesn't say it has to be good; it just says I have to deliver it. They'll rewrite it in New York anyway."

His mother answered, "Even money says your fan mail is up twenty-five per cent on this episode."

"No, thank you. I don't want you wearing yourself out writing fan mail—not at your age."

"What's wrong with my age? I used to paddle you twice a week and I can still do it. Come on; put up your dukes!"

"Too soon after breakfast."

"Sissy! Pick your way of dying—Marquis of Queensbury, dockside, or kill-quick."

"Send around your seconds; let's do this properly.

In the meantime—" He turned to his sons. "Boys, have you any plans for today?"

Castor glanced at his brother, then said cautiously, "Well, we were thinking of doing a little more shopping for ships."

"I'll go with you."

Pollux looked up sharply. "You mean we get the money?" His brother glared at him. Their father answered, "No, your money stays in the bank—where it belongs."

"Then why bother to shop?" He got an elbow in the ribs for this remark.

"I'm interested in seeing what the market has to offer," Mr. Stone answered. "Coming, Edith?"

Dr. Stone answered, "I trust your judgment, my dear."

Hazel gulped more coffee and stood up. "I'm coming along."

Buster bounced down out of his chair. "Me, too!"

Dr. Stone stopped him. "No, dear. Finish your oatmeal."

"No! I'm going, too. Can't I, Grandma Hazel?"

Hazel considered it. Riding herd on the child outside the pressurized city was a full-time chore; he was not old enough to be trusted to handle his vacuum-suit controls properly. On this occasion she wanted to be free to give her full attention to other matters. "I'm afraid not, Lowell. Tell you what, sugar, I'll keep my phone open and we'll play chess while I'm away."

Buster clouded up. "It's no fun to play chess by telephone. I can't tell what you are thinking."

Hazel stared at him. "So that's it? I've suspected it for some time. Maybe I can win a game once. No, don't start whimpering—or I'll take your slide rule away from you for a week." The child thought it over, shrugged, and his face became placid. Hazel turned to her son. "Do you suppose he really does hear thoughts?"

Her son looked at his least son. "I'm afraid to find out." He sighed and added, "Why couldn't I have been born into a nice, normal, stupid family? Your fault, Hazel."

His mother patted his arm. "Don't fret, Roger. You pull down the average."

"Hummph! Give me that spool. I'd better shoot it off to New York before I lose my nerve."

Hazel fetched it; Mr. Stone took it to the apartment phone, punched in the code for RCA New York with the combination set for highspeed transcription relay. As he slipped the spool into its socket he added, "I shouldn't do this. In addition to that 'Galactic Overlord' nonsense, Hazel, you messed up the continuity by killing off four of my standard characters."

Hazel kept her eye on the spool; it had started to revolve. "Don't worry about it. I've got it all worked out. You'll see."

"Eh? What do you mean? Are you intending to write more episodes? I'm tempted to go limp and let you struggle with it—I'm sick of it and it would serve you right. Galactic Overlords indeed!"

His mother continued to watch the spinning spool in the telephone. At highspeed relay the thirty-minute spool zipped through in thirty seconds. Shortly it went *spung!* and popped up out of the socket; Hazel breathed relief. The episode was now either in New York, or was being held automatically in the Luna City telephone exchange, waiting for a break in the live Luna-to-Earth traffic. In either case it was out of reach, as impossible to recall as an angry word.

"Certainly I plan to do more episodes," she told him. "Exactly seven, in fact."

"Huh? Why seven?"

"Haven't you figured out why I am killing off characters? Seven episodes is the end of this quarter and a new option date. This time they won't pick up your option because every last one of the characters will be dead and the story will be over. I'm taking you off the hook, son."

"*What?* Hazel, you can't do that! Adventure serials never end."

"Does it say so in your contract?"

"No, but—"

"You've been grousing about how you wanted to get off this golden treadmill. You would never have the courage to do it yourself, so your loving mother has come to your rescue. You're a free man again, Roger."

"But—" His face relaxed. "I suppose you're right. Though I would prefer to commit suicide, even literary suicide, in my own way and at my own time. Mmmm . . . see here, Hazel, when do you plan to kill off John Sterling?"

"Him? Why, Our Hero has to last until the final episode, naturally. He and the Galactic Overlord do each other in at the very end. Slow music."

"Yes. Yes, surely . . . that's the way it would have to be. But you can't do it."

"Why not?"

"Because I insist on writing that scene myself. I've hated that mealy-mouthed Galahad ever since I thought him up. I'm not going to let anyone else have the fun of killing him; he's mine!"

His mother bowed. "Your honor, sir."

Mr. Stone's face brightened; he reached for his pouch and slung it over his shoulder. "And now let's go look at some spaceships!"

"Geronimo!"

As the four left the apartment and stepped on the

slideway that would take them to the pressure lift to the surface Pollux said to his grandmother, "Hazel, what does 'geronimo' mean?"

"Ancient Druid phrase, meaning 'Let's get out of here even if we have to walk.' So pick up your feet."

III   THE SECOND-HAND MARKET

THEY STOPPED AT THE LOCKER ROOMS at East Lock and suited up. As usual, Hazel unbelted her gun and strapped it to her vacuum suit. None of the others was armed; aside from civic guards and military police no one went armed in Luna City at this late date except a few of the very old-timers like Hazel herself. Castor said, "Hazel, why do you bother with that?"

"To assert my right. Besides, I might meet a rattle-snake."

"Rattlesnakes? On the Moon? Now, Hazel!"

" 'Now, Hazel' yourself. More rattlesnakes walking around on their hind legs than ever wriggled in the dust. Anyhow, do you remember the reason the White Knight gave Alice for keeping a mouse trap on his horse?"

"Uh, not exactly."

"Look it up when we get home. You kids are ignorant. Give me a hand with this helmet."

The conversation stopped, as Buster was calling his grandmother and insisting that they start their game. Castor could read her lips through her helmet; when he had his own helmet in place and his suit radio switched on he could hear them arguing about which had the white men last game. Hazel was preoccupied thereafter as Buster, with the chess board in front of him, was intentionally hurrying the moves, whereas Hazel was kept busy visualizing the board.

They had to wait at the lock for a load of tourists, just arrived in the morning shuttle from Earth, to spill out. One of two women passengers stopped and stared at them. "Thelma," she said to her companion, "that little man—he's wearing a *gun.*"

The other woman urged her along. "Don't take notice," she said. "It's not polite." She went on, changing the subject. "I wonder where we can buy souvenir turtles around here? I promised Herbert."

Hazel turned and glared at them; Mr. Stone took her arm and urged her into the now empty lock. She continued to fume as the lock cycled. "Groundhogs! Souvenir turtles indeed!"

"Mind your blood pressure, Hazel," her son advised.

"You mind yours." She looked up at him and suddenly grinned. "I should ha' drilled her, podnuh—like this." She made a fast draw to demonstrate, then, before returning the weapon to its holster, opened the charge chamber and removed a cough drop. This she inserted through the pass valve of her helmet and caught it on her tongue. Sucking it, she continued, "Just the same, son, that did it. Your mind may not be made up; mine is. Luna is getting to be like any other ant hill. I'm going out somewhere to find elbow room, about a quarter of a billion miles of it."

"How about your pension?"

"Pension be hanged! I got along all right before I had it." Hazel, along with the other remaining Founding Fathers—and mothers—of the lunar colony, had been awarded a lifetime pension from a grateful city. This might be for a long period, despite her age, as the "normal" human life span under the biologically easy conditions of the Moon's low gravity had yet to be determined; the Luna City geriatrics clinic regularly revised the estimate upwards.

She continued, "How about you? Are you going to stay here, like a sardine in a can? Better grab your chance, son, before they run you for office again. Queen to King's Bishop Three, Lowell."

"We'll see. Pressure is down; let's get moving."

Castor and Pollux carefully stayed out of the discussion; things were shaping up.

As well as Dealer Dan's lot, the government salvage yard and that of the Bankrupt Hungarian were, of course, close by the spaceport. The Hungarian's lot sported an ancient sun-tarnished sign—BARGAINS! BARGAINS!! BARGAINS!!! GOING OUT OF BUSINESS —but there were no bargains there, as Mr. Stone decided in ten minutes and Hazel in five. The government salvage yard held mostly robot freighters without living quarters—one-trip ships, the interplanetary equivalent of discarded packing cases—and obsolete military craft unsuited for most private uses. They ended up at Ekizian's lot.

Pollux headed at once for the ship he and his brother had picked out. His father immediately called him back. "Hey, Pol! What's your hurry?"

"Don't you want to see our ship?"

"Your ship? Are you still laboring under the fancy that I am going to let you two refugees from a correction school buy that *Detroiter?*"

"Huh? Then what did we come out here for?"

"I want to look at some ships. But I am not interested in a Detroiter VII."

Pollux said, "Huh? See here, Dad, we aren't going to settle for a jumpbug. We need a—" The rest of his protest was cut off as Castor reached over and switched off his walkie-talkie; Castor picked it up:

"What sort of a ship, Dad? Pol and I have looked over most of these heaps, one time or another."

"Well, nothing fancy. A conservative family job. Let's look at that Hanshaw up ahead."

Hazel said, "I thought you said Hanshaws were fuel hogs, Roger?"

"True, but they are very comfortable. You can't have everything."

"Why not?"

Pollux had switched his radio back on immediately. He put in, "Dad, we don't want a runabout. No cargo space." Castor reached again for his belt switch; he shut up.

But Mr. Stone answered him. "Forget about cargo space. You two boys would lose your shirts if you attempted to compete with the sharp traders running around the system. I'm looking for a ship that will let the family make an occasional pleasure trip; I'm not in the market for a commercial freighter."

Pollux shut up; they all went to the Hanshaw Mr. Stone had pointed out and swarmed up into her control room. Hazel used both hands and feet in climbing the rope ladder but was only a little behind her descendants. Once they were in the ship she went down the hatch into the power room; the others looked over the control room and the living quarters, combined in one compartment. The upper or bow end was the control station with couches for pilot and co-pilot. The lower or after end had two more acceleration couches for passengers; all four couches were reversible, for the ship could be tumbled in flight, caused to spin end over end to give the ship artificial "gravity" through centrifugal force—in which case the forward direction would be "down," just the opposite of the "down" of flight under power.

Pollux looked over these arrangements with distaste. The notion of cluttering up a ship with gadgetry to coddle the tender stomachs of groundhogs disgusted him. No wonder Hanshaws were fuel hogs!

But his father thought differently. He was happily stretched out in the pilot's couch, fingering the controls. "This baby might do," he announced, "if the price is right."

Castor said, "I thought you wanted this for the family, Dad?"

"I do."

"Be pretty cramped in here once you rigged extra couches. Edith won't like that."

"You let me worry about your mother. Anyhow, there are enough couches now."

"With only four? How do you figure?"

"Me, your mother, your grandmother, and Buster. If Meade is along we'll rig something for the baby. By which you may conclude that I am really serious about you two juvenile delinquents finishing your schooling. Now don't blow your safeties!—I have it in mind that you two can use this crate to run around in—*after* you finish school. Or even during vacations, once you get your unlimited licenses. Fair enough?"

The twins gave him the worst sort of argument to answer; neither of them said anything. Their expressions said everything that was necessary. Their father went on, "See here—I'm trying to be fair and I'm trying to be generous. But how many boys your age do you know, or have even heard of, who have their own ship? None—right? You should get it through your heads that you are not supermen."

Castor grabbed at it. "How do you know that we are not 'supermen'?"

Pollux followed through with, "Conjecture, pure conjecture."

Before Mr. Stone could think of an effective answer his mother poked her head up the power room hatch. Her expression seemed to say that she had whiffed a very bad odor. Mr. Stone said, "What's the trouble, Hazel? Power plant on the blink?"

" 'On the blink,' he says! Why, I wouldn't lift this clunker at two gravities."

"What's the matter with it?"

"I never saw a more disgracefully abused— No, I won't tell you. Inspect it yourself; you don't trust my engineering ability."

"Now see here, Hazel, I've never told you I don't trust your engineering."

"No, but you don't. Don't try to sweet-talk me; I *know*. So check the power room yourself. Pretend I haven't seen it."

Her son turned away and headed for the outer door, saying huffily, "I've never suggested that you did not know power plants. If you are talking about that Gantry design, that was ten years ago; by now you should have forgiven me for being right about it."

To the surprise of the twins Hazel did not continue the argument but followed her son docilely into the air lock. Mr. Stone started down the rope ladder; Castor pulled his grandmother aside, switched off both her radio and his and pushed his helmet into contact with hers so that he might speak with her in private. "Hazel, what was wrong with the power plant? Pol and I went through this ship last week—I didn't spot anything too bad."

Hazel looked at him pityingly. "You've been losing sleep lately? It's obvious—only four couches."

"Oh." Castor switched on his radio and silently followed his brother and father to the ground.

Etched on the stern of the next ship they visited was *Cherub, Roma, Terra,* and she actually was of the Carlotti Motors *Angel* series, though she resembled very little the giant Archangels. She was short—barely a hundred fifty feet high—and slender, and she was at least twenty years old. Mr. Stone had been reluctant to inspect her. "She's too big for us," he protested, "and I'm not looking for a cargo ship."

"Too big how?" Hazel asked. " 'Too big' is a financial term, not a matter of size. And with her cargo hold empty, think how lively she'll be. I like a ship that jumps when I twist its tail—and so do you."

"Mmmm, yes," he admitted. "Well, I suppose it doesn't cost anything to look her over."

"You're talking saner every day, son." Hazel reached for the rope ladder.

The ship was old and old-fashioned and she had plied many a lonely million miles of space, but, thanks to the preservative qualities of the Moon's airless waste, she had not grown older since the last time her jets had blasted. She had simply slumbered timelessly, waiting for someone to come along and appreciate her sleeping beauty. Her air had been salvaged; there was no dust in her compartments. Many of her auxiliary fittings had been stripped and sold, but she herself was bright and clean and space-worthy.

The light Hazel could see in her son's eyes she judged to be love at first sight. She hung back and signaled the twins to keep quiet. The open airlock had let them into the living quarters; a galley-saloon, two little staterooms, and a bunkroom. The control room was separate, above them, and was a combined conn & comm. Roger Stone immediately climbed up into it.

Below the quarters was the cargo space and below that the power room. The little ship was a passenger-carrying freighter, or conversely a passenger ship with cargo space; it was this dual nature which had landed her, an unwanted orphan, in Dealer Dan's second-hand lot. Too slow when carrying cargo to compete with the express liners, she could carry too few passengers to make money without a load of freight. Although of sound construction she did not fit into the fiercely competitive business world.

The twins elected to go on down into the power room. Hazel poked around the living quarters, nodded approvingly at the galley, finally climbed up into the control room. There she found her son stretched out in the pilot's couch and fingering the controls. Hazel promptly swung herself into the co-pilot's couch, settled down in the bare rack—the pneumatic pads were missing—and turned her head toward Roger Stone. She called out, "All stations manned and ready, Captain!"

He looked at her and grinned. "Stand by to raise ship!"

She answered, "Board green! Clear from tower! Ready for count off!"

"Minus thirty! Twenty-nine—twenty-eight—" He broke off and added sheepishly, "It *does* feel good."

"You're dern tootin' it does. Let's grab ourselves a chunk of it before we're too old. This city life is getting us covered with moss."

Roger Stone swung his long legs out of the pilot's couch. "Um, maybe we should. Yes, we really should."

Hazel's booted feet hit the deck plates by his. "That's my boy! I'll raise you up to man size yet. Let's go see what the twins have taken apart."

The twins were still in the power room. Roger went down first; he said to Castor, "Well, son, how does it look? Will she raise high enough to crash?"

Castor wrinkled his forehead. "We haven't found anything wrong, exactly, but they've taken her boost units out. The pile is just a shell."

Hazel said, "What do you expect? For 'em to leave 'hot' stuff sitting in a decommissioned ship? In time the whole stern would be radioactive, even if somebody didn't steal it."

Her son answered, "Quit showing off, Hazel, Cas knows

that. We'll check the log data and get a metallurgical report later—if we ever talk business."

Hazel answered, "King's knight to queen's bishop five. What's the matter, Roger? Cold feet?"

"No, I like this ship . . . but I don't know that I can pay for her. And even if she were a gift, it will cost a fortune to overhaul her and get her ready for space."

"Pooh! I'll run the overhaul myself, with Cas and Pol to do the dirty work. Won't cost you anything but dockage. As for the price, we'll burn that bridge when we come to it."

"I'll supervise the overhaul, myself."

"Want to fight? Let's go down and find out just what inflated notions Dan Ekizian has this time. And remember—let me do the talking."

"Now wait a minute—I never said I was going to buy this bucket."

"Who said you were? But it doesn't cost anything to dicker. I can make Dan see reason."

Dealer Dan Ekizian was glad to see them, doubly so when he found that they were interested, not in the Detroiter VII, but in a larger, more expensive ship. At Hazel's insistence she and Ekizian went into his inner office alone to discuss prices. Mr. Stone let her get away with it, knowing that his mother drove a merciless bargain. The twins and he waited outside for quite a while; presently Mr. Ekizian called his office girl in.

She came out a few minutes later, to be followed shortly by Ekizian and Hazel. "It's all settled," she announced, looking smug.

The dealer smiled grudgingly around his cigar. "Your mother is a very smart woman, Mister Mayor."

"Take it easy!" Roger Stone protested. "You are both mixed up in your timing. I'm no longer mayor, thank heaven—and nothing is settled yet. What are the terms?"

Ekizian glanced at Hazel, who pursed her lips. "Well,

41

now, son," she said slowly, "it's like this. I'm too old a woman to fiddle around. I might die in bed, waiting for you to consider all sides of the question. So I bought it."

"*You?*"

"For all practical purposes. It's a syndicate. Dan puts up the ship; I wangle the cargo—and the boys and I take the stuff out to the Asteroids for a fat profit. I've always wanted to be a skipper."

Castor and Pollux had been lounging in the background, listening and watching faces. At Hazel's announcement Pollux started to speak; Castor caught his eye and shook his head. Mr. Stone said explosively, "That's preposterous! I won't let you do it."

"I'm of age, son."

"Mr. Ekizian, you must be out of your mind."

The dealer took his cigar and stared at the end of it. "Business is business."

"Well . . . at least you won't get my boys mixed up in it. That's out!"

"Mmm . . ." said Hazel. "Maybe. Maybe not. Let's ask them."

"They're not of age."

"No . . . not quite. But suppose they went into court and asked that I be appointed their guardian?"

Mr. Stone listened to this quietly, then turned to his sons. "Cas . . . Pol . . . did you frame this with your grandmother?"

Pollux answered, "No, sir."

"Would you do what she suggests?"

Castor answered, "Now, Dad, you know we wouldn't like to do anything like that."

"But you would do it, eh?"

"I didn't say so, sir."

"Hmm—" Mr. Stone turned back. "This is pure blackmail—and I won't stand for it. Mr. Ekizian, you knew that I came in here to bid on that ship. You knew that my mother was to bargain for it *as my agent*. You both knew that—but you made a deal behind my back. Now either you set that so-called deal aside and we start over—or I haul both of you down to the Better Business Bureau."

Hazel was expressionless; Mr. Ekizian examined his rings. "There's something in what you say, Mr. Stone. Suppose we go inside and talk it over?"

"I think we had better."

Hazel followed them in and plucked at her son's sleeve before he had a chance to start anything. "Roger? You really want to buy this ship?"

"I do."

She pointed to papers spread on Ekizian's desk. "Then just sign right there and stamp your thumb."

He picked up the papers instead. They contained no suggestion of the deal Hazel had outlined; instead they conveyed to him all right, title and interest in the vessel he had just inspected, and at a price much lower than he had been prepared to pay. He did some hasty mental arithmetic and concluded that Hazel had not only gotten the ship at scrap-metal prices but also must have bulldozed Ekizian into discounting the price by what it would have cost him to cut the ship up into pieces for salvage.

In dead silence he reached for Mr. Ekizian's desk stylus, signed his name, then carefully affixed his thumb print. He looked up and caught his mother's eye. "Hazel, there is no honesty in you and you'll come to a bad end."

She smiled. "Roger, you do say the sweetest things."

Mr. Ekizian sighed. "As I said, Mr. Stone, your mother is a very smart woman. I offered her a partnership."

"Then there *was* a deal?"

"Oh, no, no, not that deal—I offered her a partnership in the lot."

"But I didn't take it," Hazel added. "I want elbow room."

Roger Stone grinned and shrugged, stood up. "Well, anyway—who's skipper now?"

"You are—Captain."

As they came out both twins said, "Dad, did you buy it?"

Hazel answered, "Don't call him 'Dad'—he prefers to be called 'Captain.'"

"Oh."

"Likewise 'Oh,'" Pol repeated.

Dr. Stone's only comment was, "Yes, dear. I gave them notice on the lease." Meade was almost incoherent; Lowell was incoherent. After dinner Hazel and the twins took Meade and the baby out to see their ship; Dr. Stone—who had shown no excitement even during the Great Meteor Shower—stayed home with her husband. He spent the time making lists of things that must be attended to, both in the city and on the ship itself, before they could leave. He finished by making a list that read as follows:

> Myself—skipper
> Castor—1st officer & pilot
> Meade—2nd officer & asst. cook
> Hazel—chief engineer
> Pollux—asst. eng. & relief pilot
> Edith—ship's surgeon & cook
> Buster—"supercargo"

He stared at it for a while, then said softly to himself, "Something tells me this isn't going to work."

IV ASPECTS OF DOMESTIC ENGINEERING

MR. STONE DID NOT SHOW his ship's organization bill to the rest of the family; he knew in his heart that the twins were coming along, but he was not ready to concede it publicly. The subject was not mentioned while they were overhauling the ship and getting it ready for space.

The twins did most of the work with Hazel supervising and their father, from time to time, arguing with her about her engineering decisions. When this happened the twins usually went ahead and did it the way they thought it ought to be done. Neither of them had much confidence in the skill and knowledge of their elders; along with their great natural talent for mechanics and their general brilliance went a cocksure, half-baked conceit which led them to think that they knew a great deal more than they did.

This anarchistic and unstable condition came to a head over the overhaul of the intermediate injector sequence. Mr. Stone had decreed, with Hazel concurring, that all parts which could be disassembled would so be, interior surfaces inspected, tolerances checked, and gaskets replaced with new ones. The intermediate sequence in this model was at comparatively low pressure; the gasketing was of silicone-silica laminate rather than wrung metal.

Spare gaskets were not available in Luna City, but had to be ordered up from Earth; this Mr. Stone had done. But the old gaskets appeared to be in perfect condition, as Pollux pointed when they opened the sequence. "Hazel, why don't we put these back in? They look brand new."

His grandmother took one of the gaskets, looked it over, flexed it, and handed it back. "Lots of life left in it, that's sure. Keep it for a spare."

Castor said, "That .wasn't what Pol said. The new gaskets have to be flown from Rome to Pikes Peak, then jumped here. Might be three days, or it might be a week. And we can't do another thing until we get this mess cleaned up."

"You can work in the control room. Your father wants all new parts on everything that wears out."

"Oh, bother! Dad goes too much by the book; you've said so yourself."

Hazel looked up at her grandson, bulky in his pressure suit. "Listen, runt, your father is an A-one engineer. I'm privileged to criticize him; you aren't."

Pollux cut in hastily, "Just a sec, Hazel, let's keep personalities out of this. I want your unbiased professional opinion: are those gaskets fit to put back in, or aren't they? Cross your heart and shame the devil."

"Well . . . I say they are fit to use. You can tell your father I said so. He ought to be here any minute now; I expect he will agree." She straightened up. "I've got to go."

Mr. Stone failed to show up when expected. The twins fiddled around, doing a little preliminary work on the preheater. Finally Pollux said, "What time is it?"

"Past four."

"Dad won't show up this afternoon. Look, those gaskets are all right and, anyhow, two gets you five he'd never know the difference."

"Well, he would okay them if he saw them."

"Hand me that wrench."

Hazel did show up again but by then they had the sequence put back together and had opened up the preheater. She did not ask about the injector sequence but got down on her belly with a flashlight and mirror and inspected the preheater's interior. Her frail body, although still agile as a cricket under the Moon's weak pull, was not up to heavy work with a wrench, but her eyes were sharper—and much more experienced—than those of the twins. Presently she wiggled out. "Looks good," she announced. "We'll put it back together tomorrow. Let's go see what the cock ruined tonight." She helped them disconnect their oxygen hoses from the ship's tank and reconnect to their back packs, then the three went down out of the ship and back to Luna City.

Dinner was monopolized by a hot argument over the next installment of *The Scourge of the Spaceways.* Hazel was still writing it but the entire family, with the exception of Dr. Stone, felt free to insist on their own notions of just what forms of mayhem and violence the characters should indulge in next. It was not until his first pipe after dinner that Mr. Stone got around to inquiring about the day's progress.

Castor explained that they were about to close up the preheater. Mr. Stone nodded. "Moving right along—good! Wait a minute; you'll just have to tear it down again to put in the— Or did they send those gaskets out to the ship? I didn't think they had come in yet?"

"What gaskets?" Pollux said innocently. Hazel glanced quickly at him but said nothing.

"The gaskets for the intermediate injector sequence, of course."

"Oh, *those!*" Pollux shrugged. "They were okay, absolutely perfect to nine decimal places—so we put 'em back in."

"Oh, you did? That's interesting. Tomorrow you can take them out again—and I'll stand over you when you put the new ones in."

Castor took over. "But Dad, Hazel said they were okay!"

Roger Stone looked at his mother. "Well, Hazel?"

She hesitated. She knew that she had not been sufficiently emphatic in telling the twins that their father's engineering instructions were to be carried out to the letter; on the other hand she had told them to check with him. Or had she? "The gaskets were okay, Roger. No harm done."

He looked at her thoughtfully. "So you saw fit to change my instructions? Hazel, are you itching to be left behind?"

She noted the ominously gentle tone of his voice and checked an angry reply. "No," she said simply.

" 'No' what?"

"No, Captain."

"Not captain yet, perhaps, but that's the general idea." He turned to his sons. "I wonder if you two yahoos understand the nature of the situation?"

Castor bit his lip. Pollux looked at his twin, then back at his father. "Dad, *you're* the one who doesn't understand the nature of the situation. You're making a fuss over nothing. If it'll give you any satisfaction, we'll open it up again—but you'll simply see that we were right. If you had seen those gaskets, you would have passed them."

"Probably. Almost certainly. But a skipper's orders as to how he wants his ship gotten ready for space are not subject to change by a dockyard mechanic—which is what you both rate at the moment. Understand me?"

"Okay, so we should have waited. Tomorrow we'll open her up, you'll see that we were right and we'll close it up again."

"Wrong. Tomorrow you will go out, open it up, and bring the old gaskets back to me. Then you will both stay right here at home until the new gaskets arrive.

You can spend the time contemplating the notion that orders are meant to be carried out."

Castor said, "Now just a minute, Dad! You'll put us days behind."

Pollux added, "Not to mention the hours of work you are making us waste already."

Castor: "You can't expect us to get the ship ready if you insist on jiggling our elbows!"

Pollux: "And don't forget the money we're saving you."

Castor: "Right! It's not costing you a square shilling!"

Pollux: "And yet you pull this 'regulation skipper' act on us."

Castor: "Discouraging! That's what it is!"

"Pipe down!" Without waiting for them to comply he stood up and grasped each of them by the scruff of his jacket. Luna's one-sixth gravity permitted him to straight-arm them both; he held them high up off the floor and wide apart. They struggled helplessly, unable to reach anything.

"Listen to me," he ordered. "Up to now I hadn't quite decided whether to let you two wild men go along or not. But now my mind's made up."

There was a short silence from the two, then Pollux said mournfully, "You mean we don't go?"

"I mean you do go. You need a taste of strict ship's discipline a durn sight more than you need to go to school; these modern schools aren't tough enough for the likes of you. I mean to run a taut ship—prompt, cheerful obedience, on the bounce! Or I throw the book at you. Understand me? Castor?"

"Uh, yes, sir."

"Pollux?"

"Aye aye, sir!"

"See that you remember it. Pull a fast-talk like that on me when we're in space and I'll stuff you down each other's throat." He cracked their heads together smartly and threw them away.

The next day, on the way back from the field with the old gaskets, the twins stopped for a few minutes at the city library. They spent the four days they had to wait boning up on space law. They found it rather sobering reading, particularly the part which asserted that a commanding officer in space, acting independently, may and must maintain his authority against any who might attempt to usurp or dispute it. Some of the cited cases were quite grisly. They read of a freighter captain who, in his capacity as chief magistrate, had caused a mutineer to be shoved out an airlock, there to rupture his lungs in the vacuum of space, drown in his own blood.

Pollux made a face. "Grandpa," he inquired, "how would you like to be spaced?"

"No future in it. Thin stuff, vacuum. Low vitamin content."

"Maybe we had better be careful not to irritate Dad. This 'captain' pose has gone to his head."

"It's no pose. Once we raise ship it's legal as church on Sunday. But Dad won't space us, no matter what we do."

"Don't count on it. Dad is a very tough hombre when he forgets that he's a loving father."

"Junior, you worry too much."

"So? When you feel the pressure drop remember what I said."

It had been early agreed that the ship could not stay the *Cherub*. There had been no such agreement on what the new name should be. After several noisy arguments Dr. Stone, who herself had no special preference, suggested that they place a box on the dining table into which proposed names might be placed without debate. For one week the slips accumulated; then the box was opened.

Dr. Stone wrote them down:

Dauntless	*Icarus*
Jabberwock	*Susan B. Anthony*
H. M. S. Pinafore	*Iron Duke*
The Clunker	*Morning Star*
Star Wagon	*Tumbleweed*
Go-Devil	*Oom Paul*
Onward	*Viking*

"One would think," Roger grumbled, "that with all the self-declared big brains there are around this table someone would show some originality. Almost every name on the list can be found in the Big Register—half of them for ships still in commission. I move we strike out those tired, second-hand, used-before names and consider only fresh ones."

Hazel looked at him suspiciously. "What ones will that leave?"

"Well—"

"You've looked them up, haven't you? I thought I caught you sneaking a look at the slips before breakfast."

"Mother, your allegation is immaterial, irrelevant, and unworthy of you."

"But true. Okay; let's have a vote. Or does someone want to make a campaign speech?"

Dr. Stone rapped on the table with her thimble. "We'll vote. I've still got a medical association meeting to get to tonight." As chairman she ruled that any name receiving less than two votes in the first round would be eliminated. Secret ballot was used; when Meade canvassed the vote, seven names had gotten one vote each, none had received two.

51

Roger Stone pushed back his chair. "Agreement from this family is too much to expect. I'm going to bed. Tomorrow morning I'm going to register her as the R. S. *Deadlock*."

"Daddy, you wouldn't!" Meade protested.

"Just watch me. The R. S. *Hair Shirt* might be better. Or the R. S. *Madhouse*."

"Not bad," agreed Hazel. "It sounds like us. Never a dull moment."

"I, for one," retorted her son, "could stand a little decent monotony."

"Rubbish! We thrive on trouble. Do you want to get covered with moss?"

"What's 'moss,' Grandma Hazel?" Lowell demanded.

"Huh? It's . . . well, it's what rolling stones don't gather."

Roger snapped his fingers. "Hazel, you've just named the ship."

"Eh? Come again."

"The *Rolling Stones*. No, the *Rolling Stone*."

Dr. Stone glanced up. "I like that, Roger."

"Meade?"

"Sounds good, Daddy."

"Hazel?"

"This is one of your brighter days, son."

"Stripped of the implied insult, I take it that means 'yes.'"

"I don't like it," objected Pollux. "Castor and I plan to gather quite a bit of moss."

"It's four to three, even if you get Buster to go along with you and your accomplice. Overruled. The *Rolling Stone* it is."

Despite their great sizes and tremendous power space-ships are surprisingly simple machines. Every technology goes through three stages: first a crudely simple and quite unsatisfactory gadget; second, an enormously complicated group of gadgets designed to overcome the shortcomings of the original and achieving thereby somewhat satisfactory performance through extremely complex compromise; third, a final proper design therefrom.

In transportation, the ox cart and the rowboat represent the first stage of technology.

The second stage might well be represented by the automobiles of the middle twentieth century just before the opening of interplanetary travel. These unbelievable museum pieces were for their time fast, sleek and powerful—but inside their skins were assembled a preposterous collection of mechanical buffoonery. The prime mover for such a juggernaut might have rested in one's lap; the rest of the mad assembly consisted of afterthoughts intended to correct the uncorrectable, to repair the original basic mistake in design —for automobiles and even the early aeroplanes were "powered" (if one may call it that) by "reciprocating engines."

A reciprocating engine was a collection of miniature heat engines using (in a basically inefficient cycle) a small percentage of an exothermic chemical reaction, a reaction which was started and stopped every split second. Much of the heat was intentionally thrown away into a "water jacket" or "cooling system," then wasted into the atmosphere through a heat exchanger.

What little was left caused blocks of metal to thump foolishly back-and-forth (hence the name "reciprocating") and thence through a linkage to cause a shaft and flywheel to spin around. The flywheel (believe it if you can) had no gyroscopic function; it was used to store kinetic energy in a futile attempt to cover up the sins of reciprocation. The shaft at long last caused the wheels to turn and thereby propelled this pile of junk over the countryside.

The prime mover was used only to accelerate and to overcome "friction"—a concept then in much wider engineering use. To decelerate, stop, or turn the heroic human operator used *his own muscle power,* multiplied precariously through a series of levers.

Despite the name "automobile" these vehicles had no autocontrol circuits; control, such as it was, was exercised second by second for hours on end by a human being peering out through a small pane of dirty silica glass, and judging unassisted and often disastrously his own motion and those of other objects. In almost all cases the operator had no notion of the kinetic energy stored in his missile and could not have written the basic equation. Newton's Laws of Motion were to him mysteries as profound as the meaning of the universe.

Nevertheless millions of these mechanical jokes swarmed over our home planet, dodging each other by inches or failing to dodge. None of them ever worked right; by their nature they could not work right; and they were constantly getting out of order. Their operators were usually mightily pleased when they worked at all. When they did not, which was every few hundred miles (*hundred,* not hundred thousand), they hired a member of a social class of arcane specialists to make inadequate and always expensive temporary repairs.

Despite their mad shortcomings, these "automobiles" were the most characteristic form of wealth and the most cherished possessions of their time. Three whole generations were slaves to them.

The *Rolling Stone* was of the third stage of technology. Her power plant was nearly 100% efficient, and, save for her gyroscopes, she contained almost no moving parts—the power plant used no moving parts at all; a rocket engine is the simplest of all possible heat engines. Castor and Pollux might have found themselves baffled by the legendary Model-T Ford automobile, but the *Rolling Stone* was not nearly that complex, she was merely much larger. Many of the fittings they had to handle were very massive, but the Moon's one-sixth gravity was an enormous advantage; only occasionally did they have to resort to handling equipment.

Having to wear a vacuum suit while doing mechanic's work was a handicap but they were not conscious of it. They had worn space suits whenever they were outside the pressurized underground city since before they could remember; they worked in them and wore them without thinking about them, as their grandfather had worn overalls. They conducted the entire overhaul without pressurizing the ship because it was such a nuisance to have to be forever cycling an airlock, dressing and undressing, whenever they wanted anything outside the ship.

An IBM company representative from the city installed the new ballistic computer and ran it in, but after he had gone the boys took it apart and checked it throughout themselves, being darkly suspicious of any up-check given by a manufacturer's employee. The ballistic computer of a spaceship has to be right; without perfect performance from it a ship is a mad robot, certain to crash and kill its passengers. The new computer was of the standard "I-tell-you-three-times" variety, a triple brain each third of which was capable of solving the whole problem; if one triplet failed, the other two would outvote it and cut it off from action, permitting thereby at least one perfect landing and a chance to correct the failure.

The twins made personally sure that the multiple brain was sane in all its three lobes, then, to their disgust, their father and grandmother checked everything that they had done.

The last casting had been x-rayed, the last metallurgical report had been received from the space port laboratories, the last piece of tubing had been reinstalled and pressure tested; it was time to move the *Rolling Stone* from Dan Ekizian's lot to the port, where a technician of the Atomic Energy Commission—a great monkey with a Ph.D.—would install and seal the radioactive bricks which fired her "boiler." There, too, she would take on supplies and reactive mass, stabilized monatomic hydrogen; in a pinch the *Rolling Stone* could eat anything, but she performed best on "single-H."

The night before the ship was to be towed to the space port the twins tackled their father on a subject dear to their hearts—money. Castor made an indirect approach. "See here, Dad, we want to talk with you seriously."

"So? Wait till I phone my lawyer."

"Aw, Dad! Look, we just want to know whether or not you've made up your mind where we are going?"

"Eh? What do you care? I've already promised you that it will be some place new to you. We won't go to Earth, nor to Venus, not this trip."

"Yes, but *where?*"

"I may just close my eyes, set up a prob on the computer by touch, and see what happens. If the prediction takes us close to any rock bigger than the ship, we'll scoot off and have a look at it. That's the way to enjoy traveling."

Pollux said, "But, Dad, you can't load a ship if you don't know where it's going."

Castor glared at him; Roger Stone stared at him. "Oh," he said slowly, "I begin to see. But don't worry about it. As skipper, it is my responsibility to see that we have whatever we need aboard before we blast."

Dr. Stone said quietly, "Don't tease them, Roger."

"I'm not teasing."

"You're managing to tease me, Daddy," Meade said suddenly. "Let's settle it. I vote for Mars."

"It's not subject to vote."

Hazel said, "The deuce it ain't!"

"Pipe down, Mother. Time was, when the senior male member of a family spoke, everybody did what he—"

"Roger, if you think I am going to roll over and play dead—"

"I said, 'pipe down.' But everybody in this family thinks it's funny to try to get around Pop. Meade sweet-talks me. The twins fast-talk me. Buster yells until he gets what he wants. Hazel bullies me and pulls seniority." He looked at his wife. "You, too, Edith. You give in until you get your own way."

"Yes, dear."

"See what I mean? You all think papa is a schnook. But I'm not. I've got a soft head, a pliable nature, and probably the lowest I.Q. in the family, but this clambake is going to be run to suit me."

"What's a 'clambake'?" Lowell wanted to know.

"Keep your child quiet, Edith."

"Yes, dear."

"I'm going on a picnic, a *wanderjahr*. Anyone who wants to come along is invited. But I refuse to deviate by as much as a million miles from whatever trajectory suits me. I bought this ship from money earned in spite of the combined opposition of my whole family; I did not touch one thin credit of the money I hold in trust for our two young robber barons—and I don't propose to let them run the show."

Dr. Stone said quietly, "They merely asked where we were going. I would like to know, too."

"So they did. But why? Castor, you want to know so that you can figure a cargo, don't you?"

"Well—yes. Anything wrong with that? Unless we know what market we're taking it to, we won't know what to stock."

"True enough. But I don't recall authorizing any such commercial ventures. The *Rolling Stone* is a family yacht."

Pollux cut in with, "For the love of Pete, Dad! With all that cargo space just going to waste, you'd think that—"

"An empty hold gives us more cruising range."

"But—"

"Take it easy. This subject is tabled for the moment. What do you two propose to do about your educations?"

Castor said, "I thought that was settled. You said we could go along."

"That part is settled. But we'll be coming back this way in a year or two. Are you prepared to go down to Earth to school then—and stay there—until you get your degrees?"

The twins looked at each other; neither one of them said anything. Hazel butted in: "Quit being so offensively orthodox, Roger. I'll take over their educations. I'll give them the straight data. What they taught me in school durn near ruined me, before I got wise and started teaching myself."

Roger Stone looked bleakly at his mother. "You would teach them, all right. No, thanks, I prefer a somewhat more normal approach."

" 'Normal!' Roger, that's a word with no meaning."

"Perhaps not, around here. But I'd like the twins to grow up as near normal as possible."

"Roger, have you ever met any normal people? I never have. The so-called normal man is a figment of the imagination; every member of the human race, from Jojo the cave man right down to that final culmination of civilization, namely me, has been as eccentric as a pet coon—once you caught him with his mask off."

"I won't dispute the part about yourself."

"It's true for everybody. You try to make the twins 'normal' and you'll simply stunt their growth."

Roger Stone stood up. "That's enough. Castor, Pollux—come with me. Excuse us, everybody."

"Yes, dear."

"Sissy," said Hazel. "I was just warming up to my rebuttal."

He led them into his study, closed the door. "Sit down."

The twins did so. "Now we can settle this quietly. Boys, I'm quite serious about your educations. You can do what you like with your lives—turn pirate or get elected to the Grand Council. But I won't let you grow up ignorant."

Castor answered, "Sure, Dad, but we do study. We study all the time. You've said yourself that we are better engineers than half the young snots that come up from Earth."

"Granted. But it's not enough. Oh, you can learn most things on your own but I want you to have a formal, disciplined, really sound grounding in mathematics."

"Huh? Why, we cut our teeth on differential equations!"

Pollux added, "We know Hudson's Manual by heart. We can do a triple integration in our heads faster than Hazel can. If there's one thing we *do* know, it's mathematics."

Roger Stone shook his head sadly. "You can count

on your fingers but you can't reason. You probably think that the interval from zero to one is the same as the interval from ninety-nine to one hundred."

"Isn't it?"

"Is it? If so, can you prove it?" Their father reached up to the spindles on the wall, took down a book spool, and inserted it into his study projector. He spun the selector, stopped with a page displayed on the wall screen. It was a condensed chart of the fields of mathematics invented thus far by the human mind. "Let's see you find your way around that page."

The twins blinked at it. In the upper left-hand corner of the chart they spotted the names of subjects they had studied; the rest of the array was unknown territory; in most cases they did not even recognize the names of the subjects. In the ordinary engineering forms of the calculus they actually were adept; they had not been boasting. They knew enough of vector analysis to find their way around unassisted in electrical engineering and electronics; they knew classical geometry and trigonometry well enough for the astrogating of a space ship, and they had enough of non-Euclidean geometry, tensor calculus, statistical mechanics, and quantum theory to get along with an atomic power plant.

But it had never occurred to them that they had not yet really penetrated the enormous and magnificent field of mathematics.

"Dad," asked Pollux in a small voice, "what's a 'hyper-ideal'?"

"Time you found out."

Castor looked quickly at his father. "How many of these things have *you* studied, Dad?"

"Not enough. Not nearly enough. But my sons should know more than I do."

It was agreed that the twins would study mathematics intensively the entire time the family was in space, and not simply under the casual supervision of their father and grandmother but formally and systematically through I.C.S. correspondence courses ordered up from Earth. They would take with them spools enough to keep them busy for at least a year and mail their completed lessons from any port they might touch. Mr. Stone was satisfied, being sure in his heart that any person skilled with mathematical tools could learn anything else he needed to know, with or without a master.

"Now, boys, about this matter of cargo—"

The twins waited; he went on: "I'll lift the stuff for you—"

"Gee, Dad, that's swell!"

"—at cost."

The twins suddenly looked cautious. "How do you figure 'cost'?" Castor asked.

"You figure it and I'll check your figures. Don't try to flummox me or I'll stick on a penalty. If you're going to be businessmen, don't confuse the vocation with larceny."

"Right, sir. Uh . . . we still can't order until we know where we are going."

"True. Well, how would Mars suit you, as the first stop?"

"Mars?" Both boys got far-away looks in their eyes; their lips moved soundlessly.

"Well? Quit figuring your profits; you aren't there yet."

"Mars? Mars is fine, Dad!"

"Very well. One more thing: fail to keep up your studies and I won't let you sell a tin whistle."

"Oh, we'll study!" The twins got out while they were ahead. Roger Stone looked at the closed door with a fond smile on his face, an expression he rarely let them see. Good boys! Thank heaven he hadn't been saddled with a couple of obedient, well-behaved little nincompoops!

When the twins reached their own room Castor got down the general catalog of Four Planets Export. Pollux said, "Cas?"

"Don't bother me."

"Have you ever noticed that Dad always gets pushed around until he gets his own way?"

"Sure. Hand me that slide rule."

V   BICYCLES AND BLAST-OFF

THE *Rolling Stone* WAS MOVED over to the space port by the port's handling & spotting crew—over the protests of the twins, who wanted to rent a tractor and dolly and do it themselves. They offered to do so at half price, said price to be applied against freightage on their trade goods to Mars.

"Insurance?" inquired their father.

"Well, not exactly," Pol answered.

"We'd carry our own risk," added Castor. "After all, we've got assets to cover it."

But Roger Stone was not to be talked into it; he preferred, not unreasonably, to have the ticklish job done by bonded professionals. A spaceship on the ground is about as helpless and unwieldy as a beached whale. Sitting on her tail fins with her bow pointed at the sky and with her gyros dead a ship's precarious balance is protected by her lateral jacks, slanting down in three directions. To drag her to a new position requires those jacks to be raised clear of the ground, leaving the ship ready to topple, vulnerable to any jar. The *Rolling Stone* had to be moved thus through a pass in the hills to the port ten miles away. First she was jacked higher until her fins were two feet off the ground, then a broad dolly was backed under her; to this she was clamped. The bottom handler ran the tractor; the top handler took position in the control room. With his eyes on a bubble level, his helmet hooked by wire phone to his mate, he nursed a control stick which let him keep the ship upright. A hydraulic mercury capsule was under each fin of the ship; by tilting the stick the top handler could force pressure into any capsule to offset any slight irregularity in the road.

The twins followed the top handler up to his station. "Looks easy," remarked Pol while the handler tested his gear with the jacks still down.

"It is easy," agreed the handler, "provided you can out-guess the old girl and do the opposite of what she does—only do it first. Get out now; we're ready to start."

"Look, Mister," said Castor, "we want to learn how. We'll hold still and keep quiet."

"Not even strapped down—you might twitch an eyebrow and throw me half a degree off."

"Well, for the love of Pete!" complained Pollux. "Whose ship do you think this is?"

"Mine, for the time being," the man answered without rancor. "Now do you prefer to climb down, or simply be kicked clear of the ladder?"

The twins climbed out and clear, reluctantly but promptly. The *Rolling Stone,* designed for the meteoric speeds of open space, took off for the space port at a lively two miles an hour. It took most of a Greenwich day to get her there. There was a bad time in the pass when a slight moonquake set her to rocking, but the top handler had kept her jacks lowered as far as the terrain permitted. She bounced once on number-two jack, then he caught her and she resumed her stately progress.

Seeing this, Pollux admitted to Castor that he was glad they had not gotten the contract. He was beginning to realize that this was an esoteric skill, like glassblowing or chipping flint arrowheads. He recalled stories of the Big Quake of '31 when nine ships had toppled.

No more temblors were experienced save for the

microscopic shivers Luna continually experiences under the massive tidal strains of her eighty-times-heavier cousin Terra. The *Rolling Stone* rested at last on a launching flat on the east side of Leyport, her jet pointed down into splash baffles. Fuel bricks, water, and food, and she was ready to go—anywhere.

The mythical average man needs three and a half pounds of food each day, four pounds of water (for drinking, not washing), and thirty-four pounds of air. By the orbit most economical of fuel the trip to Mars from the Earth-Moon system takes thirty-seven weeks. Thus it would appear that the seven rolling Stones would require some seventy-five thousand pounds of consumable supplies for the trip, or about a ton a week.

Fortunately the truth was brighter or they would never have raised ground. Air and water in a space ship can be used over and over again with suitable refreshing, just as they can be on a planet. Uncounted trillions of animals for uncounted millions of years have breathed the air of Terra and drunk of her streams, yet air of Earth is still fresh and her rivers still run full. The Sun sucks clouds up from the ocean brine and drops it as sweet rain; the plants swarming over the cool green hills and lovely plains of Earth take the carbon dioxide of animal exhalation from the winds and convert it into carbohydrates, replacing it with fresh oxygen.

With suitable engineering a spaceship can be made to behave in the same way.

Water is distilled; with a universe of vacuum around the ship low-temperature, low-pressure distillation is cheap and easy. Water is no problem—or, rather, shortage of water is no problem. The trick is to get rid of excess, for the human body creates water as one of the by-products of its metabolism, in "burning" the hydrogen in food. Carbon dioxide can be replaced by oxygen through "soilless gardening"—hydroponics. Short-jump ships, such as the Earth-Moon shuttles, do not have such equipment, any more than a bicycle has staterooms or a galley, but the *Rolling Stone,* being a deep-space vessel, was equipped to do these things.

Instead of forty-one and a half pounds of supplies per person per day the *Rolling Stone* could get along with two; as a margin of safety and for luxury she carried about three, or a total of about eight tons, which included personal belongings. They would grow their own vegetables en route; most foods carried along would be dehydrated. Meade wanted them to carry shell eggs, but she was overruled both by the laws of physics and by her mother—dried eggs weigh so very much less.

Baggage included a tossed salad of books as well as hundreds of the more usual film spools. The entire family, save the twins, tended to be old-fashioned about books; they liked books with covers, volumes one could hold in the lap. Film spools were not quite the same.

Roger Stone required his sons to submit lists of what they proposed to carry to Mars for trade. The first list thus submitted caused him to call them into conference. "Castor, would you mind explaining this proposed manifest to me?"

"Huh? What is there to explain? Pol wrote it up. I thought it was clear enough."

"I'm afraid it's entirely too clear. Why all this copper tubing?"

"Well, we picked it up as scrap. Always a good market for copper on Mars."

"You mean you've already bought it?"

"Oh, no. We just put down a little to hold it."

"Same for the valves and fittings I suppose?"

"Yes, sir."

"That's good. Now these other items—cane sugar, wheat, dehydrated potatoes, polished rice. How about those?"

Pollux answered. "Cas thought we ought to buy hardware; I favored foodstuffs. So we compromised."

"Why did you pick the foods you did?"

"Well, they're all things they grow in the city's air-conditioning tanks, so they're cheap. No Earth imports on the list, you noticed."

"I noticed."

"But most of the stuff we raise here carries too high a percentage of water. You wouldn't want to carry *cucumbers* to Mars, would you?"

"I don't want to carry anything to Mars; I'm just going for the ride." Mr. Stone put down the cargo list, picked up another. "Take a look at this."

Pollux accepted it gingerly. "What about it?"

"I used to be a pretty fair mechanic myself. I got to wondering just what one could build from the 'hardware' you two want to ship. I figure I could build a fair-sized still. With the 'foodstuffs' you want to take a man would be in a position to make anything from vodka to grain alcohol. But I don't suppose you two young innocents noticed that?"

Castor looked at the list. "Is that so?"

"Hmm— Tell me: did you plan to sell this stuff to the government import agency, or peddle it on the open market?"

"Well, Dad, you know you can't make much profit unless you deal on the open market."

"So I thought. You didn't expect me to notice what the stuff was good for—and you didn't expect the customs agents on Mars to notice, either." He looked them over. "Boys, I intend to try to keep you out of prison until you are of age. After that I'll try to come to see you each visiting day." He chucked the list back at them.

"Guess again. And bear in mind that we raise ship Thursday—and that I don't care whether we carry cargo or not."

Pollux said, "Oh, for pity's sake, Dad! Abraham Lincoln used to sell whiskey. They taught us that in history. And Winston Churchill used to drink it."

"And George Washington kept slaves," his father agreed. "None of which has anything to do with you two. So scram!"

They left his study and passed through the living room; Hazel was there. She cocked a brow at them. "Did you get away with it?"

"No."

She stuck out a hand, palm up. "Pay me. And next time don't bet that you can outsmart your Pop. He's my boy."

Cas and Pol settled on bicycles as their primary article of export. On both Mars and Luna prospecting by bicycle was much more efficient than prospecting on foot; on the Moon the old-style rock sleuth with nothing but his skis and Shank's ponies to enable him to scout the area where he had landed his jumpbug had almost disappeared; all the prospectors took bicycles along as a matter of course, just as they carried climbing ropes and spare oxygen. In the Moon's one-sixth gravity it was an easy matter to shift the bicycle to one's back and carry it over any obstacle to further progress.

Mars' surface gravity is more than twice that of Luna, but it is still only slightly more than one-third Earth normal, and Mars is a place of flat plains and very gentle slopes; a cyclist could maintain fifteen to twenty miles an hour. The solitary prospector, deprived of his traditional burro, found the bicycle an acceptable and reliable, if somewhat less congenial, substitute. A miner's bike would have looked odd in the streets of

Stockholm; over-sized wheels, doughnut sand tires, towing yoke and trailer, battery trickle charger, two-way radio, saddle bags, and Geiger-counter mount made it not the vehicle for a spin in the park—but on Mars or on the Moon it fitted its purpose the way a canoe fits a Canadian stream.

Both planets imported their bicycles from Earth—until recently. Lunar Steel Products Corporation had lately begun making steel tubing, wire, and extrusions from native ore; Sears & Montgomery had subsidized an assembly plant to manufacture miner's bikes on the Moon under the trade name "Lunocycle" and Looney bikes, using less than twenty per cent by weight of parts raised up from Earth, undersold imported bikes by half.

Castor and Pollux decided to buy up second-hand bicycles which were consequently flooding the market and ship them to Mars. In interplanetary trade cost is always a matter of where a thing is gravity-wise —not how far away. Earth is a lovely planet but all her products lie at the bottom of a very deep "gravity well," deeper than that of Venus, enormously deeper than Luna's. Although Earth and Luna average exactly the same distance from Mars in miles, Luna is about five miles per second "closer" to Mars in terms of fuel and shipping cost.

Roger Stone released just enough of their assets to cover the investment. They were still loading their collection of tired bikes late Wednesday afternoon, with Cas weighing them in, Meade recording for him, and Pol hoisting. Everything else had been loaded; trial weight with the crew aboard would be taken by the port weightmaster as soon as the bicycles were loaded. Roger Stone supervised the stowing, he being personally responsible for the ship being balanced on take off.

Castor and he went down to help Pol unload the last flat. "Some of these seem hardly worth shipping," Mr. Stone remarked.

"Junk, if you ask me," added Meade.

"Nobody asked you," Pol told her.

"Keep a civil tongue in your head," Meade answered sweetly, "or go find yourself another secretary."

"Stow it, Junior, admonished Castor. "Remember she's working free. Dad, I admit they aren't much to look at, but wait a bit. Pol and I will overhaul them and paint them in orbit. Plenty of time to do a good job—like new."

"Mind you don't try to pass them off as new. But it looks to me as if you had taken too big a bite. When we get these inside and clamped down, there won't be room enough in the hold to swing a cat, much less do repair work. If you were thinking of monopolizing the living space, consider it vetoed."

"Why would anyone want to swing a cat?" asked Meade. "The cat wouldn't like it. Speaking of that, why don't we take a cat?"

"No cats," her father replied. "I traveled with a cat once and I was in executive charge of its sand box. No cats."

"Please, Cap'n Daddy! I saw the prettiest little kitten over at the Haileys' yesterday and—"

"No cats. And don't call me 'Captain Daddy.' One or the other, but the combination sounds silly."

"Yes, Captain Daddy."

"We weren't planning on using the living quarters," Castor answered. "Once we are in orbit we'll string 'em outside and set up shop in the hold. Plenty of room."

A goodly portion of Luna City came out to see them off. The current mayor, the Honorable Thomas Beasley, was there to say good-by to Roger Stone; the few surviving members of the Founding Fathers turned out to honor Hazel. A delegation from the Junior League and what appeared to be approximately half of the male members of the senior class of City Tech showed up to mourn Meade's departure. She wept and hugged them all, but kissed none of them; kissing while wearing a space suit is a futile, low-caloric business.

The twins were attended only by a dealer who wanted his payment and wanted it now and wanted it in full.

Earth hung in half phase over them and long shadows of the Obelisk Mountains stretched over most of the field. The base of the *Rolling Stone* was floodlighted; her slender bow thrust high above the circle of brightness. Beyond her, marking the far side of the field, the peaks of Rodger Young Range were still shining in the light of the setting Sun. Glorious Orion glittered near Earth; north and east of it, handle touching the horizon, was the homely beauty of the Big Dipper. The arching depth of sky and the mighty and timeless monuments of the Moon dwarfed the helmeted, squatty figures at the base of the spaceship.

A searchlight on the distant control tower pointed at them; blinked red three times. Hazel turned to her son. "Thirty minutes, Captain."

"Right." He whistled into his microphone. "Silence, everyone! Please keep operational silence until you are underground. Thanks for coming, everybody. Good-by!"

" 'Bye, Rog!" "Good trip, folks!" "Aloha!" "Hurry back—"

Their friends started filing down a ramp into one of the field tunnels; Mr. Stone turned to his family. "Thirty minutes. Man the ship!"

"Aye aye, sir."

Hazel started up the ladder with Pollux after her. She stopped suddenly, backed down and stepped on his fingers. "Out of my way, youngster!" She jumped down and ran toward the group disappearing down the ramp. "Hey, Tom! Beasley! Wait! Half a mo—"

The mayor paused and turned around; she thrust a package into his hand. "Mail this stuff for me?"

"Certainly, Hazel."

"That's a good boy. 'Bye!"

She came back to the ship; her son inquired, "What was the sudden crisis, Hazel?"

"Six episodes. I stay up all night getting them ready . . . then I didn't even notice I still had 'em until I had trouble climbing with one hand."

"Sure your head's on tight?"

"None of your lip, boy."

"Get in the ship."

"Aye aye, sir."

Once they were all inboard the port's weightmaster made his final check, reading the scales on the launching flat under each fin, adding them together. "Two and seven-tenths pounds under, Captain. Pretty close figuring." He fastened trim weights in that amount to the front of the ladder. "Take it up."

"Thank you, sir." Roger Stone hauled up the ladder, gathered in the trim weights, and closed the door of the airlock. He let himself into the ship proper, closed and dogged the inner door behind him, then stuck his head up into the control room. Castor was already in the co-pilot's couch. "Time?"

"Minus seventeen minutes, Captain."

"She tracking?" He reached out and set the trim weights on a spindle at the central axis of the ship.

"Pretty as could be." The main problem and the exact second of departure had been figured three weeks earlier; there is only one short period every twenty-six months when a ship may leave the Luna-Terra system for Mars by the most economical orbit. After trial weight had been taken the day before Captain Stone had figured his secondary problem, i.e., how much thrust for how long a period was required to put this particular ship into that orbit. It was the answer to this second problem which Castor was now tracking in the automatic pilot.

The first leg of the orbit would not be toward Mars, but toward Earth, with a second critical period, as touchy as the take off, as they rounded Earth. Captain Stone frowned at the thought, then shrugged; that worry had to come later. "Keep her tracking. I'm going below."

He went down into the power room, his eyes glancing here and there as he went. Even to a merchant skipper, to whom it is routine, the last few minutes before blast-off are worry-making. Blast-off for a spaceship has a parachute-jump quality; once you jump it is usually too late to correct any oversights. Space skippers suffer nightmares about misplaced decimal points.

Hazel and Pollux occupied the couches of the chief and assistant. Stone stuck his head down without going down. "Power room?"

"She'll be ready. I'm letting her warm slowly."

Dr. Stone, Meade, and Buster were riding out the lift in the bunkroom, for company; he stuck his head in. "Everybody okay?"

His wife looked up from her couch. "Certainly, dear. Lowell has had his injection." Buster was stretched out on his back, strapped down and sleeping. He alone had never experienced acceleration thrust and free falling; his mother had decided to drug him lest he be frightened.

Roger Stone looked at his least son. "I envy him."

Meade sat up. "Head pretty bad, Daddy?"

"I'll live. But today I regard farewell parties as much overrated affairs, especially for the guest of honor."

The horn over his head said in Castor's voice, "Want me to boost her, Dad? I feel fine."

"Mind your own business, co-pilot. She still tracking?"

"Tracking, sir. Eleven minutes."

Hazel's voice came out of the horn. " 'The wages of sin are death.' "

"Look who's talking! No more unauthorized chatter over the inter-com. That's an order."

"Aye aye, Captain."

He started to leave; his wife stopped him. "I want you to take this, dear." She held out a capsule.

"I don't need it."

"Take it."

"Yes, Doctor darling." He swallowed it, made a face, and went up to the control room. As he climbed into his couch he said, "Call tower for clearance."

"Aye aye, sir. *Rolling Stone*, Luna City registry, to Tower—request clearance to lift according to approved plan."

"*Tower to Rolling Stone—you are cleared to lift.*"

"*Rolling Stone to Tower—roger!*" Castor answered.

Captain Stone looked over his board. All green, except one red light from power room which would not wink green until he told his mother to unlock the safety on the cadmium damper plates. He adjusted the microvernier on his tracking indicator, satisfied himself that the auto-pilot was tracking to perfection as Castor had reported. "All stations, report in succession—power room!"

"She's sizzling, Skipper!" came back Hazel's reply.

"Passengers!"

"We're ready, Roger."

"Co-pilot!"

"Clear and green, sir! Check off completed. Five minutes."

"Strap down and report!"

"Power gang strapped."—"We're strapped, dear."—"Strapped, sir—all stations."

"Power room, unlock for lift."

The last red light on his board winked green as Hazel reported, "Power board unlocked, Skipper. Ready to blast."

Another voice followed hers, more softly: "Now I lay me down to sleep—"

"Shut up, Meade!" Roger Stone snapped. "Co-pilot, commence the count!"

Castor started singsonging: "Minus two minutes ten . . . minus two minutes . . . minus one minute fifty . . . minus one minute forty—"

Roger Stone felt his blood begin to pound and wished heartily that he had had the sense to come home early, even if the party had been in his honor.

"Minus one minute! . . . minus fifty-five . . . minus fifty—"

He braced his right hand with his forefinger over the manual firing key, ready to blast if the auto-pilot should fail—then quickly took it away. This was no military vessel! If it failed to fire, the thing to do was to cancel—not risk his wife and kids with imperfect machinery. After all, he held only a private license—

"Minus thirty-five . . . *half minute!*"

His head felt worse. Why leave a warm apartment to bounce around in a tin covered-wagon?

"Twenty-*eight*, twenty-*sev'n*, twenty-*six*—"

Well, if anything went wrong, at least there wouldn't be any little orphans left around. The whole Stone family was here, root and branch. The rolling Stones—

"Nine*teen* . . . eigh*teen* . . . seven*teen*—"

He didn't fancy going back and meeting all those people who had just come out to say good-by—telling them, "It's like this: we swung and we missed—"

"Twelve! Eleven! and ten! and nine!"

He again placed his forefinger over the manual button, ready to stab.

"And *five!*

"And *four!*

"And *three!*

"And *two!*

"And—" Castor's chant was blanked out by the blazing "white noise" of the jet; the *Rolling Stone* cast herself into the void.

VI BALLISTICS AND BUSTER

BLASTING OFF FROM LUNA is not the terrifying and oppressive experience that a lift from Earth is. The Moon's field is so weak, her gravity well so shallow, that a boost of one-g would suffice—just enough to produce Earth-normal weight.

Captain Stone chose to use two gravities, both to save time and to save fuel by getting quickly away from Luna—"quickly" because any reactive mass spent simply to hold a spaceship up against the pull of a planet is an "overhead" cost; it does nothing toward getting one where one wants to go. Furthermore, while the *Rolling Stone* would operate at low thrust she could do so only by being very wasteful of reactive mass, i.e., by not letting the atomic pile heat the hydrogen hot enough to produce a really efficient jet speed.

So he caused the *Stone* to boost at two gravities for slightly over two minutes. Two gravities—a mere nothing! The pressure felt by a wrestler pinned to the mat by the body of his opponent—the acceleration experience by a child in a schoolyard swing—hardly more than the push resulting from standing up very suddenly.

But the Stone family had been living on Luna; all the children had been born there—two gravities was twelve times what they were used to.

Roger's headache, which had quieted under the sedative his wife had prescribed for him, broke out again with renewed strength. His chest felt caved in; he fought for breath and he had to read and reread the accelerometer to convince himself that the ship had not run wild.

After checking over his board and assuring himself that all was going according to plan even if it did feel like a major catastrophe he turned his head heavily. "Cas? You all right?"

Castor gasped, "Sure, Skipper . . . tracking to flight plan, sir."

"Very well, sir." He turned his face to his inter-com mike. "Edith—"

There was no answer. "*Edith!*"

This time a strained voice replied, "Yes, dear."

"*Are you all right?*"

"Yes, dear. Meade and I . . . are all right. The baby is having a bad time."

He was about to call the power room when Castor reminded him of the passage of time. "Twenty seconds! Nineteen! Eighteen—"

He turned his eyes to the *brennschluss* timer and poised his hand on the cut-off switch, ready to choke the jet if the auto-pilot should fail. Across from him Castor covered him should *he* fail; below in the power room Hazel was doing the same thing, hand trembling over the cut-off.

As the timer flashed the last half second, as Castor shouted, "*Brennschluss!*", three hands slammed at three switches—but the auto-pilot had beaten them to it. The jet gasped as its liquid food was suddenly cut off from it; damper plates quenched the seeking neutrons in the atomic pile—and the *Stone* was in free orbit, falling toward Earth in a sudden, aching silence broken only by the whispering of the air-conditioner.

Roger Stone reswallowed his stomach. "Power room!" he rasped. "Report!"

He could hear Hazel sighing heavily. "Okay, son," she said feebly, "but mind that top step—it's a dilly!"

"Cas, call the port. Get a doppler check."

"Aye aye, sir." Castor called the radar & doppler station at Leyport. The *Rolling Stone* had all the usual radar and piloting instruments but a spaceship cannot possibly carry equipment of the size and accuracy of those mounted as pilot aids at all ports and satellite stations. "*Rolling Stone* to *Luna Pilot*—come in, *Luna Pilot*." While he called he was warming up their own radar and doppler-radar, preparing to check the performance of their own instruments against the land-based standards. He did this without being told, it being a co-pilot's routine duty.

"*Luna Pilot* to *Rolling Stone*."

"*Rolling Stone* to *Luna Pilot*—request range, bearing, and separation rate, and flight plan deviations, today's flight fourteen—plan as filed; no variations."

"We're on you. Stand by to record."

"Standing by," answered Castor and flipped the switch on the recorder. They were still so close to the Moon that the speed-of-light lag in transmission was unnoticeable.

A bored voice read off the reference time to the nearest half second, gave the double coordinates of their bearing in terms of system standard—corrected back to where the Moon *had been* at their blast-off—then gave their speed and distance relative to Luna with those figures also corrected back to where the Moon had been. The corrections were comparatively small since the Moon ambles along at less than two-thirds of a mile per second, but the corrections were utterly necessary. A pilot who disregarded them would find himself fetching up thousands or even millions of miles from his destination.

The operater added, "Deviation from flight plan negligible. A very pretty departure, *Rolling Stone*."

Castor thanked him and signed off. "In the groove, Dad!"

"Good. Did you get our own readings?"

"Yes, sir. About seven seconds later than theirs."

"Okay. Run 'em back on the flight line and apply the vectors. I want a check." He looked more closely at his son; Castor's complexion was a delicate chartreuse. "Say, didn't you take your pills?"

"Uh, yes, sir. It always hits me this way at first. I'll be all right."

"You look like a week-old old corpse."

"You don't look so hot yourself, Dad."

"I don't feel so hot, just between us Can you work that prob, or do you want to sack in for a while?"

"Sure I can!"

"Well . . . mind your decimal places."

"Aye aye, Captain."

"I'm going aft." He started to unstrap, saying into the inter-com as he did so, "All hands, unstrap at will. Power room, secure the pile and lock your board."

Hazel answered, "I heard the flight report, Skipper. Power room secured."

"Don't anticipate my orders, Hazel—unless you want to walk back."

She answered, "I expressed myself poorly, Captain. What I mean to say is, we are now securing the power room, as per your orders, sir. There—it's done. Power room secured!"

"Very well, Chief." He smiled grimly, having noted by the tell-tales on his own board that the first report was the correct one; she had secured as soon as she had known they were in the groove. Just as he had feared: playing skipper to a crew of rugged individualists was not going to be a picnic. He grasped the center stanchion, twisted around so that he faced aft and floated through the hatch into the living quarters.

He wiggled into the bunkroom and checked himself by a handhold. His wife, daughter, and least child were all unstrapped. Dr. Stone was manipulating the child's chest and stomach. He could not see just what she was doing but it was evident that Lowell had become violently nauseated—Meade, glassy-eyed herself, was steadying herself with one hand and trying to clean up the mess with the other. The boy was still unconscious.

Roger Stone felt suddenly worse himself. "Good grief!"

His wife looked over her shoulder. "Get my injection kit," she ordered. "In the locker behind you. I've got to give him the antidote and get him awake. He keeps trying to swallow his tongue."

He gulped. "Yes, dear. Which antidote?"

"Neocaffeine—one c.c. *Move!*"

He found the case, loaded the injector, handed it to Dr. Stone. She pressed it against the child's side. "What else can I do?" he asked.

"Nothing."

"Is he in any danger?"

"Not while I have an eye on him. Now get out and ask Hazel to come here."

"Yes, dear. Right away." He swam on aft, found his mother sitting in midair, looking pleased with herself. Pollux was still loosely secured to his control couch. "Everything all right back here?" he asked.

"Sure. Why not? Except my assistant, maybe. I believe he wants off at the next stop."

Pollux growled, "I'm feeling okay. Quit riding me."

Roger Stone said, "Edith could use your help, Mother. Buster has thrown up all over the bunkroom."

"Why, the little devil! He didn't have a thing to eat today; I rode herd on him myself."

"You must have let him out of your sight for a few

minutes, from the evidence. Better go give Edith a hand."

"To hear is to obey, Master." She kicked one heel against the bulkhead behind her and zipped out the hatch. Roger turned to his son.

"How's it going?"

"I'll be all right in a couple of hours. It's just one of those things you have to go through with, like brushing your teeth."

"Check. I'd like to rent a small planet myself. Have you written up the engineering log?"

"Not yet."

"Do so. It will take your mind off your stomach." Roger Stone went forward again and looked into the bunkroom. Lowell was awake and crying; Edith had him sheeted to a bunk to give him a feeling of pressure and stability.

The child wailed, "Mama! Make it hold *still!*"

"Shush, dear. You're all right. Mother is here."

"I want to go *home!*"

She did not answer but caressed his forehead. Roger Stone backed hastily out and pulled himself forward.

By supper time all hands except Lowell were over the effects of free fall—a sensation exactly like stepping off into an open elevator shaft in the dark. Nevertheless no one wanted much to eat; Dr. Stone limited the menu to a clear soup, crackers, and stewed dried apricots. Ice cream was available but there were no takers.

Except for the baby none of them had any reason to expect more than minor and temporary discomfort from the change from planet-surface weight to the endless falling of free orbit. Their stomachs and the semicircular canals of their ears had been through the ordeal before; they were inured to it, salted.

Lowell was not used to it; his physical being rebelled against it, nor was he old enough to meet it calmly and without fear. He cried and made himself worse, alternating that with gagging and choking. Hazel and Meade took turns trying to quiet him. Meade finished her skimpy dinner and relieved the watch; when Hazel came into the control room where they were eating Roger Stone said, "How is he now?"

Hazel shrugged. "I tried to get him to play chess with me. He spit in my face."

"He must be getting better."

"Not so you could notice it."

Castor said, "Gee whiz, Mother, can't you dope him up till he gets his balance?"

"No," answered Dr. Stone, "I'm giving him the highest dosage now that his body mass will tolerate."

"How long do you think it will take him to snap out of it?" asked her husband.

"I can't make a prediction. Ordinarily children adapt more readily than adults, as you know, dear—but we know also that some people never do adapt. They simply are constitutionally unable to go out into space."

Pollux let his jaw sag. "You mean Buster is a natural-born *groundhog?*" He made the word sound like both a crippling disability and a disgrace.

"Pipe down," his father said sharply.

"I mean nothing of the sort," his mother said crisply. "Lowell is having a bad time but he may adjust very soon."

There was glum silence for some minutes. Pollux refilled his soup bag, got himself some crackers, and eased back to his perch with one leg hooked around a stanchion. He glanced at Castor; the two engaged in a conversation that consisted entirely of facial expressions and shrugs. Their father looked at them and looked away; the twins often talked to each other that way; the code—if it was a code—could not be read by anyone else. He turned to his wife. "Edith, do you honestly think there is a chance that Lowell may not adjust?"

"A chance, of course." She did not elaborate, nor did she need to. Spacesickness like seasickness does not itself kill, but starvation and exhaustion do.

Castor whistled. "A fine time to find it out, after it's too late. We're already in orbit for Mars."

Hazel said sharply, "You know better than that, Castor."

"Huh?"

"Of course, dopy," his twin answered. "We'll have to tack back."

"Oh." Castor frowned. "I forgot for the moment that this was a two-legged jump." He sighed. "Well, that's that. I guess we go back." There was one point and one only at which they could decide to return to the Moon. They were falling now toward Earth in a conventional "S-orbit," practically a straight line. They would pass very close to Earth in an hyperboloid at better than five miles per second, Earth relative. To continue to Mars they planned to increase this speed by firing the jet at the point of closest approach, falling thereby into an ellipsoid, relative to the Sun, which would let them fall to a rendezvous with Mars.

They could reverse this maneuver, check their plunging progress by firing the jet against their motion and thereby force the *Stone* into an ellipsoid relative to Earth, a curve which, if correctly calculated, would take them back to Luna, back home before their baby brother could starve or wear himself out with retching. "Yep, that's that," agreed Pollux. He suddenly grinned. "Anybody want to buy a load of bicycles? Cheap?"

"Don't be in too big a hurry to liquidate," his father told him, "but we appreciate your attitude. Edith, what do you think?"

"I say we mustn't take any chances," announced Hazel. "That baby is sick."

Dr. Stone hesitated. "Roger, how long is it to perigee?"

He glanced at his control board. "About thirty-five hours."

"Why don't you prepare both maneuvers? Then we will not have to decide until it's time to turn ship."

"That makes sense. Hazel, you and Castor work the homing problem; Pol and I will work the Mars vector. First approximations only; we'll correct when we're closer. Everyone work independently, then we'll swap and check. Mind your decimals!"

"*You* mind *yours*," Hazel answered.

Castor gave his father a sly grin. "You picked the easy one, eh, Dad?"

His father looked at him. "Is it too hard for you? Do you want to swap?"

"Oh, no, sir! I can do it."

"Then get on with it—and bear in mind you are a crew member in space."

"Aye aye, sir."

He had in fact "picked the easy one"; the basic tack-around-Earth-for-Mars problem had been solved by the big computers of Luna Pilot Station before they blasted off. To be sure, Luna Pilot's answer would have to be revised to fit the inevitable errors, or deviations from flight plan, that would show up when they reached perigee rounding Earth—they might be too high, too low, too fast, too slow, or headed somewhat differently from the theoretical curve which had been computed for them. In fact they could be sure to be wrong in all three factors; the tiniest of errors at blast-off had a quarter of a million miles in which to multiply.

But nothing could be done to compute the corrections for those errors for the next fifteen or twenty hours; the deviations had to be allowed to grow before they could be measured accurately.

But the blast back to shape an ellipsoid home to Luna was a brand-new, unpremeditated problem. Captain Stone had not refused it out of laziness; he intended to do both problems but had kept his intention to himself. In the meantime he had another worry; strung out behind him were several more ships, all headed for Mars. For the next several days there would be frequent departures from the Moon, all ships taking advantage of the one favorable period in every twenty-six months when the passage to Mars was relatively "cheap", i.e., when the minimum-fuel ellipse tangent to both planets' orbits would actually make rendezvous with Mars rather than arrive foolishly at some totally untenanted part of Mars' orbit. Except for military vessels and super-expensive passenger ships, all traffic for Mars left at this one time.

During the four-day period bracketing the ideal instant of departure ships leaving Leyport paid a fancy premium for the privilege over and above the standard service fee. Only a large ship could afford such a fee; the saving in cost of single-H reactive mass had to be greater than the fee. The *Rolling Stone* had departed just before the premium charge went into effect; consequently she had trailing her like beads on a string a round dozen of ships, all headed down to Earth, to tack around her toward Mars.

If the *Rolling Stone* vectored back and shaped course for Luna rather than Mars, there was a possibility of traffic trouble.

Collisions between spaceships are almost unheard of; space is very large and ships are very tiny. But they are possible, particularly when many ships are doing much the same thing at the same time and the same region of space. Spacemen won't forget the *Rising Star* and the patrol vessel *Trygve Lie*—four hundred and seven dead, no survivors.

Ships for Mars would be departing Luna for the next three days and more; the *Rolling Stone*, in rounding Earth and heading back to Luna (toward where Luna would be on her arrival) would cut diagonally across their paths. Besides these hazards, there were Earth's three radio satellites and her satellite space station; each ship's flight plan, as approved by Luna Pilot Station, took into consideration these four orbits, but the possible emergency maneuver of the *Rolling Stone* had had no such safety check. Roger Stone mentally chewed his nails at the possibility that Traffic Control might refuse permission for the *Rolling Stone* to change its approved flight plan—which they would do if there was the slightest possibility of collision, sick child or no.

And Captain Stone would ignore their refusal, risk collision and take his child home—there to lose his pilot's license certainly and to face a stiff sentence from the Admiralty court possibly.

Besides the space station and the radio satellites there were the robot atom-bomb peace rockets of the Patrol, circling the Earth from pole to pole, but it was most unlikely that the *Rolling Stone*'s path would intersect one of their orbits; they moved just outside the atmosphere, lower than a spaceship was allowed to go other than in landing, whereas in order to tack the *Rolling Stone* would necessarily go inside the orbits of the radio satellites and that of the space station—wait a minute! Roger Stone thought over that last idea. Would it be possible to match in with the space station instead of going back to Luna?

If he could, he could get Lowell back to weight a couple of days sooner—in the spinning part of the space station!

The ballistic computer was not in use; Castor and

Hazel were still in the tedious process of setting up their problems. Captain Stone moved to it and started making a rough set-up directly on the computer itself, ignoring the niceties of ballistics, simply asking the machine, "Can this, or can this not, be done?"

Half an hour later he gave up, let his shoulders sag. Oh, yes, he could match in with the space station's orbit—but at best only at a point almost a hundred degrees away from the station. Even the most lavish expenditure of reaction mass would not permit him to reach the station itself.

He cleared the computer almost violently. Hazel glanced toward him. "What's eating you, son?"

"I thought we might make port at the station. We can't."

"I could have told you that."

He did not answer but went aft. Lowell, he found, was as sick as ever.

Earth was shouldering into the starboard port, great and round and lovely; they were approaching her rapidly, less than ten hours from the critical point at which they must maneuver, one way or the other. Hazel's emergency flight plan, checked and rechecked by the Captain, had been radioed to Traffic Control. They were all resigned to a return to Luna; nevertheless Pollux was, with the help of Quito Pilot, Ecuador, checking their deviations from their original flight plan and setting up the problem of preparing a final ballistic for Mars.

Dr. Stone came into the control room, poised near the hatch, caught her husband's eye and beckoned him to come with her. He floated after her into their stateroom. "What is it?" he asked. "Is Lowell worse?"

"No he's better."

"Eh?"

"Dear, I don't think he was spacesick at all."

"What's that?"

"Oh, a little bit, perhaps. But I think his symptoms were largely allergy; I think he is sensitive to the sedative."

"Huh? I never heard of anyone being sensitive to that stuff before."

"Neither have I, but there can always be a first time. I withdrew the drug several hours ago since it did not seem to help him. His symptoms eased off gradually and his pulse is better now."

"Is he okay? Is it safe to go on to Mars?"

"Too early to say. I'd like to keep him under observation another day or two."

"But—Edith, you know that's impossible! I've got to maneuver." He was wretched from strain and lack of sleep; neither had slept since blast-off more than twenty-four hours earlier.

"Yes, I know. Give me thirty minutes warning before you must have an answer. I'll decide then."

"Okay. I'm sorry I snapped at you."

"Dear Roger!"

Before they were ready to "round the corner" on their swing past Earth the child was much better. His mother kept him under a light hypnotic for several hours; when he woke from it he demanded food. She tried letting him have a few mouthfuls of custard; he choked on the first bite but that was simply mechanical trouble with no-gravity—on the second bite he learned how to swallow and kept it down.

He kept several more down and was still insisting that he was starved when she made him stop. Then he demanded to be untied from the couch. His mother gave in on this but sent for Meade to keep him under control and in the bunkroom. She pulled herself forward and found her husband. Hazel and Castor were at the computer; Castor was reading off to her a problem program while she punched the keys; Pollux was taking a doppler reading on Earth. Edith drew Roger Stone away from them and whispered, "Dear, I guess we can relax. He has eaten—and he didn't get sick."

"Are you sure? I wouldn't want to take even a slight chance."

She shrugged. "How can I be sure? I'm a doctor, not a fortune-teller."

"What's your decision?"

She frowned. "I would say to go on to Mars."

"It's just as well." He sighed. "Traffic turned down my alternate flight plan. I was just coming back to tell you."

"Then we have no choice."

"You know better than that. I'd rather tell it to the judge than read the burial service. But I have one more card up my sleeve."

She looked her query; he went on, "The *War God* is less than ten thousand miles behind us. If necessary, by using our mass margin, in less than a week I could match with her and you and the baby could transfer. She's a 'tumbling pigeon' since they refitted her—anything from Luna-surface to a full gravity."

"I hadn't thought of that. Well, I don't think it will be necessary but it's a comfort to know that there is help close by." She frowned. "I would not like to leave you and the children to shift for yourselves—and besides, it's risky to use your margin; you may need it badly when we approach Mars."

"Not if we handle the ship properly. Don't you worry; Hazel and I will get it there if we have to get out and push."

Pollux had stopped what he was doing and had been trying to overhear his parents' conversation. He was unsuccessful; they had had too many years' practice in keeping the kids from hearing. But he could see their intent expressions and the occasional frowns; he signaled his twin.

Castor said, "Hold it, Hazel. Time out to scratch. What goes, Pol?"

" 'Now is the time for all good men.' " He nodded toward their parents.

"Right. I'll do the talking." They moved aft.

Roger Stone looked at them and frowned. "What is it, boys? We're busy."

"Yes, sir. But this seems like a salubrious time to make an announcement."

"Yes?"

"Pol and I vote to go back home."

"Huh?"

"We figure that there's no percentage in taking a chance with Buster."

Pol added, "Sure, he's a brat, but look how much you've got invested in him."

"If he died on us," Castor went on, "it would spoil all the fun."

"And even if he didn't, who wants to clean up after him for weeks on end?"

"Right," agreed Pol. "Nobody likes to play room steward to a sick groundhog."

"And if he *did* die, the rest of you would blame us for the rest of our lives."

"Longer than that," Pol added.

"Don't worry about that 'negat' from Traffic. Hazel and I are working out a skew path that will let us miss the *Queen Mary* with minutes to spare—seconds anyhow. Course it may scare 'em a little."

"*Quiet!*" said Captain Stone. "One at a time—Castor, let me get this straight: do I understand that you and your brother are sufficiently concerned about your younger brother's welfare that you want to return to Luna in any case?"

"Yes, sir."

"Even if your mother decides that it is safe for him to continue?"

"Yes, sir. We talked it over. Even if he's looking pretty good now, he was one sick pup and anybody that sick might not make it to Mars. It's a long haul. We don't want to risk it."

Hazel had come aft and listened; now she said, "Nobility ill-becomes you, Cas. You were more convincing with the other routine."

"You butt out of this, Mother. Pol?"

"Cas told you. Shucks, we can make other trips."

Roger Stone looked at his sons. "I must say," he said slowly, "that it is surprising and gratifying to find so much family solidarity in this aggregation of individualists. Your mother and I will remember it with pride. But I am glad to say that it is unnecessary. We will continue for Mars."

Hazel scowled at him. "Roger, did you bump your head on the take-off? This is no time to take a chance; we take the kid back to Luna. I've talked with the boys and they mean it. So do I."

Castor said, "Dad, if you're afraid of the skew orbit, I'll pilot. I know—"

"*Silence!*" When he got it he went on as if to himself, "It says right here in the book to give orders, not explanations, and never to let them be argued. So help me, I'm going to run a taut ship if I have to put my own mother in irons." He raised his voice. "All hands! Prepare for maneuvering. Departure for Mars, gravity-well procedure."

Edith Stone said softly to Hazel, "The baby is all right, Mother. I'm sure." Then she turned to her sons. "Castor, Pollux—come here, dears."

"But Dad said—"

"I know. Come here first." She kissed each of them and said, "Now man your stations."

Meade appeared at the hatch, towing Lowell behind her like a toy balloon. He seemed cheerful and his face was cheerfully smeared with chocolate. "What's all the racket about?" she demanded. "You not only woke us; you must be disturbing people three ships behind."

VII IN THE GRAVITY WELL

A GRAVITY-WELL MANEUVER involved what appears to be a contradiction in the law of conservation of energy. A ship leaving the Moon or a space station for some distant planet can go faster on less fuel by dropping first toward Earth, then performing her principal acceleration while as close to Earth as possible. To be sure, a ship gains kinetic energy (speed) in falling toward Earth, but one would expect that she would lose exactly the same amount of kinetic energy as she coasted away from Earth.

The trick lies in the fact that the reactive mass or "fuel" is itself *mass* and as such has potential energy of position when the ship leaves the Moon. The reactive mass used in accelerating near Earth (that is to say, at the bottom of the gravity well) has lost its energy of position by falling down the gravity well. That energy has to go somewhere, and so it does—into the ship, as kinetic energy. The ship ends up going faster for the same force and duration of thrust than she possibly could by departing directly from the Moon or from a space station. The mathematics of this is somewhat baffling—but it works.

Captain Stone put both the boys in the power room for this maneuver and placed Hazel as second pilot. Castor's feelings were hurt but he did not argue, as the last discussion of ship's discipline was still echoing. The pilot has his hands full in this maneuver, leaving it up to the co-pilot to guard the auto-pilot, to be ready to fire manually if need be, and to watch for *brennschluss*. It is the pilot's duty to juggle his ship on her gyros and flywheel with his eyes glued to a measuring telescope, a "coelostat," to be utterly sure to the extreme limit of the accuracy of his instruments that his ship is aimed exactly right when the jet fires.

In the passage from Earth to Mars a mistake in angle of one minute of arc, one sixtieth of a degree, will amount to—at the far end—about fifteen thousand miles. Such mistakes must be paid for in reactive mass by maneuvering to correct, or, if the mistake is large enough, it will be paid for tragically and inexorably with the lives of captain and crew while the ship plunges endlessly on into the empty depths of space.

Roger Stone had a high opinion of the abilities of his twins, but, on this touchy occasion, he wanted the co-pilot backing him up to have the steadiness of age and experience. With Hazel riding the other couch he could give his whole mind to his delicate task.

To establish a frame of reference against which to aim his ship he had three stars, Spica, Deneb, and Fomolhaut, lined up in his scope, their images brought together by prisms. Mars was still out of sight beyond the bulging breast of Earth, nor would it have helped to aim for Mars; the road to Mars is a long curve, not a straight line. One of the images seemed to drift a trifle away from the others; sweating, he unclutched his gyros and nudged the ship by flywheel. The errant image crept back into position. "Doppler?" he demanded.

"In the groove."

"Time?"

"About a minute. Son, keep your mind on your duck shooting and don't fret."

He wiped his hands on his shirt and did not answer. For some seconds silence obtained, then Hazel said quietly, "Unidentified radar-beacon blip on the screen, sir. Robot response and a string of numbers."

"Does it concern us?"

"Closing north and starboard. Possible collision course."

Roger Stone steeled himself not to look at his own screen; a quick glance would tell him nothing that Hazel had not reported. He kept his face glued to the eyeshade of the coelostat. "Evasive maneuver indicated?"

"Son, you're as likely to dodge into it as duck away from it. Too late to figure a ballistic."

He forced himself to watch the star images and thought about it. Hazel was right, one did not drive a spaceship by the seat of the pants. At the high speeds and tight curves at the bottom of a gravity well, close up to a planet, an uncalculated maneuver might bring on a collision. Or it might throw them into an untenable orbit, one which would never allow them to reach Mars.

But what could it be? Not a spaceship, it was unmanned. Not a meteor, it carried a beacon. Not a bomb rocket, it was too high. He noted that the images were steady and stole a glance, first at his own screen, which told him nothing, and then through the starboard port.

Good heavens! he could *see* it!

A great gleaming star against the black of space . . . growing—growing!

"Mind your scope, son," said Hazel. "Nineteen seconds."

He put his eye back to the scope; the images were steady. Hazel continued, "It seems to be drawing ahead slightly."

He had to look. As he did so something flashed up and obscured the starboard port and at once was visible in the portside port—visible but shrinking rapidly. Stone had a momentary impression of a winged torpedo shape.

"*Whew!*" Hazel sighed. "They went that-a-way, podnuh!" She added briskly, "All hands, brace for accelera-

him and stuff him out of the lock. We can explain and correct the ship's mass factor tomorrow."

"I was not sick!"

Pollux said, "Meade had quite a bit of sack time on the leg down. Maybe you can talk her into taking him off our hands?"

"I'll try."

Meade was awake; she considered it. "Cash?"

"Sis, don't be that way!"

"Well . . . three days' dishwashing?"

"Skinflint! It's a deal; come take charge of the body."

Meade had to use the bunkroom as a nursery; the boys went forward and slept in the control room, each strapping himself loosely to a control couch as required by ship's regulations to avoid the chance of jostling instruments during sleep.

VIII   THE MIGHTY ROOM

CAPTAIN STONE HAD ALL HANDS with the exception of Dr. Stone and Lowell compute their new orbit. They all worked from the same data, using readings supplied by Traffic Control and checked against their own instruments. Roger Stone waited until all had finished before comparing results."

"What do you get, Hazel?"

"As I figure, Captain, you won't miss Mars by more than a million miles or so."

"I figure it right on."

"Well, now that you mention it, so do I."

"Cas? Pol? Meade?"

The twins were right together to six decimal places and checked with their father and grandmother to five, but Meade's answer bore no resemblance to any of the others. Her father looked it over curiously. "Baby girl, I can't figure out how you got this out of the computer. As near as I can tell you have us headed for Proxima Centauri."

Meade looked at it with interest. "Is that so? Tell you what: let's use mine and see what happens. It ought to be interesting."

"But not practical. You have us going faster than light."

"I *thought* the figures were a bit large."

Hazel stuck out a bony forefinger. "That ought to be a minus sign, hon."

"That's not all that's wrong," announced Pollux. "Look at this—" He held out Meade's programming sheet.

"That will do, Pol," his father interrupted. "You are not called on to criticize Meade's astrogation."

"But—"

"Stow it."

"I don't mind, Daddy," Meade put in. "I knew I was wrong." She shrugged. "It's the first one I've ever worked outside of school. Somehow it makes a difference when it's real."

"It certainly does—as every astrogator learns. Never mind, Hazel has the median figures. We'll log hers."

Hazel shook hands with herself. "The winnah and still champeen!"

Castor said, "Dad, that's final? No more maneuvers until you calculate your approach to Mars?"

"Of course not. No changes for six months at least. Why?"

"Then Pol and I respectfully request the Captain's permission to decompress the hold and go outside. We want to get to work on our bikes."

"Never mind the fake military-vessel phraseology. But I have news for you." He took a sheet of paper out of his belt pouch. "Just a moment while I make a couple of changes." He wrote on it, then fastened it to the control room bulletin board. It read:

SHIP'S ROUTINE

0700   Reveille (optional for Edith, Hazel & Buster)

0745   Breakfast (Meade cooks. Twins wash dishes)

0900   School C & P, math

Meade, astrogation, coached by Hazel

Lowell, reeling, writhing, and fainting in coils—or whatever his mother deems necessary.

1200   End of morning session

1215   Lunch

1300   School C & P, math

Hydroponics chores, Meade

1600   End of afternoon session

1800 Dinner—All Hands initial ship's maintenance schedule

SATURDAY ROUTINE—turn to after breakfast and clean ship, Hazel in charge. Captain's inspection at 1100. Personal laundry in afternoon.

SUNDAY ROUTINE—meditation, study, and recreation. Make & Mend in afternoon

Hazel looked it over. "Where are we headed, Rog? Botany Bay? You forgot to set a time to flog the peasants."

"It seems very reasonable to me."

"Possibly. Six gets you ten it won't last a week."

"Done. Let's see your money."

The twins had read it with dismay. Pollux blurted out, "But Dad! You haven't left us any time to repair our bikes—do you want us to lose our investment?"

"I've assigned thirty hours of study a week. That leaves one hundred and thirty-eight other hours. How you use them is your business as long as you keep our agreement about studying."

Castor said, "Suppose we want to start math at eight-thirty and again right after lunch? Can we get out of school that much earlier?"

"I see no objection."

"And suppose we study evenings sometimes? Can we work up some velvet?"

Their father shrugged. "Thirty hours a week—any reasonable variations in the routine will be okay, provided you enter in the log the exact times."

"Now that that's settled," Hazel commenced, "I regret to inform you, Captain, that there is one other little item on that Procrustean program that will have to be canceled, for the time being at least. Much as I would enjoy inducting our little blossom into the mysteries of astrogation I don't have the time right now. You'll have to teach her yourself."

"Why?"

" 'Why' the man asks? You should know better than anyone. *The Scourge of the Spaceways,* that's why. I've got to hole up and write like mad for the next three or four weeks; I've got to get several months of episodes ahead before we get out of radio range."

Roger Stone looked at his mother sadly. "I knew it was bound to come, Hazel, but I didn't expect it to hit you so young. The mental processes dull, the mind tends to wander, the—"

"Whose mind does what? Why you young—"

"Take it easy. If you'll look over your left shoulder out the starboard port and squint your eyes, you might imagine that you see a glint on the *War God.* It can't be much over ten thousand miles away."

"What's that got to do with me?" she demanded suspiciously.

"Poor Hazel! We'll take good care of you. Mother, we're riding in orbit with several large commercial vessels; every one of them has burners powerful enough to punch through to Earth. We won't *ever* be out of radio contact with Earth."

Hazel stared out the port as if she could actually spot the *War God.* "Well, I'll be dogged," she breathed. "Roger, lead me to my room—that's a good boy. It's senile decay, all right. You'd better take back your show; I doubt if I can write it."

"Huh uh! You let them pick up that option; you've *got* to write it. Speaking of *The Scum of the Waste Spaces,* I've been meaning to ask you a couple of questions about it and this is the first spare moment we've had. In the first place, why did you let them sign us up again?"

"Because they waved too much money under my nose, as you know full well. It's an aroma we Stones have hardly ever been able to resist."

"I just wanted to make you admit it. You were going to get me off the hook—remember? So you swallowed it yourself."

"More bait."

"Surely. Now the other point: I don't see how you dared to go ahead with it, no matter how much money they offered. The last episode you showed me, while you had killed off the Galactic Overlord you had also left Our Hero in a decidedly untenable position. Sealed in a radioactive sphere, if I remember correctly, at the bottom of an ammonia ocean on Jupiter. The ocean was swarming with methane monsters, whatever they are, each hypnotized by the Overlord's mind ray to go after John Sterling at the first whiff—and him armed only with his Scout knife. How did you get him out of it?"

"We found a way," put in Pol. "If you assume—"

"Quiet, infants. Nothing to it, Roger. By dint of super-human effort Our Hero extricated himself from his predicament and—"

"That's no answer."

"You don't understand. I open the next episode on Ganymede. John Sterling is telling Special Agent Dolores O'Shanahan about his adventure. He's making light of it, see? He's noble so he really wouldn't want to boast to a girl. Just as he is jokingly disparaging his masterly escape the next action starts and it's so fast and so violent and so bloody that our unseen audience doesn't have time to think about it until the commercial. And by then they've got too much else to think about."

Roger shook his head. "That's literary cheating."

"Who said this was literature. I've got three new sponsors."

"Hazel," asked Pollux, "where have you got them now? What's the situation?"

Hazel glanced at the chronometer. "Roger, does that schedule take effect today? Or can we start fresh tomorrow?"

He smiled feebly. "Tomorrow, I guess."

"If this is going to degenerate into a story conference, I'd better get Lowell. I get my best ideas from Lowell, he's just the mental age of my average audience."

"If I were Buster, I would resent that."

"Quiet!" She slithered to the hatch and called out, "Edith! May I borrow your wild animal for a while?"

Meade said, "I'll get him, Grandmother. But wait for me."

She returned quickly with the child. Lowell said, "What do you want, Grandma Hazel? Bounce tag?"

She gathered him in an arm. "No, son—blood. Blood and gore. We're going to kill off some villains."

"Swell!"

"Now as I recall it—and mind you, I was only there once—I left them lost in the Dark Nebula. Their food is gone and so is the Q-fuel. They've made a temporary truce with their Arcturian prisoners and set them free to help—which is safe enough because they are silicon-chemistry people and can't eat humans. Which is about what they are down to; the real question is—who gets barbecued for lunch? They need the help of the Arcturian prisoners because the Space Entity they captured in the last episode and imprisoned in an empty fuel tank has eaten its way through all but the last bulkhead and *it* doesn't have any silly prejudices about body chemistry. Carbon or silicon; it's all one to it."

"I don't believe that's logical," commented Roger Stone. "If it's own chemistry was based—"

"Out of order," ruled Hazel. "Helpful suggestions only, please. Pol? You seem to have a gleam in your eye."

"This Space Entity jigger—can he stand up against radar wave lengths?"

"Now we're getting somewhere. But we've got to complicate it a bit. Well, Meade?"

The twins started moving their bicycles outside the following day. The suits they wore were the same ones they had worn outdoors on the Moon, with the addition of magnetic boots and small rocket motors. These latter were strapped to their backs with the nozzles sticking straight from their waists. An added pressure bottle to supply the personal rocket motor was mounted on the shoulders of each boy but, being weightless, the additional mass was little handicap.

"Now remember," their father warned them, "those boost units are strictly for dire emergency. Lifelines at all times. And don't depend on your boots when you shift lines, snap on the second line before you loose the first."

"Shucks, Dad, we'll be careful."

"No doubt. But you can expect me to make a surprise inspection at any time. One slip on a safety precaution and it's the rack and thumb screws, plus fifty strokes of bastinado."

"No boiling oil?"

"Can't afford it. See here, you think I'm joking. If one of you should happen to get loose and drift away from the ship, don't expect me to come after you. One of you is a spare anyway."

"Which one?" asked Pollux. "Cas, maybe?"

"Sometimes I think it's one, sometimes the other. Strict compliance with ship's orders will keep me from having to decide at this time."

The cargo hatch had no airlock; the twins decompressed the entire hold, then opened the door, remembering just in time to snap on their lines as the door opened. They looked out and both hesitated. Despite their lifelong experience with vacuum suits on the face of the Moon this was the first time either one had ever been outside a ship in orbit.

The hatch framed endless cosmic night, blackness made colder and darker by the unwinking diamond stars many light-years away. They were on the night side of the *Stone;* there was nothing but stars and the swallowing depths. It was one thing to see it from the safety of Luna or through the strong quartz of a port; it was quite another to see it with nothing at all between one's frail body and the giddy cold depths of eternity.

Pollux said, "Cas, I don't like this."

"There's nothing to be afraid of."

"Then why are my teeth chattering?"

"Go ahead; I'll keep a tension on your line."

"You are too good to me, dear brother—a darn sight too good! *You* go and I'll keep a tension on *your* line."

"Don't be silly! Get on out there."

"After you, Grandpa."

"Oh, well!" Castor grasped the frame of the hatch and swung himself out. He scrambled to click his magnetic boots to the side of the ship but the position was most awkward, the suit was cumbersome, and he had no gravity to help him. Instead, he swung around and his momentum pulled his fingers loose from the smooth frame. His floundering motions bumped the side of the ship and pushed him gently away. He floated out, still floundering, until his line checked him three or four feet from the side. "Pull me in!"

"Put your feet down, clumsy!"

"I can't. Pull me in, you red-headed moron!"

"Don't call me 'red-headed.' " Pollux let out a couple of feet more line.

"Pol, quit fooling. I don't like this."

"I thought you were brave, Grandpa?"

Castor's reply was incoherent. Pollux decided that it had gone far enough; he pulled Castor in and, while holding firmly to a hatch dog himself, he grabbed one of Castor's boots and set it firmly against the side; it clicked into place. "Snap on your other line," he ordered.

Castor, still breathing heavily, looked for a padeye in the side of the ship. He found one nearby and walked over to it, picking up his feet as if he walked in sticky mud. He snapped his second line to the ring of the padeye and straightened up. "Catch," Pollux called out and sent his own second line snaking out to his twin.

Castor caught it and fastened it beside his own. "All set?" asked Pollux. "I'm going to unsnap us in here."

"All secure." Castor moved closer to the hatch.

"Here I come."

"So you do." Castor gave Pollux's line a tug; Pollux came sailing out of the hatch—and Castor let him keep on sailing. Castor checked the line gently through his fingers, soaking up the momentum, so that Pollux reached the end of the fifty-foot line and stayed there without bouncing back.

Pollux had been quite busy on the way out but to no effect—sawing vacuum is futile. When he felt himself snubbed to a stop he quit struggling. "Pull me back!"

"Say 'uncle.' "

Pollux said several other things, some of which he had picked up dockside on Luna, plus some more colorful expressions derived from his grandmother. "You had better get off this ship," he concluded, "because I'm coming down this line and take your helmet off." He made a swipe for the line with one hand; Castor flipped it away.

"Say 'even-Steven' then."

Pollux had the line now, having remembered to reach for his belt where it was hooked instead of grabbing for the bight. Suddenly he grinned. "Okay—'even-Steven.'"

"Even-Steven it is. Hold still; I'll bring you in." He towed him in gently, grabbing Pol's feet and clicking them down as he approached. "You looked mighty silly out there," he commented when Pollux was firm to the ship's side.

His twin invoked their ritual. "Even-Steven!"

"My apologies, Junior. Let's get to work."

Padeyes were spaced about twenty feet apart all over the skin of the ship. They had been intended for convenience in rigging during overhauls and to facilitate outside inspections while underway; the twins now used them to park bicycles. They removed the bicycles from the hold half a dozen at a time, strung on a wire loop like a catch of fish. They fastened each clutch of bikes to a padeye; the machines floated loosely out from the side like boats tied up to an ocean ship.

Stringing the clusters of bicycles shortly took them over the "horizon" to the day side of the ship. Pollux was in front, carrying six bicycles in his left hand. He stopped suddenly. "Hey, Grandpa! Get a load of this!"

"Don't look at the Sun," Castor said sharply.

"Don't be silly. But come see this."

Earth and Moon swam in the middle distance in slender crescent phase. The *Stone* was slowly dropping behind Earth in her orbit, even more slowly drifting outward away from the Sun. For many weeks yet Earth would appear as a ball, a disc, before distance cut her down to a brilliant star. Now she appeared about as large as she had from Luna but she was attended by Luna herself. Her day side was green and dun and lavished with cottony clouds; her night side showed the jewels of cities.

But the boys were paying no attention to Earth; they were looking at the Moon. Pollux sighed. "Isn't she beautiful?"

"What's the matter, Junior? Homesick?"

"No. But she's beautiful, just the same. Look, Cas, whatever ships we ever own, let's always register them out of Luna City. Home base."

"Suits. Can you make out the burg?"

"I think so."

"Probably just a spot on your helmet. I can't. Let's get back to work."

They had used all the padeyes conveniently close to the hatch and were working aft when Pollux said, "Wups! Take it easy. Dad said not to go aft of frame 65."

"Shucks, it must be 'cool' back to 90, at least. We've used the jet less than five minutes."

"Don't be too sure; neutrons are slippery customers. And you know what a stickler Dad is, anyway."

"He certainly is," said a third voice.

They did not jump out of their boots because they were zipped tight. Instead they turned around and saw their father standing, hands on hips, near the passenger airlock. Pollux gulped and said, "Howdy, Dad."

"You sure gave us a start," Castor added sheepishly.

"Sorry. But don't let me disturb you; I just came out to enjoy the view." He looked over their work. "You've certainly got my ship looking like a junkyard."

"Well, we had to have room to work. Anyhow, who's to see?"

"In this location you have the Almighty staring down the back of your neck. But I don't suppose He'll mind."

"Say, Dad, Pol and I sort of guessed that you wouldn't want us to do any welding inside the hold?"

"You sort of guessed correctly—not after what happened in the *Kong Christian*."

"So we figured we could jury-rig a rack for welding out here. Okay?"

"Okay. But it's too nice a day to talk business." He raised his open hands to the stars and looked out. "Swell place. Lots of elbow room. Good scenery."

"That's the truth! But come around to the Sun side if you want to see something."

"Right. Here, help me shift my lines." They walked around the hull and into the sunlight. Captain Stone, Earth born, looked first at the mother planet. "Looks like a big storm is working up around the Philippines."

Neither of the twins answered; weather was largely a mystery to them, nor did they approve of weather. Presently he turned to them and said softly, "I'm glad we came, boys. Are you?"

"Oh, you bet!" "Sure!" They had forgotten how cold and unfriendly the black depths around them had seemed only a short time before. Now it was an enormous room, furnished in splendor, though not yet fully inhabited. It was their own room, to live in, to do with as they liked.

They stood there for quite a long time, enjoying it. At last Captain Stone said, "I've had all the sun I can stand for a while. Let's work around back into the shade." He shook his head to dislodge a drop of sweat from his nose.

"We ought to get back to work anyhow."

"I'll help you; we'll get done faster."

The *Rolling Stone* swung on and outward toward Mars; her crew fell into routine habits. Dr. Stone was handy at weightless cooking, unusually skillful, in fact, from techniques she had picked up during a year's interneship in the free-fall research clinic in Earth's station. Meade was not so skilled but very little can be done to ruin breakfast. Her father supervised her hydroponics duties, supplementing thereby the course she had had in Luna City High School. Dr. Stone split the care of her least child with his grandmother and used her leisure placidly collating some years of notes for a paper "On the Cumulative Effects of Marginal Hypoxia."

The twins discovered that mathematics could be even more interesting than they had thought and much more difficult—it required even more "savvy" than they thought they had (already a generous estimate) and they were forced to stretch their brains. Their father caught up on the back issues of *The Reactomotive World* and studied his ship's manual but still had plenty of time to coach them and quiz them. Pollux, he discovered, was deficient in the ability to visualize a curve on glancing at an equation.

"I don't understand it," he said. "You got good marks in analytical geometry."

Pollux turned red. "What's biting you?" his father demanded.

"Well, Dad, you see it's this way—"

"Go on."

"Well, I didn't *exactly* get good marks in analyt."

"Eh? What is this? You both got top marks; I remember clearly."

"Well, now, you see— Well, we were awfully busy that semester and, well, it seemed logical. . . ." His voice trailed off.

"Out with it! Out with it!"

"Cas took both courses in analyt," Pollux blurted out, "and I took both courses in history. But I did read the book."

"Oh, my!" Roger Stone sighed. "I suppose it's covered by the statute of limitations by this time. Anyhow, you are finding out the hard way that such offenses carry their own punishments. When you need it, you don't know it worth a hoot."

"Yessir."

"But an extra hour a day for you, just the same—until you can visualize instantly from the equation a four-coordinate hypersurface in a non-Euclidean continuum—standing on your head in a cold shower."

"Yessir."

"Cas, what course did you fudge? Did you read the book?"

"Yes, sir. It was medieval European history, sir."

"Hmm . . . You're equally culpable, but I'm not too much concerned with any course that does not require a slide rule and tables. You coach your brother."

"Aye aye, sir."

"If you are pinched for time, I'll give you a hand with those broken-down bicycles, though I shouldn't."

The twins pitched into it, hard. At the end of two weeks Roger Stone announced himself satisfied with Pollux's proficiency in analytical geometry. They moved on to more rarefied heights . . . the complex logics of matrix algebra, frozen in beautiful arrays . . . the tensor calculus that unlocks the atom . . . the wild and wonderful field equations that make Man king of the universe . . . the crashing, mind-splitting intuition of Forsyte's Solution that had opened the 21st century and sent mankind another mighty step toward the stars. By the time Mars shone larger in the sky than Earth they had gone beyond the point where their father could coach them; they plowed on together.

They usually studied together, out of the same book, floating head to head in their bunkroom, one set of feet pointed to celestial south, the other pair to the north. The twins had early gotten into the habit of reading the same book at the same time; as a result either of them could read upside down as easily as in the conventional attitude. While so engaged Pollux said to his brother, "You ought to go into research rather than business. After all, money isn't everything."

"No," agreed Castor, "there are also stocks, bonds, and patent rights, not to mention real estate and chattels."

"I'm serious."

"We'll do both. I've finished this page; flip the switch when you're ready."

The *War God*, riding in a slightly different orbit, had been gradually closing on them until she could be seen as a "star" by naked eye—a variable star that winked out and flared up every sixteen seconds. Through the *Stone's* coelostat the cause could easily be seen; the *War God* was tumbling end over end, performing one full revolution every thirty-two seconds to provide centrifugal "artificial gravity" to coddle the tender stomachs of her groundhog passengers. Each half revolution the Sun's rays struck her polished skin at the proper angle to flash a dazzling gleam at the *Stone*. Through the 'scope the reflection was bright enough to hurt the eyes.

The observation turned out to be both ways. A radio message came in; Hazel printed it and handed it with a straight face to her son: "WAR GOD TO ROLLING STONE—PVT—ROG OLD BOY, I HAVE YOU IN THE SCOPE. WHAT IN SPACE HAVE YOU GOT ON YOU? FUNGUS? OR SEA WEEDS? YOU LOOK LIKE A CHRISTMAS TREE. P. VANDENBERGH, MASTER."

Captain Stone glared at the message stat. "Why, that fat Dutchman! I'll 'fungus' him. Here, Mother, send this: 'Master to Master—private message: In that drunken tumbling pigeon how do you keep your eye to a scope? Do you enjoy playing nursemaid to a litter of groundhogs? No doubt the dowagers fight over a chance to eat at the captain's table. Fun, I'll bet. R. Stone, Master.' "

The answer came back: "ROGER DODGER YOU OLD CODGER, I'VE LIMITED MY TABLE TO FEMALE PASSENGERS CIRCA AGE TWENTY SO I CAN KEEP AN EYE ON THEM—PREFERENCE GIVEN TO BLONDES AROUND FIFTY KILOS MASS. COME OVER FOR DINNER. VAN."

Pollux looked out the port, caught the glint on the *War God*. "Why don't you take him up, Dad? I'll bet I could make it across on my suit jet with one spare oxy bottle."

"Don't be silly. We haven't that much safety line, even at closest approach. Hazel, tell him: 'Thanks a million but I've got the prettiest little girl in the system cooking for me right now.' "

Meade said, "Me, Daddy? I thought you didn't like my cooking?"

"Don't give yourself airs, snub nose. I mean your mother, of course."

Meade considered this. "But I look like her, don't I?"

"Some. Send it, Hazel."

"RIGHT YOU ARE! MY RESPECTS TO EDITH. TRUTHFULLY, WHAT IS THAT STUFF? SHALL I SEND OVER WEEDKILLER, OR BARNACLE REMOVER? OR COULD WE BEAT IT TO DEATH WITH A STICK?"

"Why not tell him, Dad?" Castor inquired.

"Very well, I will. Hazel, send: 'Bicycles: want to buy one?' "

To their surprise Captain Vandenbergh answered: "MAYBE. GOT A RALEIGH 'SANDMAN'?"

"Tell him, 'Yes!' " Pollux put in. "A-number-one condition and brand-new tires. A bargain."

"Slow up there," his father interrupted. "I've seen your load. If you've got a bike in first-class condition, Raleigh or any other make, you've got it well hidden."

"Aw, Dad, it will be—by the time we deliver."

"What do you suppose he wants a bicycle for, dear?" Dr. Stone asked. "Prospecting? Surely not."

"Probably just sightseeing. All right, Hazel, you can send it—but mind you, boys, I'll inspect that vehicle myself; Van trusts me."

Hazel pushed herself away from the rig. "Let the boys tell their own whoppers. I'm getting bored with this chit-chat."

Castor took over at the key, started to dicker. The passenger skipper, it developed, really was willing to buy a bicycle. After a leisurely while they settled on a price well under Castor's asking price, attractively under the usual prices on Mars, but profitably over what the boys had paid on Luna—this for delivery F.O.B. Phobos, circum Mars.

Roger Stone exchanged affectionate insults and gossip with his friend from time to time over the next several days. During the following week the *War God* came within phone range, but the conversations dropped off and stopped; they had exhausted topics of conversation. The *War God* had made her closest approach and was pulling away again; they did not hear from her for more than three weeks.

The call was taken by Meade. She hurried aft to the hold where her father was helping the twins spray enamel on reconditioned bicycles. "Daddy, you're wanted on the phone! *War God,* master to master—official."

"Coming." He hurried forward and took the call. "*Rolling Stone,* Captain Stone speaking."

"Oh. You're rig..........................

"I suppose so."

"Then let's get busy."

"As you say, sir. You know, Roger, if the *War God* comes in with an unidentified and uncontrolled disease aboard, they'll never let her make port at Mars. They'll swing her in a parking orbit, fuel her up again, and send her back at next optimum."

"What of it? It's nothing to me if fat tourists and a bunch of immigrants are disappointed."

"Check. But I was thinking of something else. With Van and the first officer sick, maybe about to check in, if the second officer comes down with it, too, the *War God* might not even get as far as a parking orbit."

Roger Stone did not have to have the thought elaborated; a ship approaching a planet, unless maneuvered at the last by a skilled pilot, can do one of only two things—crash, or swing on past and out endlessly into empty space to take up a comet-like orbit which arrives nowhere ever.

He covered his face with his hands. "What do I do, Mother?"

"You are captain, son."

He sighed. "I suppose I knew it all along."

"Yes, but you had to struggle with it first." She kissed him. "Orders, son?"

"Let's get to it. It's a good thing we didn't waste any margin in departure."

"That it is."

When Hazel told the others the news Castor asked, "Does Dad want us to compute a ballistic?"

"No."

"A good thing—for we've got to get those bikes into take care of Lowell and keep him out of the way. But you won't be bringing the bikes inboard."

"What? You can't balance the ship for maneuvers with them where they are. Besides, the first blast would probably snap the wires and change your mass factor."

"Cas, where are your brains? Can't you see the situation? We jettison."

"Huh? We throw away our *bikes*? After dragging almost to Mars?"

"Your bikes, all our books, and everything else we can do without. The rough run-through on the computer made that clear as quartz; it's the only way we can do this maneuver and still be sure of having a safe margin for homing in. Your father is checking over the weight schedule right now."

"But—" Castor's face suddenly relaxed and became impassive. "Aye aye, ma'am."

The twins were suiting up but had not yet gone outside when Pollux was struck by a notion. "Cas? We cut the bikes loose; then what happens?"

"We charge it off to experience—and try to recover from Four-Planets Transit. They won't pay up, of course."

"Use your skull. Where do the bikes end up?"

"Huh? Why, at *Mars!*"

"Right. Or pretty near. In the orbit we're in now, they swing in mighty close and then head down Sunside again. Suppose, on closest approach, we are standing there waiting to snag 'em?"

"Not a chance. It will take us just as long to get to Mars—and in a different orbit, same as the *War God's.*"

"Yes, but just supposing. You know, I wish I had a

spare radar beacon to hang on them. Then if we could reach them, we'd know where they were."

"Well, we haven't got one. Say! Where did you put that used reflecting foil?"

"Huh? Oh, I see. Grandpa, sometimes your senile decay is not quite so noticeable." The *Stone* had started out, of course, covered on one side of her living quarters by mirror-bright aluminum foil. As she drifted farther and farther from the Sun, reflecting the Sun's heat had grown less necessary, absorbing it more desirable. To reduce the load on the ship's heating and cooling system, square yards of it were peeled up and taken inside to store from week to week.

"Let's ask Dad."

Hazel stopped them at the hatch to the control room. "He's at the computer. What's the complaint?"

"Hazel, the reflecting foil we've been salvaging—is it on the jettison list?"

"Certainly. We'll pick up some more on Mars for the trip back. Why?"

"A radar corner—that's why!" They explained the plan.

She nodded. "A long chance, but it makes sense. See here, wire everything we jettison to the bikes. We might get it all back."

"Sure thing!" The twins got busy. While Pollux gathered together the bunches of bicycles, all but a few in good repair and brave with new paint, Castor constructed a curious geometrical toy. With 8-gauge wire, aluminum foil, and sticky tape he made a giant square of foil, edged and held flat with wire. This he bisected at right angles with a second square. The two squares he again bisected at the remaining possible right angle with a third square. The result was eight shiny right-angled corners facing among them in all possible directions—a radar reflector. Each corner would bounce radar waves directly back to source, a principle easily illustrated with a rubber ball and any room or box corner. The final result was to step up the effectiveness of radar from an inverse fourth-power law to an inverse square law—in theory, at least. In practice it would be somewhat less than perfectly efficient but the radar response of the assembly would be increased enormously. A mass so tagged would stand out on a radar screen like a candle in a cave.

This flimsy giant kite Castor anchored to the ball of bicycles and other jetsam with an odd bit of string. No stronger link was necessary; out here no vagrant wind would blow it away, no one would cut it loose. "Pol," he said, "go bank on the port and tell 'em we're ready."

Pollux walked forward and did so, rapping on the quartz first to attract his grandmother's attention, then tapping code to report. While he was gone Castor attached a piece of paper reading:

NOT FOR SALVAGE

This cargo is in free transit by intention. The undersigned owner intends to recover it and warns all parties not to claim it as abandoned. U.P. Rev. Stat. #193401

> Roger Stone, Master
> P.Y. *Rolling Stone*, Luna

When Pollux came back he said, "Hazel says go ahead but take it easy."

"Of course." Castor untwisted the single wire that held the ungainly mass to the ship, then stood back and watched it. It did not move. He reached out and gave it the gentlest shove with his little finger, then continued watching. Slowly, slowly it separated from the ship. He wished to disturb its orbit as little as possible, to make it easy to find. The petty vector he had placed on it—an inch a minute was his guess—would act for all the days from there to Mars; he wanted the final sum to remain small.

Pollux twisted around and picked out the winking gleam of the *War God*. "Will the jet be clear of it when we swing ship?" he asked anxiously.

"Quit worrying. I already figured that."

The maneuver to be performed was of the simplest—point to point in space in a region which could be treated as free of gravity strain since the two ships were practically the same distance from the Sun and Mars was too far away to matter. There were four simple steps: cancellation of the slight vector difference between the two ships (the relative speed with which the *War God* was pulling away), acceleration toward the *War God*, transit of the space between them, deceleration to match orbits and lie dead in space relative to each other on arrival.

Steps one and two would be combined by vector addition; step three was simply waiting time. The operation would be two maneuvers, two blasts on the jet.

But step three, the time it would take to reach the *War God*, could be enormously cut down by lavish use of reactive mass. Had time been no object they could have, as Hazel put it, closed the gap "by throwing rocks off the stern." There was an infinite number of choices, each requiring different amounts of reactive mass. One choice would have saved the bicycles and their personal possessions—but it would have stretched the transit time out to over two weeks.

This was a doctor's emergency call—Roger Stone elected to jettison.

But he did not tell the twins this and he did not require them to work a ballistic. He did not care to let them know of the choice between sacrificing their capital or letting strangers wait for medical attention. After all, he reflected, the twins were pretty young.

Eleven hours from blast time the *Stone* hung in space close by the *War God*. The ships were still plunging toward Mars at some sixteen miles per second; relative to each other they were stationary—except that the liner continued her stately rotation, end over end. Dr. Stone, her small figure encumbered not only with space suit, pressure bottles, radio, suit jet, and life lines, but also with a Santa Claus pack of surgical supplies, stood with her husband on the side of the *Stone* nearest the liner. Not knowing exactly what she might need she had taken all that she believed could be spared from the stock of their own craft—drugs, antibiotics, instruments, supplies.

The others had been kissed good-by inside and told to stay there. Lowell had cried and tried to keep his mother from entering the lock. He had not been told what was going on, but the emotions of the others were contagious.

Roger Stone was saying anxiously, "Now see here, the minute you have this under control, back you come —you hear?"

She shook her head. "I'll see you on Mars, dearest."

"No indeed! You—"

"No, Roger. I might act as a carrier. We can't risk it."

"You might act as a carrier coming back to us on Mars, too. Don't you *ever* expect to come back?"

She ignored the rhetorical question. "On Mars there will be hospitals. But I can't risk a family epidemic in space."

"Edith! I've a good mind to refuse to—"

"They're ready for me, dear. See?"

Over their heads, two hundred yards away, a passenger lock on the rotation axis of the mighty ship had opened; two small figures spilled silently out, flipped neatly to boot contact, stood on the ship's side, their heads pointing "down" at Mr. and Mrs. Stone. Roger Stone called into his microphone, *"War God!"*

"War God aye aye!"

"Are you ready?"

"Whenever you are."

"Stand by for transfer."

Acting Captain Rowley had proposed sending a man over to conduct Dr. Stone across the gap. She had refused, not wishing to have anyone from the infected ship in contact with the *Rolling Stone*. Now she said, "Are my lines free for running, Roger?"

"Yes, dearest." He had bent several lines together, one end to her waist, the other to a padeye.

"Will you do my boots, dear?"

He kneeled and unzipped her magnetic boots without speaking, his voice have become uncertain. He straightened and she put her arms around him. They embraced awkwardly, hampered by the suits, hampered by the extra back pack she carried. "Adios, my darling," she said softly. "Take care of the children."

"Edith! Take care of yourself!"

"Yes, dear. Steady me now."

He slipped his hands to her hips; she stepped out of the boots, was now held against the ship only by his hands.

"Ready! One! Two!" They crouched down together. "Three!" She jumped straight away from the ship, her lines snaking after her. For long, long seconds she sailed straight out over his head, closing the gap between her and the liner. Presently it became evident that she had not leaped quite straight; her husband got ready to haul her back in.

But the reception committee was ready for that exigency. One of them was swinging a weighted line around his head; he let the end of it swing farther and farther out. As she started to move past the side of the *War God* he swung it against her safety line; the weighted end wrapped itself around her line. Back at the *Rolling Stone* Roger Stone snubbed her line and stopped her; the man on the liner gently pulled her in.

The second man caught her and snapped a hook to her belt, then unfastened the long line from the *Stone*. Before she entered the lock she waved, and the door closed.

Roger Stone looked at the closed door for a moment, then pulled in the line. He let his eyes drop to the pair of little boots left standing empty beside him. He pulled them loose, held them to him, and plodded back to his own airlock.

IX   ASSETS RECOVERABLE

THE TWINS KEPT OUT OF THEIR FATHER'S WAY for the next several days. He was unusually tender and affectionate with all of them but he never smiled and his mood was likely to flare suddenly and unexpectedly into anger. They stayed in their bunkroom and pretended to study—they actually did study some of the time. Meade and Hazel split the care of Lowell between them; the child's feeling of security was damaged by the absence of his mother. He expressed it by temper tantrums and demands for attention.

Hazel took over the cooking of lunch and dinner; she was no better at it than Meade. She could be heard twice a day, burning herself and swearing and complaining that she was not the domestic type and never had had any ambitions that way. Never!

Dr. Stone phoned once a day, spoke briefly with her husband, and begged off from speaking to anyone else for the reason that she was much too busy. Roger Stone's explosions of temper were most likely to occur shortly after these daily calls.

Hazel alone had the courage to quiz him about the calls. On the sixth day at lunch she said, "Well, Roger? What was the news today? Give."

"Nothing much. Hazel, these chops are atrocious."

"They ought to be good; I flavored 'em with my own blood." She held out a bandaged thumb. "Why don't you try cooking? But back on the subject. Don't evade me, boy."

"She thinks she's on the track of something. So far as she can tell from their medical records, nobody has caught it so far who is known to have had measles."

Meade said, "Measles? People don't die of *that,* do they?"

"Hardly ever," agreed her grandmother, "though it can be fairly serious in an adult."

"I didn't say it was measles," her father answered testily, "nor did your mother. She thinks it's related to measles, a mutant strain maybe—more virulent."

"Call it 'neomeasles,' " suggested Hazel. "That's a good question-begging tag and it has an impressive scientific sound to it. Any more deaths, Roger?"

"Well, yes."

"How many?"

"She wouldn't say. Van is still alive, though, and she says that he is recovering. She *told* me," he added, as if trying to convince himself, "that she thought she was learning how to treat it."

"Measles," Hazel said thoughtfully. "You've never had it, Roger."

"No."

"Nor any of the kids."

"Of course not," put in Pollux. Luna City was by long odds the healthiest place in the known universe; the routine childhood diseases of Earth had never been given a chance to establish.

"How did she sound, Son?"

"Dog tired." He frowned. "She even snapped at me."

"Not Mummy!"

"Quiet, Meade." Hazel went on, "I've had measles, seventy or eighty years ago. Roger, I had better go over and help her."

He smiled without humor. "She anticipated that. She said to tell you thanks but she had all the unskilled help she could use."

" 'Unskilled help!' I like that! Why, during the epidemic of '93 there were times when I was the only woman in the colony able to change a bed. Hummph!"

Hazel deliberately waited around for the phone call the next day, determined to get a few words at least with her daughter-in-law. The call came in about the usual time; Roger took it. It was not his wife.

"Captain Stone? Turner, sir—Charlie Turner. I'm the third engineer. Your wife asked me to phone you."

"What's the matter? She busy?"

"Quite busy."

"Tell her to call me as soon as she's free. I'll wait by the board."

"I'm afraid that's no good, sir. She was quite specific that she would not be calling you today. She won't have time."

"Fiddlesticks! It will only take her thirty seconds. In a big ship like yours you can hook her in wherever she is."

The man sounded embarrassed. "I'm sorry, sir. Dr. Stone gave strict orders not to be disturbed."

"But confound it, I—"

"I'm very sorry, sir. Good-by." He left him sputtering into a dead circuit.

Roger Stone remained quiet for several moments, then turned a stricken face to his mother. "She's caught it."

Hazel answered quietly, "Don't jump to conclusions, Son." But in her own heart she had already reached the same conclusion. Edith Stone had contracted the disease she had gone to treat.

The same barren stall was given Roger Stone on the following day; by the third day they gave up the pretense. Dr. Stone was ill, but her husband was not to worry. She had already, before she gave into it herself, progressed far enough in standardizing a treatment that all the new cases—hers among them—were doing nicely. So they said.

No, they would not arrange a circuit to her bed. No, he could not talk to Captain Vandenbergh; the Captain was still too ill.

"I'm coming over!" Roger Stone shouted.

Turner hesitated. "That's up to you, Captain. But if you do, we'll have to quarantine you here. Dr. Stone's written orders."

Roger Stone switched off. He knew that that settled it; in matters medical Edith was a Roman judge—and he could not abandon his own ship, his family, to get to Mars by themselves. One frail old woman, two cocksure half-trained student pilots—no, he had to take his ship in.

They sweated it out. The cooking got worse, when anyone bothered to cook. It was seven endless, Earth-standard days later when the daily call was answered by, "Roger—hello, darling!"

"Edith! Are you all right?"

"Getting that way."

"What's your temperature?"

"Now, darling, I won't have you quack-doctoring me. My temperature is satisfactory, as is the rest of my physical being. I've lost a little weight, but I could stand to—don't you think?"

"No, I don't. Listen—you come home! You hear me?"

"Roger dearest! I can't and that's settled. This entire ship is under quarantine. But how is the rest of my family?"

"Oh, shucks, fine, fine! We're all in the pink!"

"Stay that way. I'll call you tomorrow. Bye, dear."

Dinner that night was a celebration. Hazel cut her thumb again, but not even she cared.

The daily calls, no longer a nagging worry but a

pleasure, continued. It was a week later that Dr. Stone concluded by saying, "Hold on, dear. A friend of yours wants to speak with you."

"Okay, darling. Love and stuff—good-by."

"Roger Dodger?" came a bass voice.

"Van! You squareheaded bay window! I knew you were too mean to die."

"Alive and kicking, thanks to your wonderful wife. But no longer with a bay window; I haven't had time to regrow it yet."

"You will."

"No doubt. But I was asking the good doctor about something and she couldn't give me much data. Your department. Rog, how did this speed run leave you for single-H? Could you use some go-juice?"

Captain Stone considered it. "Have you any surplus, Captain?"

"A little. Not much for this wagon, but it might be quite a lot for a kiddie cart like yours."

"We had to jettison, did you know?"

"I know—and I'm sorry. I'll see that a claim is pushed through promptly. I'd advance it myself, Captain, if alimony on three planets left me anything to advance."

"Maybe it won't be necessary." He explained about the radar reflector. "If we could nudge back into the old groove we just might get together with our belongings."

Vandenbergh chuckled. "I want to meet those kids of yours again; they appear to have grown up a bit in the last seven years."

"Don't. They'll steal your bridgework. Now about this single-H: how much can you spare?"

"Enough, enough, I'm sure. This caper is worth trying, just for the sport. I'm sure it has never been done before. Never."

The two ships, perfectly matched to eye and almost so by instrument, nevertheless had drifted a couple of miles apart while the epidemic in the liner raged and died out. The undetectable gravitational attraction between them gave them mutual escape velocity much less than their tiny residual relative motion. Up to now nothing had been done about it since they were still in the easiest of phone range. But now it was necessary to pump reactive mass from one to the other.

Roger Stone threw a weight fastened to a light messenger line as straight and as far as he could heave. By the time it was slowed to a crawl by the drag of the line a crewman from the *War God* came out after it on his suit jet. In due course the messenger line brought over a heavier line which was fastened to the smaller ship. Hand power alone took a strain on the line. While the mass of *Rolling Stone* was enormous by human muscle standards, the vector involved was too small to handle by jet and friction was nil. In warping in a spaceship the lack of brakes is a consideration more important than power, as numerous dents to ships and space stations testify.

As a result of that gentle tug, two and a half days later the ships were close enough to permit a fuel hose to be connected between them. Roger and Hazel touched the hose only with wrench and space-suit gauntlet, not enough contact to affect the quarantine even by Dr. Stone's standards. Twenty minutes later even that connection was broken and the *Stone* had a fresh supply of jet juice.

And not too soon. Mars was a ruddy gibbous moon, bulging ever bigger in the sky; it was time to prepare to maneuver.

"There it is!" Pollux was standing watch on the radar screen; his yelp brought his grandmother floating over.

"More likely a flock of geese," she commented. "Where?"

"Right there. Can't you see it?"

Hazel grudgingly conceded that the blip might be real. The next several hours were spent in measuring distance, bearing, and relative motion by radar and doppler and in calculating the cheapest maneuver to let them match with the errant bicycles, baggage, and books. Roger Stone took it as easily as he could, being hurried somewhat by the growing nearness of Mars. He finally settled them almost dead in space relative to the floating junk pile, with a slight drift which would bring them within three hundred yards of the mass—so he calculated—at closest approach a few hours hence.

They spent the waiting time figuring the maneuvers to rendezvous with Mars. The *Rolling Stone* would not, of course, land on Mars but at the port on Phobos. First they must assume an almost circular ellipse around Mars matching with Phobos, then as a final maneuver they must settle the ship on the tiny moon—simple maneuvers made fussy by one thing only; Phobos has a period of about ten hours; the *Stone* would have to arrive not only at the right place with the right speed and direction, but also at the right time. After the bicycles were taken aboard the ship would have to be nursed along while still fairly far out if she were to fall to an exact rendezvous.

Everybody worked on it but Buster, Meade working under Hazel's tutelage. Pollux continued to check by radar their approach to their cargo. Roger Stone had run through and discarded two trial solutions and was roughing out another which, at last, seemed to be making sense when Pollux announced that his latest angulation of the radar data showed that they were nearly as close as they would get.

His father unstrapped himself and floated to a port.

"Where is it? Good heavens, we're practically sitting on it. Let's get busy, boys."

"I'm coming, too," announced Hazel.

"Me, too!" agreed Lowell.

Meade reached out and snagged him. "That's what you think, Buster. You and Sis are going to play a wonderful game called, 'What's for dinner?' Have fun, folks." She headed aft, towing the infant against his opposition.

Outside the bicycles looked considerably farther away. Cas glanced at the mass and said, "Maybe I ought to go across on my suit jet, Dad? It would save time."

"I strongly doubt it. Try the heaving line, Pol."

Pollux snapped the light messenger line to a padeye. Near the weighted end had been fastened a half a dozen large hooks fashioned of 6-gauge wire. His first heave seemed to be strong enough but it missed the cluster by a considerable margin.

"Let me have it, Pol," Castor demanded.

"Let him be," ordered their father. "So help me, this is the last time I'm going into space without a proper line-throwing gun. Make note of that, Cas. Put it on the shopping list when we go inside."

"Aye aye, sir."

The second throw was seen to hit the mass, but when Pol heaved in the line came away, the hooks having failed to catch. He tried again. This time the floating line came taut.

"Easy, now!" his father cautioned. "We don't want a bunch of bikes in our lap. There—'vast heaving. She's started." They waited.

Castor became impatient and suggested that they give the line another tug. His father shook his head. Hazel added, "I saw a green hand at the space station try to hurry a load that way. Steel plate, it was."

"What happened?"

"He had started it with a pull; he thought he could stop it with a shove. They had to amputate both legs but they saved his life." Castor shut up.

A few minutes later the disorderly mass touched down, bending a handlebar of one bike that got pinched but with no other damage. The twins and Hazel swarmed over the mass, working free on their safety lines and clicking on with their boots only to pass bicycles into the hold, where Roger Stone stowed them according to his careful mass distribution schedule.

Presently Pollux came across Castor's "Not for Salvage" warning. "Hey, Cas! Here's your notice."

"It's no good now." Nevertheless he accepted it and glanced at it. Then his eyes snapped wider.

An endorsement had been added at the bottom:

"Sez you!
    "The Galactic Overlord."

Captain Stone came out to investigate the delay, took the paper and read it. He looked at his mother. "Hazel!"

"Me? Why, I've been right here in plain sight the whole time. How could I have done it?"

Stone crumpled the paper. "I do not believe in ghosts, inside straights, nor 'Galactic Overlords.' "

If Hazel did it, no one saw her and she never admitted it. She persisted in the theory that the Galactic Overlord wasn't really dead after all. To prove it, she revived him in her next episode.

X PHOBOS PORT

MARS HAS TWO READY-MADE space stations, her two tiny, close-in moons—Phobos and Deimos, the dogs of the War God, Fear and Panic. Deimos is a jagged, ragged mass of rock; a skipper would be hard put to find a place to put down a ship. Phobos was almost spherical and fairly smooth as we found her; atomic power has manicured her into one big landing field all around her equator—a tidying-up that may have been over-hasty; by one very plausible theory the Martian ancients used her themselves as a space station. The proof, if such there be, may lie buried under the slag of Phobos port.

The *Rolling Stone* slid inside the orbit of Deimos, blasted as she approached the orbit of Phobos and was matched in with Phobos, following an almost identical orbit around Mars only a scant five miles from that moon. She was falling now, falling *around* Mars but falling *toward* Phobos, for no vector had been included as yet to prevent that. The fall could not be described as a headlong plunge; at this distance, one radius of Phobos, the moon attracted the tiny mass of the spaceship with a force of less than three ten-thousandths of one Earth-surface gravity. Captain Stone had ample time in which to calculate a vector which would let him land; it would take the better part of an hour for the *Stone* to sink to the surface of the satellite.

However he had chosen to do it the easy way, through outside help. The jet of the *Rolling Stone*, capable of blasting at six gravities, was almost too much of a tool for the thin gravity field of a ten-mile rock—like swatting a fly with a pile-driver. A few minutes after they had ceased blasting, a small scooter rocket up from Phobos matched with them and anchored to their airlock.

The spacesuited figure who swam in removed his helmet and said, "Permission to board, sir? Jason Thomas, port pilot—you asked for pilot-and-tow?"

"That's right, Captain Thomas."

"Just call me Jay. Got your mass schedule ready?"

Roger Stone gave it to him; he looked it over while they looked him over. Meade thought privately that he looked more like a bookkeeper than a dashing spaceman—certainly nothing like the characters in Hazel's show. Lowell stared at him gravely and said, "Are you a Martian, Mister?"

The port pilot answered him with equal gravity. "Sort of, son."

"Then where's your other leg?"

Thomas looked startled, but recovered. "I guess I'm a cut-rate Martian."

Lowell seemed doubtful but did not pursue the point. The port official returned the schedule and said, "Okay, Captain. Where are your outside control-circuit jacks?"

"Just forward of the lock. The inner terminals are here on the board."

"Be a few minutes." He went back outside, moving very rapidly. He was back inside in less than ten minutes.

"That's all the time it took you to mount auxiliary rockets?" Roger Stone asked incredulously.

"Done it a good many times. Gets to be a routine. Besides, I've got good boys working with me." Quickly he plugged a small portable control board to the jacks pointed out to him earlier, and tested his controls. "All set." He glanced at the radar screen. "Nothing to do but loaf for a bit. You folks immigrating?"

"Not exactly. It's more of a pleasure trip."

"Now ain't that nice! Though it beats me what pleasure you expect to find on Mars." He glanced out the port where the reddish curve of Mars pushed up into the black.

"We'll do some sightseeing I expect."

"More to see in the State of Vermont than on this whole planet. I know." He looked around. "This your whole family?"

"All but my wife." Roger Stone explained the situation.

"Oh, yes! Read about it in the daily *War Cry*. They got the name of your ship wrong, though."

Hazel snorted in disgust. "Newspapers!"

"Yes, mum. I put the *War God* down just four hours ago. Berths 32 & 33. She's in quarantine, though." He pulled out a pipe. "You folks got static precipitation?"

"Yes," agreed Hazel. "Go ahead and smoke, young man."

"Thanks on both counts." He made almost a career of getting it lighted; Pollux began to wonder when he intended to figure his ballistic.

But Jason Thomas did not bother even to glance at the radar screen; instead he started a long and meandering story about his brother-in-law back Earthside. It seemed that this connection of his had tried to train a parrot to act as an alarm clock.

The twins knew nothing of parrots and cared less. Castor began to get worried. Was this moron going to crash the *Stone?* He began to doubt that Thomas was a pilot of any sort. The story ambled on and on. Thomas interrupted himself to say, "Better hang on, everybody. And somebody ought to hold the baby."

"I'm not a baby," Lowell protested.

"I wish I was one, youngster." His hand sought his control panel as Hazel gathered Lowell in. "But the joke of the whole thing was—" A deafening rumble shook the ship, a sound somehow more earsplitting than their own jet. It continued for seconds only; as it died Thomas continued triumphantly: "—the bird never did learn to tell time. Thanks, folks. The office'll bill you." He stood up with a catlike motion, slid across the floor without lifting his feet. "Glad to have met you. G'bye!"

They were down on Phobos.

Pollux got up from where he had sprawled on the deckplates—and bumped his head on the overhead. After that he tried to walk like Jason Thomas. He had weight, real weight, for the first time since Luna, but it arounted to only two ounces in his clothes. "I wonder how high I can jump here?" he said.

"Don't try it," Hazel advised. "Remember the escape velocity of this piece of real estate is only sixty-six feet a second."

"I don't think a man could jump that fast."

"There was Ole Gunderson. He dived right around Phobos—a free circular orbit thirty-five miles long. Took him eighty-five minutes. He'd have been traveling yet if they hadn't grabbed as he came back around."

"Yes, but wasn't he an Olympic jumper or something? And didn't he have to have a special rack or some such to take off from?"

"You wouldn't have to jump," Castor put in. "Sixty-six feet a second is forty-five miles an hour, so the circular speed comes out a bit more than thirty miles an hour. A man can run twenty miles an hour back home, easy. He could certainly get up to forty-five here."

Pollux shook his head. "No traction."

"Special spiked shoes—and maybe a tangent launching ramp for the last hundred yards—then *whoosh!* off the end and you're gone for good."

"Okay, you try it, Grandpa. I'll wave good-by to you."

Roger Stone whistled loudly. "Quiet, please! If you armchair athletes are quite through, I have an announcement to make."

"Do we go groundside now, Dad?"

"Not if you don't quit interrupting me. I'm going over to the *War God*. Anyone who wants to come along, or wishes to take a stroll outside may do so—just as long as you settle the custody of Buster among you. Wear your boots; I understand they have steel strip walkways for the benefit of transients."

Pollux was the first one suited up and into the lock, where he was surprised to find the rope ladder still rolled up. He wondered about Jason Thomas and decided that he must have jumped . . . a hundred-odd feet of drop wouldn't hurt a man's arches here. But when he opened the outer door he discovered that it was quite practical to walk straight down the side of the ship like a fly on a wall. He had heard of this but had not quite believed it, not on a *planet* . . . well, a moon.

The others followed him, Hazel carrying Lowell. Roger Stone stopped when they were down and looked around. "I could have sworn," he said with a puzzled air, "that I spotted the *War God* not very far east of us just before we landed."

"There is something sticking up over there," Castor said, pointing north. The object was a rounded dome swelling up above the extremely near horizon—a horizon only two hundred yards away for Castor's height of eye. The dome looked enormous but it grew rapidly smaller as they approached it and finally got it entirely above the horizon. The sharp curvature of the little globe played tricks on them; it was so small that if was possible to see that it was curved, but the habit of thinking of anything over the horizon as distant stayed with them.

Before they reached the dome they encountered one of the steel walking strips running across their path, and on it a man. He was spacesuited as they were and was carrying with ease a large coil of steel line, a hand-powered winch, and a ground anchor with big horns. Roger Stone stopped him. "Excuse me, friend, but could you tell me the way to the R.S. *War God?* Berths thirty-two and -three, I believe she is."

"Off east there. Just follow this strip about five miles; you'll raise her. Say, are you from the *Rolling Stone?*"

"Yes. I'm her master. My name's Stone, too."

"Glad to know you, Captain. I'm just on my way out to respot your ship. You'll find her in berth thirteen, west of here when you come back."

The twins looked curiously at the equipment he was carrying. "Just with that?" asked Castor, thinking of the ticklish problem it had been to move the *Stone* on Luna.

"Did you leave your gyros running?" asked the port jockey.

"Yes," answered Captain Stone.

"I won't have any trouble. See you around." He headed out to the ship. The family party turned east along the strip; the traction afforded by their boot magnets against steel made much easier walking. Hazel put Lowell down and let him run.

They were walking toward Mars, a great arc of which filled much of the eastern horizon. The planet rose appreciably as they progressed; like Earth in the Lunar sky Mars never rose nor set for any particular point of the satellite's surface—but they were moving over the curve of Phobos so rapidly that their own walking made it rise. About a mile farther along Meade spotted the bow of the *War God* silhouetted against the orange-red face of Mars. They hurried, but it was another three miles before they had her in sight down to her fins.

At last they reached her—to find a temporary barrier of line and posts around her and signs prominently displayed: "WARNING!—QUARANTINE—no entrance by order of Phobos Port Authority."

"I can't read," said Hazel.

Roger Stone pondered it. "The rest of you stay here, or go for a walk—whatever you please. I'm going in. Mind you stay off the field proper."

"Shucks," answered Hazel, "there's plenty of time to see a ship coming in and run for it, the way they float in here. That's all the residents do. But don't you want me to come with you, boy?"

"No, it's my pidgin." He left them at the barrier, went toward the liner. They waited. Hazel passed the time by taking a throat lozenge from her gun and popping it in through her mouth valve; she gave one to Lowell. Presently they saw Roger walk up the side of the ship to a view port. He stayed there quite a while, then walked down again.

When he got back to them his face was stormy. Hazel said, "No go, I take it?"

"None at all. Oh, I saw Van and he rapped out some irrelevant insults. But he did let me see Edith—through the port."

"How did she look?"

"Wonderful, just wonderful! A little bit thinner perhaps, but not much. She blew a kiss for all of you." He paused and frowned. "But I can't get in and I can't get her out."

"You can't blame Van," Hazel pointed out. "It would mean his ticket."

"I'm not blaming anybody! I'm just mad, that's all."

"Well, what next?"

He thought about it. "The rest of you do what you like for the next hour or so. I'm going to the administration building—it's that dome back there. I'll meet you all at the ship—berth thirteen."

The twins elected to walk on east while Meade and Hazel returned at once to the ship—Buster was getting restless. The boys wanted a really good look at Mars. They had watched it through the *Stone*'s ports, of course, on the approach—but this was different . . . more real, somehow—not framed like a television shot. Three more miles brought all of it in sight, or all of it that was illuminated, for the planet was in half phase to them, the Sun being at that point almost overhead.

They studied the ruddy orange deserts, the olive green fertile stretches, the canals stretching straight as truth across her flat landscape. The south polar cap was tipped slightly toward them; it had almost disappeared. Facing them was the great arrowhead of Syrtis Major.

They agreed that it was beautiful, almost as beautiful as Luna—more beautiful perhaps than Earth in spite of Earth's spectacular and always changing cloud displays. But after a while they grew bored with it and headed back to the ship.

They found berth thirteen without trouble and walked up into the ship. Meade had dinner ready; Hazel was playing with Buster. Their father came in just as they were ready to eat. "You," announced Hazel, "looked as if you had bribed a chairwarmer."

"Not quite." He hesitated, then said, "I'm going into quarantine with Edith. I'll come out when she does."

"But Daddy—" protested Meade.

"I'm not through. While I'm gone Hazel takes command. She is also head of this family."

"I always have been," Hazel said smugly.

"Please, Mother. Boys, if she finds it necessary to break your arms, please be advised that the action is authorized in advance. You understand me?"

"Yes, sir."—"Aye aye, sir."

"Good. I'm going to pack now and leave."

"But Daddy!" Meade objected, almost in tears, "aren't you even going to wait for dinner?"

He stopped and smiled. "Yes, sugar pie. You are getting to be a good cook, did you know?"

Castor glanced at Pollux, then said, "Uh, Dad, let me get this straight. We are simply to wait here in the ship—on this under-sized medicine ball—until you and Mother get out of hock?"

"Why, yes—no, that isn't really necessary. I simply hadn't thought about it. If Hazel is willing, you can close down the ship and go down to Mars. Phone us your address and we'll join you there. Yes, I guess that's the best scheme."

The twins sighed with relief.

"*War God*, commanding officer speaking. Captain, can you—"

"Just a moment. This does not sound like Captain Vandenbergh."

"It isn't. This is Rowley, Second Officer. I—"

"I understood that your captain wanted me, officially. Let me speak with him."

"I'm trying to explain, Captain." The officer sounded strained and irritable. "I *am* the commanding officer. Both Captain Vandenbergh and Mr. O'Flynn are on the binnacle list."

"Eh? Sorry. Nothing serious, I hope?"

"I'm afraid it is, sir. Thirty-seven cases on the sick list this morning—and four deaths."

"Great Scott, man! What is it?"

"I don't know, sir."

"Well, what does your medical officer *say* it is?"

"That's it, sir. The Surgeon died during the mid-watch."

"Oh—"

"Captain, can you possibly match with us? Do you have enough maneuvering margin?"

"What? Why?"

"You have a medical officer aboard. Haven't you?"

"Huh? But she's my wife!"

"She's an M.D., is she not?"

Roger Stone remained silent for a long moment. Then he said, "I'll call you back shortly, sir."

It was a top level conference, limited to Captain Stone, Dr. Stone, and Hazel. First, Dr. Stone insisted on calling the *War God* and getting a full report on symptoms and progress of the disease. When she switched off her husband said, "Well, Edith, what is it?"

"I don't know. I'll have to see it."

"Now, see here, I'm not going to have you risking—"

"I'm a doctor, Roger."

"You're not in practice, not now. And you are the mother of a family. It's quite out of the ques—"

"I am a doctor, Roger."

He sighed heavily. "Yes, dear."

"The only thing to be determined is whether or not you can match in with the *War God*. Have you two reached an answer?"

"We'll start computing."

"I'm going aft and check over my supplies." She frowned. "I didn't expect to have to cope with an epidemic."

When she was gone Roger turned his face, twisted with indecision, to Hazel. "What do you think, Mother?"

"Son, you don't stand a chance. She takes her oath seriously. You've known that a long time."

"*I* haven't taken the Hippocratic oath! If I won't move the ship, there's nothing she can do about it."

"You're not a doctor, true. But you're a master in space. I guess the 'succor & rescue' rule might apply."

"The devil with rules! This is *Edith*."

"Well," Hazel said slowly, "I guess I might stack the Stone family up against the welfare of the entire human race in a pinch myself. But I can't decide it for you."

"I won't let her do it! It's not *me*. There's Buster—he's no more than a baby still; he needs his mother."

"Yes, he does."

"That settles it. I'm going aft and tell her."

"Wait a minute! If that's your decision, Captain, you won't mind me saying that's the wrong way to do it."

"Eh?"

"The only way you'll get it past your wife is to get on that computer and come out with the answer you're looking for . . . an answer that says it's physically im-

XI "WELCOME TO MARS!"

ROGER STONE PROMPTLY CAUGHT the epidemic disease and had to be nursed through it—and thereby extended the quarantine time. It gave the twins that much more time in which to exercise their talent for trouble. The truncated family went from Phobos down to Marsport by shuttle—not the sort of shuttle operating between Pikes Peak and Earth's station, but little glider rockets hardly more powerful than the ancient German war rockets. Mars' circular-orbit speed is only a trifle over two miles per second.

Nevertheless the fares were high . . . and so were freight charges. The twins had unloaded their cargo, moved it to the freight lots between the customs shed and the administration building, and arranged for it to follow them down, all before they boarded the shuttle. They had been horrified when they were presented with the bill—payable in advance. It had come to more than the amount they had paid their father for the added ship's costs of boosting the bicycles all the way to Mars.

Castor was still computing their costs and possible profits as the five Stones were strapping down for the trip down to Marsport. "Pol," he said fretfully, "we'd better by a darn sight get a good price for those bikes."

"We will, Grandpa, we will. They're good bikes."

The shuttle swooped to a landing on the Grand Canal and was towed into a slip, rocking gently the while. The twins were glad to climb out; they had never before been in a water-borne vehicle and it seemed to them an undependable if not outright dan-

145

gerous mode of travel. The little ship was unsealed with a soft sigh and they were breathing the air of Mars. It was thin but the pressure was not noticeably lower than that they had maintained in the *Rolling Stone*—a generation of the atmosphere project had made skin suits and respirators unnecessary. It was not cold; the Sun was right at the zenith.

Meade sniffed as she climbed to the dock. "What's the funny smell, Hazel?"

"Fresh air. Odd stuff, isn't it? Come on, Lowell." They all went inside the Hall of Welcome, that being the only exit from the dock. Hazel looked around, spotted a desk marked "Visas" and headed for it. "Come on, kids. Let's stick together."

The clerk looked over their papers as if he had never seen anything of the sort before and didn't want to now. "You had your physical examinations at Phobos port?" he said doubtfully.

"See for yourself. They're all endorsed."

"Well . . . you don't have your property declaration filled out for immigration."

"We're not immigrants; we're visitors."

"Why didn't you say so? You haven't posted a bond; all terrestrial citizens have to post bonds."

Pollux looked at Castor and shook his head. Hazel counted up to ten and replied, "We're not terrestrials; we're citizens of Luna Free State—and entitled to full reciprocity under the treaty of '07. Look it up and see."

"Oh." The clerk looked baffled and endorsed and stamped their papers. He stuck them in the stat machine, then handed them back. "That'll be five pounds."

"Five pounds?"

"Pounds Martian, of course. If you apply for citizenship it's returnable."

Hazel counted it out. Pollux converted the figure into System credit in his head and swore under his breath; he was beginning to think that Mars was the Land of the Fee. The clerk recounted the money, then reached for a pile of pamphlets, handed them each one. "Welcome to Mars," he said, smiling frigidly. "I know you'll like it here."

"I was beginning to wonder," Hazel answered, accepting a pamphlet.

"Eh?"

"Never mind. Thank you."

They turned away. Castor glanced at his pamphlet; it was titled:

WELCOME TO MARS!!!

Compliments
of the Marsport
Chamber of Commerce &
Booster Club

He skimmed the table of contents: What to See—Where to Eat—And Now to Sleep—"When in Rome—"—In Ancient Times—Souvenirs? Of course!—Business Opportunities—Facts & Figures about Marsport, Fastest Growing City in the System.

The inside, he found, contained more advertising space than copy. None of the pictures were stereo. Still, it was free; he stuck it in his pouch.

They had not gotten more than ten steps away when the clerk suddenly called out, "Hey! Madam! Just a moment, please—come back!"

Hazel turned around and advanced on him, her mouth set grimly. "What's biting you, bub?"

He pointed to her holster. "That gun. You can't wear that—not in the city limits."

"I can't, eh?" She drew it, opened the charge chamber, and offered it to him with a sudden grin. "Have a cough drop?"

A very pleasant lady at the Traveler's Aid desk, after determining that they really did not want to rent an ancient Martian tower believed to be at least a million years old but sealed and airconditioned nevertheless, made out for them a list of housekeeping apartments for rent. Hazel had vetoed going to any of the tourist hotels even for one night, after telephoning three and getting their rates. They tramped through a large part of the city, searching. There was no public transit system; many of the inhabitants used powered roller skates, most of them walked. The city was laid out in an oblong checkerboard with the main streets parallel to the canal. Except for a few remaining pressurized domes in "Old Town" the buildings were all one-story prefabricated boxlike structures without eaves or windows, all of depressing monotony.

The first apartment turned out to be two little stalls in the back of a private home—share refresher with family. The second was large enough but was in sniffing range of a large plastics plant; one of its exhalations seemed to be butyl mercaptan though Hazel insisted it put her more in mind of a dead goat. The third—but none of them approached the standard of comfort they had enjoyed on the Moon, nor even that of the *Rolling Stone*.

Hazel came out of the last one they had looked at, jumped back suddenly to keep from being run over by a delivery boy pulling a large hand truck, caught her breath and said, "What'll it be, children? Pitch a tent, or go back up to the *Stone?*"

Pollux protested, "But we can't do that. We've got to sell our bicycles."

"Shut up, Junior," his brother told him. "Hazel, I thought there was one more? 'Casa' something?"

"Casa Mañana Apartments, way out south along the

canal—and likely no better than the rest. Okay, troops, mush on!"

The buildings thinned out and they saw some of the heliotropic Martian vegetation, spreading greedy hands to the Sun. Lowell began to complain at the walk. "Carry me, Grandma Hazel!"

"Nothing doing, pet," she said emphatically, "your legs are younger than mine."

Meade stopped. "My feet hurt, too."

"Nonsense! This is just a shade over one-third gravity."

"Maybe so, but it's twice what it is back home and we've been in free fall for half a year and more. Is it much farther?"

"Sissy!"

The twins' feet hurt, too, but they would not admit it. They alternated taking Buster piggy-back the rest of the way. Casa Mañana turned out to be quite new and, by their suddenly altered standards, acceptable. The walls were of compacted sand, doubled against the bitter nights; the roof was of sheet metal sandwich with glass-wool core for insulation. It was a long, low building which made Hazel think of chicken coops but she kept the thought to herself. It had no windows but there were sufficient glow tubes and passable air ducting.

The apartment which the owner and manager showed to them consisted of two tiny cubicles, a refresher, and a general room. Hazel looked them over. "Mr. d'Avri, don't you have something a bit larger?"

"Well, yes, ma'am, I do—but I hate to rent larger ones to such a small family with the tourist season just opening up. I'll bring in a cot for the youngster."

She explained that two more adults would be coming. He considered this. "You don't know how long the *War God* will be quarantined?"

"Not the slightest."

"Then why don't we play that hand after it's dealt? We'll accommodate you somehow; that's a promise."

Hazel decided to close the deal; her feet were killing her. "How much?"

"Four hundred and fifty a month—four and a quarter if you take a lease for the whole season."

At first Hazel was too surprised to protest. She had not inquired rents at the other places since she had not considered renting them. "Pounds or credits?" she said feebly.

"Why, pounds, of course."

"See here, I don't want to buy this du—this place. I just want to use it for a while."

Mr. d'Avril looked hurt. "You needn't do either one, ma'am. With ships arriving every day now I'll have my pick of tenants. My prices are considered very reasonable. The Property Owners' Association has tried to get me to up 'em—and that's a fact."

Hazel dug into her memory to recall how to compare a hotel price with a monthly rental—add a zero to the daily rate; that was it. Why, the man must be telling the truth!—if the hotel rates she had gotten were any guide. She shook her head. "I'm just a country girl, Mr. d'Avril. How much did this place cost to build?"

Again he looked hurt. "You're not looking at it properly, ma'am. Every so often we have a big load of tourists dumped on us. They stay awhile, then they go away and we have no rent coming in at all. And you'd be surprised how these cold nights nibble away at a house. We can't build the way the Martians could."

Hazel gave up. "Is that season discount you mentioned good from now to Venus departure?"

"Sorry, ma'am. It has to be the whole season." The next favorable time to shape an orbit for Venus was ninety-six Earth-standard days away—ninety-four Mars days—whereas the "whole season" ran for the next fifteen months, more than half a Martian year before Earth and Mars would again be in a position to permit a minimum-fuel orbit.

"We'll take it by the month. May I borrow your stylus? I don't have that much cash on me."

Hazel felt better after dinner. The Sun was down and the night would soon be too bitter for any human not in a heated suit, but inside Casa Mañana it was cozy, even though cramped. Mr. d'Avril, for an extra charge only mildly extortionate, had consented to plug in television for them and Hazel was enjoying for the first time in months one of her own shows. She noted that they had rewritten it in New York as usual, and, again as usual, she found the changes no improvement. But she could recognize some of the dialogue and most of the story line.

That Galactic Overlord—he was a baddy, he was! Maybe she should kill him off again.

They could try to find a cheaper place tomorrow. At least as long as the show kept up its audience rating the family wouldn't starve, but she hated to think of Roger's face when he heard what rent he was paying. Mars! All right to visit, maybe, but no place to live. She frowned.

The twins were whispering in their own cubicle about some involved financial dealing; Meade was knitting quietly and watching the screen. She caught Hazel's expression. "What were you thinking about, Grandmother?"

"*I* know what she's thinking about!" announced Lowell."

"If you do, keep it to yourself. Nothing much, Meade —that pipsqueak clerk. Imagine the nerve of him, saying I couldn't pack a gun!"

XII FREE ENTERPRISE

THE TWINS STARTED OUT to storm the marts of trade next morning after breakfast. Hazel cautioned them, "Be back in time for dinner. And try not to commit any capital crimes."

"What are they here?"

"Um, let me see. Abandonment without shelter . . . pollution of the water supply . . . violation of treaty regulations with the natives—I think that's about all."

"Murder?"

"Killing is largely a civil matter here—but they stick you for the prospective earnings of your victim for whatever his life expectancy was. Expensive. Very expensive, if the prices we've run into are any guide. Probably leave you indentured the rest of your life."

"Hmm— We'll be careful. Take note of that, Pol. Don't kill anybody."

"*You* take note of it. You're the one with the bad temper."

"Back sharp at six, boys. Have you adjusted your watches?"

"Pol slowed his down; I'm leaving mine on Greenwich rate."

"Sensible."

"Pol!" put in Lowell. "Cas! Take me along!"

"Can't do it, sprout. Business."

"Take me! I want to see a Martian. Grandma Hazel, *when* am I going to see a Martian?"

She hesitated. Ever since an unfortunate but instructive incident forty years earlier a prime purpose of the planetary government had been to keep humans as far away from the true Martians as possible—tourists most especially. Lowell had less chance of getting his wish than a European child visiting Manhattan would have of seeing an American Indian. "Well, Lowell, it's like this—"

The twins left hastily, not wishing to be drawn into what was sure to be a fruitless debate.

They soon found the street catering to the needs of prospectors. They picked a medium-sized shop displaying the sign of Angelo & Sons, Ltd., General Outfitters, which promised "Bedrolls, Geiger Counters, Sand Cycles, Assaying Service, Black-Light Lamps, Firearms, Hardware-Ironmongery—Ask for It; We've Got It or Can Get it."

Inside they found a single shopkeeper leaning against a counter while picking his teeth and playing with something that moved on the counter top. Pollux glanced curiously at it; aside from the fact that it was covered with fur and seemed to be roughly circular, he could not make out what it was. Some sort of Martian dingus probably. He would investigate later—business first.

The shopkeeper straightened up and remarked with professional cheer, "Good morning, gentlemen. Welcome to Mars."

"How did you know?" asked Castor.

"Know what?"

"That we had just gotten here."

"Eh? That's hard to say. You've still got some free fall in your walk and—oh, I don't know. Little things that add up automatically. You get to know."

Pollux shot Castor a glance of warning; Castor nodded. This man's ancestors, he realized subconsciously, had plied the Mediterranean, sizing up customers, buying cheap and selling dear. "You're Mr. Angelo?"

"I'm Tony Angelo. Which one did you want?"

"Uh, no one in particular, Mr. Angelo. We were just looking around."

"Help yourselves. Looking for souvenirs?"

"Well, maybe."

"How about this?" Mr. Angelo reached into a box behind him and pulled out a battered face mask. "A sandstorm mask with the lenses pitted by the sands of Mars. You can hang it up in your parlor and tell a real thriller about how it got that way and how lucky you are to be alive. It won't add much to your baggage weight allowance and I can let you have it cheap—I'd have to replace the lenses before I could sell it to the trade."

Pollux was beginning to prowl the stock, edging toward the bicycles; Castor decided that he should keep Mr. Angelo engaged while his brother picked up a few facts. "Well, I don't know," he replied. "I wouldn't want to tell a string of lies about it."

"Not lies, just creative storytelling. After all, it could have happened—it did happen to the chap that wore it; I know him. But never mind." He put the mask back. "I've got some honest-to-goodness Martian gems, only K'Raath Himself knows how old—but they are very expensive. And I've got some others that can't be told from the real ones except in a laboratory under polarized light; *they* come from New Jersey and aren't expensive at all. What's your pleasure?"

"Well, I don't know," Castor repeated. "Say, Mr. Angelo, what is this? At first I thought it was a fur cap; now I see it's alive." Castor pointed to the furry heap on the counter. It was slowly slithering toward the edge.

The shopkeeper reached out and headed it back to the middle. "That? That's a 'flat cat.' "

" 'Flat cat?' "

"It has a Latin name but I never bothered to learn

it." Angelo tickled it with a forefinger; it began to purr like a high-pitched buzzer. It had no discernible features, being merely a pie-shaped mass of sleek red fur a little darker than Castor's own hair. "They're affectionate little things and many of the sand rats keep them for pets—a man has to have someone to talk to when he's out prospecting and a flat cat is better than a wife because it can't talk back. It just purrs and snuggles up to you. Pick it up."

Castor did so, trying not to seem gingerly about it. The flat cat promptly plastered itself to Castor's shirt, fattened its shape a little to fit better the crook of the boy's arm, and changed his purr to a low throbbing which Castor could feel vibrate in his chest. He looked down and three beady little eyes stared trustfully back up at him, then closed and disappeared completely. A little sigh interrupted the purrs and the creature snuggled closer.

Castor chuckled. "It *is* like a cat, isn't it?"

"Except that it doesn't scratch. Want to buy it?"

Castor hesitated. He found himself thinking of Lowell's anxiety to see a "real Martian." Well, this was a "Martian," wasn't it? A sort of a Martian. "I wouldn't know how to take care of it."

"No trouble at all. In the first place they're cleanly little beasties—no problem that way. And they'll eat anything; they *love* garbage. Feed it every week or so and let it have all the water it will take every month or six weeks—it doesn't matter really; if it isn't fed or watered it just slows down until it is. Doesn't hurt it a bit. And you don't even have to see that it keeps warm. Let me show you." He reached out and took the flat cat back, jiggled it in his hand. It promptly curled up into a ball.

"See that? Like everything else on Mars, it can wrap itself up when the weather is bad. A real survivor type."

The shopkeeper started to mention another of its survival characteristics, then decided it had no bearing on the transaction. "How about it? I'll make you a good price."

Castor decided that Lowell would love it—and besides, it was a legitimate business expense, chargeable to good will. "How much?"

Angelo hesitated, trying to estimate what the traffic would bear, since a flat cat on Mars had roughly the cash value of still another kitten on a Missouri farm. Still, the boys must be rich or they wouldn't be here—just in and with spending money burning holes in their pockets, no doubt. Business had been terrible lately anyhow. "A pound and a half," he said firmly.

Castor was surprised at how reasonable the price was. "That seems like quite a lot," he said automatically.

Angelo shrugged. "It likes you. Suppose we say a pound?"

Castor was again surprised, this time at the speed and the size of the mark-down. "I don't know," he murmured.

"Well . . . ten per cent off for cash."

Out of the corner of his eye Castor could see that Pollux had finished inspecting the rack of bicycles and was coming back. He decided to clear the decks and establish that good will, if possible, before Pol got down to business. "Done." He fished out a pound note, received his change, and picked up the flat cat. "Come to papa, Fuzzy Britches." Fuzzy Britches came to papa, snuggled up and purred.

Pollux came back, stared at the junior Martian. "What in the world?"

"Meet the newest member of the family. We just bought a flat cat."

"We?" Pollux started to protest that it was no folly of

his, but caught the warning in Castor's eye in time. "Uh, Mr. Angelo, I don't see any prices marked?"

The shopkeeper nodded. "That's right. The sand rats like to haggle and we accommodate them. It comes to the same thing in the long run. We always settle at list; they know it and we know it, but it's part of their social life. A prospector doesn't get much."

"That Raleigh Special over there—what's the list on it?" Pollux had picked it because it looked very much like the sand cycle their father had delivered for them to Captain Vandenbergh when he had gone into quarantine.

"You want to buy that bike?"

Castor shook his head a sixteenth of an inch; Pollux answered, "Well, no, I was just pricing it. I couldn't take it Sunside, you know."

"Well, seeing that there are no regular customers around, I'll tell you. List is three hundred and seventy-five—and a bargain!"

"Whew! That seems high."

"A bargain. She's a real beauty. Try any of the other dealers."

"Mr. Angelo," Castor said carefully, "suppose I offered to sell you one just like it, not new but reconditioned as good as new and looking new, for just half that?"

"Eh? I'd probably say you were crazy."

"I mean it. I've got it to sell. You might as well have the benefit of the low price as one of your competitors. I'm not going to offer it retail; this is for dealers."

"Mmm . . . you didn't come in here to buy souvenirs, did you?"

"No, sir."

"If you had come to me with that proposition four months ago, and could have backed it up, I'd have jumped at it. Now . . . well, no."

"Why not? It's a good bike I'm offering you. A real bargain."

"I'm not disputing it." He reached out and stroked the flat cat. "Shucks, it can't hurt anything to tell you why. Come along."

He led them into the rear, past shelves crammed with merchandise, and on out behind the store. He waved a hand at stacks of merchandise that looked all too familiar. "See that? Second-hand bikes. That shed back there is stuffed with 'em; that's why I've got these stored in the open."

Castor tried to keep surprise and dismay out of his voice. "So you've got second-hand bikes," he said, "all beat-up and sand pitted. I've got second-hand bikes that look like new and will wear like new—and I can sell them cheaper than you can sell these, a lot cheaper. Don't you want to bid on them, at least?"

Angelo shook his head. "Brother, I admit that I didn't take you for a jobber. But I have bad news for you. You can't sell them to me; you can't sell them to my competitors; you can't sell them anywhere."

"Why not?"

"Because there aren't any retail customers."

"Huh?"

"Haven't you heard of the Halleujah Node? Didn't you notice I didn't have any customers? Three fourths of the sand rats on Mars are swarming into town—but they're not buying, leastwise not bicycles. They're stocking up for the Asteroids and kicking in together to charter ships. That's why I have used bikes; I had to take them back on chattel mortages—and that's why you can't sell bikes. Sorry—I'd like to do business with you."

The twins had heard of the Halleujah, all right—the news had reached them in space: a strike of both uranium and core metal out in the Asteroids. But they had given it only intellectual attention, the Asteroids no longer figuring into their plans.

"Two of my brothers have already gone," Angelo went on, "and I might give it a whirl myself if I weren't stuck with the store. But I'd close and reopen as strictly a tourist trap if I could unload my present stock. That's how bad things are."

They crept out into the street as soon as they could do so gracefully. Pollux looked at Castor. "Want to buy a bicycle, sucker?"

"Thanks, I've got one. Want to buy a flat cat?"

"Not likely. Say, let's go over to the receiving dock. If any tourists are coming in, we might find another sucker to unload that thing on. We might even show a small profit—on flat cats, that is."

"No, you don't. Fuzzy Britches is for Buster—that's settled. But let's go over anyway; our bikes might be down."

"Who cares?"

"I do. Even if we can't sell them, we can ride a couple of them. My feet hurt."

Their shipment was not yet down from Phobos but it was expected about an hour hence. They stopped in the Old Southern Dining Room & Soda Fountain across from the Hall of Welcome. There they nursed sodas, petted Fuzzy Britches, and considered their troubles. "I don't mind losing the money so much—" Castor started in.

"I do!"

"Well, so do I. But what really hurts is the way Dad will laugh when he finds out. And what he'll say."

"Not to mention Hazel."

"Yes, Hazel. Junior, we've just got to figure out some way of picking up some money before we have to tell them."

"With what? Our capital is gone. And Dad wouldn't let us touch any more of our money even if he were here—which he isn't."

"Then it has to be a way without capital."

"Not many. Not for real money."

"Hazel makes plenty credits without capital."

"You aren't suggesting that we write a television serial?" Pollux sounded almost shocked.

"Of course not. We don't have a customer for one. But there must be a way. Start thinking."

After a glum silence Pollux said, "Grandpa, did you notice that announcement in the Hall of Welcome of the Mars chess championship matches next month?"

"No. Why?"

"People bet on 'em here—same as race horses Earthside."

"I don't like bets. You can lose."

"Sometimes. But suppose we entered Buster?"

"Huh? Are you crazy? Enter him against the best players on Mars?"

"Why not? Hazel used to be Luna champion, but Buster beats her regularly."

"But you know why. He reads her mind."

"That's precisely what I am talking about."

Castor shook his head. "It wouldn't be honest, Junior."

"Since when did they pass a law against telepathy?"

"Anyhow, you don't know for certain that he does read her mind. And you don't know that he could read a stranger's mind. And it would take plenty cash to set up a good bet—which we haven't got. And besides, we might lose. No."

"Okay, okay, it was just a thought. You produce one."

Castor frowned. "I don't have one. Let's go back over and see if our bikes are in. If they are, let's treat ourselves to a day off and go sightseeing. We might as well get some use out of those bikes; they cost us enough." He stood up.

Pollux sat still and stared at his glass. Castor added, "Come on."

Pollux said, "Sit down, Grandpa. I think I'm getting an idea."

"Don't frighten it."

"Quiet." Presently Pollux said, "Grandpa, you and I have just arrived here. We want to go sightseeing—so we immediately think of our bikes. Why wouldn't tourists like to do the same thing—and pay for it?"

"Huh?" Castor thought about it. "There must be some catch in it—or somebody would have done it long before this."

"Not necessarily. It has only been the past few years that you could get a tourist visa to Mars; you came as a colonist or you didn't come at all. I'd guess that nobody has thought of shipping bikes to Mars for tourists. Bikes cost plenty and they have been imported just for prospectors—for *work*, because a sand rat could cover four or five times as much territory on a sand cycle as on foot. I'll bet nobody here has ever thought of them for pleasure."

"What do you want us to do? Paint a sign and then stand under it, shouting, 'Bicycles! Get your bicycle here! You can't see the sights of Mars without a bicycle.'"

Pollux thought it over. "We could do worse. But we would do better to try to sell somebody else on it, somebody who has the means to get it going. Shucks, we couldn't even rent a lot for our bike stand."

"There's the soft point in the whole deal. We tell somebody and what does he do? He doesn't buy our bikes; he goes to Tony Angelo and makes a deal with him to put Angelo's bikes to work, at a lower cost."

"Use your head, Grandpa. Angelo and the other dealers won't rent their new machines to tourists; they cost too much. And tourists won't rent that junk Angelo has in his back lot, they're in a holiday mood; they'll go for something new and shiny and cheerful. And for rental purposes, remember, our bikes aren't just practically new; they *are* new. Anybody who rents anything knows it has been used before; he's satisfied if it looks new."

Castor stood up again. "Okay, you've sold me. Now let's see if you can sell it to somebody else. Pick a victim."

"Sit down; what's your hurry? Our benefactor is probably right under this roof."

"Huh?"

"What's the first thing a tourist sees when he first comes out of the Hall of Welcome? The Old Southern Dining Room, that's what. The bike stand ought to be right out in front of this restaurant."

"Let's find the owner."

Joe Pappalopoulis was in the kitchen; he came out wiping his hands on his apron. "What's the matter, boys? You don't like your soda?"

"Oh, the sodas were swell! Look, Mr. Pappalopoulis, can you spare us a few minutes?"

"Call me 'Poppa'; you wear yourself out. Sure."

"Thanks. I'm Cas Stone; this is my brother Pol. We live on Luna and we came in with a load you might be interested in."

"You got a load of imported food? I don't use much. Just coffee and some flavors."

"No, no, not food. How would you like to add a new line that would fit right in with your restaurant business? Twice as much volume and only one overhead."

The owner took out a knife and began to pare his nails. "Keep talking."

Pollux took over, explained his scheme with infectious enthusiasm. Pappalopoulis looked up from time to time, said nothing. When Pollux seemed to be slowing down Castor took over; "Besides renting them by the hour, day, or week, you set up sightseeing tours and charge extra for those."

"The guides don't cost you any salary; you make 'em pay for the concession and then allow them a percentage of the guide fee."

"They rent their own bikes from you, too."

"No overhead; you've already got the best spot in town. You just arrange to be out in front every time a shuttle comes down and maybe pay one of your guides a commission on rentals he makes to watch the stand in between times."

"But the best deal is the long-term lease. A tourist uses a bike one day; you point out to him how cheap he can get it for the full time of his stay—and you get the full price of the bike back in one season. From then on you're operating on other people's money."

The restaurateur put his knife away and said, "Tony Angelo is a good businessman. Why don't I buy second-hand bikes from him—cheap?"

Castor took the plunge. "Go look at his bikes. Just look at them, sand pits and worn-out tires and all. Then we'll meet his price—with better bikes."

"Any price he names?"

"Any firm price, not a phony. If his price is really low, we'll buy his bikes ourselves." Pollux looked a warning but Castor ignored it. "We can undersell any legitimate price he can afford to make—with better merchandise. Let's go see his bikes."

Pappalopoulis stood up. "I've seen bikes in from the desert. We go see yours."

"They may not be down yet." But they were down.

Joe Poppa looked them over without expression, but the twins were very glad of the hours they had spent making them brave with paint, gaudy with stripes, polish and new decals.

Castor picked out three he knew to be in tiptop shape and said, "How about a ride? I'd like to do some sightseeing myself—free."

Pappalopoulis smiled for the first time. "Why not?"

They rode north along the canal clear to the power pile station, then back to the city, skirted it, and right down Clarke Boulevard to the Hall of Welcome and the Old Southern Dining Room. After they had dismounted and returned the vehicles to the pile, Castor signaled Pollux and waited silently.

The café owner said nothing for several moments. At last he said, "Nice ride, boys. Thanks."

"Don't mention it."

He stared at the heap of bikes. "How much?"

Castor named a price. Pappalopoulis shook his head sadly. "That's a lot of money."

Before Pollux could name a lower price Castor said, "Make it easy on yourself. We'd rather be cut in on the gravy but we thought you might prefer to own them yourselves. So let's make it a partnership; you run the business, we put up the bikes. Even split on the gross and you absorb the overhead. Fair enough?"

Pappalopoulis reached over and stroked the flat cat. "Partnerships make quarrels," he said thoughtfully.

"Have it your own way," Castor answered. "Five per cent for cash."

Pappalopoulis pulled out a roll that would have choked a medium-large Venerian sand hog. "I buy 'em."

The twins spent the afternoon exploring the city on foot and looking for presents for the rest of the family. When they started home their way led them back through the square between the receiving station and Poppa's restaurant. The sign now read:

THE OLD SOUTHERN DINING ROOM

AND

TOURIST BUREAU

Sodas   Souvenirs   Candy

Sightseeing Trips

BICYCLES RENTED

Guide Service

See the Ancient Martian Ruins!!!

Pollux looked at it. "He's a fast operator, all right. Maybe you should have insisted on a partnership."

"Don't be greedy. We turned a profit, didn't we?"

"I told you we would. Well, let's get Fuzzy Britches home to Buster."

XIII CAVEAT VENDOR

Fuzzy Britches was not an immediate success with Lowell. "Where's its legs?" he said darkly. "If it's a Martian, it ought to have three legs."

"Well," argued Castor, "some Martians don't have legs."

"Prove it!"

"This one doesn't. That proves it."

Meade picked Fuzzy Britches up; it immediately began to buzz—whereupon Lowell demanded to hold it. Meade passed it over. "I don't see," she remarked, "why anything as helpless as that would have such bright colors."

"Think again, honey lamb," advised Hazel. "Put that thing out on the desert sand and you would lose it at ten feet. Which might be a good idea."

"No!" answered Lowell.

" 'No' what, dear?"

"Don't you lose Fuzzy Britches. He's mine." The child left carrying the flat cat and cooing a lullaby to it. Fuzzy Britches might lack legs but it knew how to win friends; anyone who picked it up hated to put it down. There was something intensely satisfying about petting the furry thing. Hazel tried to analyze it but could not.

No one knew when the quarantine of the *War God* would be lifted. Therefore Meade was much surprised one morning to return to Casa Mañana and find her father in the general room. "Daddy!" she yelled, swarming over him. "When did you get down?"

"Just now."

"Mummy, too?"

"Yes. She's in the 'fresher."

Lowell stood in the doorway, watching them impassively. Roger Stone loosed himself from his daughter and said, "Good morning, Buster."

"Good morning, Daddy. This is Fuzzy Britches. He's a Martian. He's also a flat cat."

"Glad to know you, Fuzzy Britches. Did you say 'flat cat'?"

"Yes."

"Very well. But it looks more like a wig."

Dr. Stone entered, was subjected to the same treatment by Meade, then turned to Lowell. He permitted her to kiss him, then said, "Mama, this is Fuzzy Britches. Say hello to him."

"How do you do, Fuzzy Britches? Meade, where are your brothers? And your grandmother?"

Meade looked upset. "I was afraid you would get around to that. The twins are in jail again."

Roger Stone groaned. "Oh, no, not again! Edith, we should have stayed on Phobos."

"Yes, dear."

"Well, let's face it. What is the charge this time, Meade?"

"Fraud and conspiring to evade the customs duties."

"I feel better. The last time but one, you'll remember, it was experimenting with atomics inside the city limits and without license. But why aren't they out on bail? Or is there something worse you haven't told us?"

"No, it's just that the court has tied up their bank account and Hazel wouldn't get them bond. She said they were safer where they were."

"Good for Hazel!"

"Daddy, if we hurry we can get back downtown for the hearing. I'll tell you and Mummy about it on the way."

The "fraud" part of it came from Mr. Pappalopoulis; the rest of it came straight from the planetary government. Mars, being in a state of expanding economy, just beginning to be self-supporting and only recently of declared sovereignty, had a strongly selective tariff. Being forced to import much and having comparatively little to export which could not be had cheaper Earthside, all her economic statutes and regulations were bent toward relieving her chronic credit gap. Articles not produced on Mars but needed for her economy came in duty free; articles of luxury or pleasure carried very high rates; articles manufactured on Mars were completely protected by embargo against outside competition.

Bicycles were classed by the Import Commission as duty free since they were necessary to prospecting—but bicycles used for pleasure became "luxury items." The customs authorities had gotten around to noticing the final disposition of the cargo of the *Rolling Stone*. "Of course somebody put them up to it," continued Meade, "but Mr. Angelo swears he didn't do it and I believe him. He's nice."

"That's clear enough. What's the fraud angle?"

"Oh, that!" The bicycles had at once been impounded for unpaid duty penalties and costs whereupon their new owner had sworn an information charging fraud. "He's getting a civil suit, too, but I think Hazel has it under control. Mr. Poppa says he just wants his bicycles back; he's losing business. He's not mad at anybody."

"I would be," Roger Stone answered grimly. "I intend to skin those two boys with a dull knife. What makes Hazel think she can square Mr. Pappa-et-cetera? Just what, I'd like to know?"

"She got a temporary court order freeing the bicycles to Mr. Poppa pending the outcome of the hearing; she had to put up a delivery bond on the bicycles. So

Mr. Poppa dropped the fraud matter and is waiting on the civil suit to see if he's hurt."

"Hmm— My bank account feels a little better anyway. Well, dear, we might as well go down and get it over with. There doesn't seem to be anything here that a long check book can't cover."

"Yes, dear."

"Remind me to buy a pair of Oregon boots on the way home. Meade, how much is this tariff?"

"Forty per cent."

"Not too bad. They probably made more profit than that."

"But that's not all, Daddy. Forty per cent, plus another forty per cent penalty—plus confiscation of the bicycles."

"Plus two weeks in pillory, I hope?"

"Don't do anything hasty, Daddy. Hazel is arguing the case."

"Since when was she admitted to the bar?"

"I don't know, but it seems to be all right. She got that court order."

"Dear," said Dr. Stone, "shouldn't the boys have a regular lawyer? Your mother is a wonderful person, but she is sometimes just a bit impetuous."

"If you mean she's as crazy as a skew orbit, I agree with you. But I'm betting on Hazel anyhow. We'll let her have her turn at the board. It probably won't cost me much more."

"As you say, dear."

They slipped into the back of the courtroom, which appeared to be a church on some other days. Hazel was up front, talking to the judge. She saw them come in but did not appear to recognize them. The twins, looking very sober, were sitting together near the bench; they recognized their parents but took their cue from their grandmother.

"May it please the court," said Hazel, "I am a stranger here in a strange land. I am not skilled in your laws nor sophisticate in your customs. If I err, I pray the court to forgive me in advance and help me back to the proper path."

The judge leaned back and looked at her. "We were over all that earlier this morning."

"Sure, Judge, but it looks good in the record."

"Do you expect to get me reversed?"

"Oh, no! We'll settle the whole thing right here and now, I'd guess."

"I wouldn't venture to guess. I told you this morning that I would advise you as to the law, if need be. As to courtroom formalities, this is a frontier. I can remember the time when, if one of us became involved in a misadventure which caused public disapproval, the matter was settled by calling a town meeting and taking a show of hands—and I've no doubt that as much justice was dispensed that way as any other. Times have changed but I don't think you will find this court much bothered by etiquette. Proceed."

"Thanks, Judge. This young fellow here—" She hooked a thumb at the prosecutor's table. "—would have you believe that my boys cooked up a nefarious scheme to swindle the citizens of this nation out of their rightful and lawful taxes. I deny that. Then he asks you to believe that, having hatched this Machiavellian plot, they carried it through and got away with it, until the hand of justice, slow but sure, descended on them and grabbed them. That's a pack of nonsense, too."

"One moment. I thought you stipulated this morning to the alleged facts?"

"I admitted that my boys didn't pay duty on those bikes. I didn't admit anything else. They didn't pay duty because nobody asked them to pay."

"I see your point. You'll have to lay a foundation

for that and get it in by proper evidence later. I can see that this is going to be a little involved."

"It needn't be, if we'll all tell the truth and shame the devil." She paused and looked puzzled. "Warburton . . . Warburton . . ." she said slowly, "your name is Warburton, Judge? Any kinfolk on Luna?"

The judge squared his shoulders. "I'm a hereditary citizen of the Free State," he said proudly. "Oscar Warburton was my grandfather."

"That's it!" agreed Hazel. "It's been bothering me all morning—but the numbers didn't click into place until I noticed your profile just now. I knew your granddaddy well. I'm a Founding Father, too."

"How's that? There weren't any Stones on the roster."

"Hazel Meade Stone."

"You're Hazel Meade? But you can't be—you must be dead!"

"Take another look, Judge. I'm Hazel Meade."

"Well, by the breath of K'Raath! Excuse me, ma'am. We must get together when this is over." He straightened up again. "In the meantime I trust you realize that this in no way affects the case before us?"

"Oh, naturally not! But I must say it makes me feel better to know who's sitting on this case. Your granddaddy was a just man."

"Thank you. And now shall we proceed?"

The young prosecutor was on his feet. "May it please the court!"

"May what please the court?"

"We feel that this is most irregular. We feel that under the circumstances the only proper procedure is for this court to disqualify itself. We feel—"

"Cut out that 'we' stuff, Herbert. You're neither an editor nor a potentate. Motion denied. You know as well as I do that Judge Bonelli is laid up sick. I don't propose to clutter up the calendar on the spurious theory that I can't count fingers in front of my face." He glanced at the clock. "In fact, unless one of you has new facts to produce—facts, not theories—I'm going to assume that you have both stipulated to the same body of facts. Objection?"

"Okay with me, Judge."

"No objection," the prosecutor said wearily.

"You may continue, ma'am. I think we ought to wind this up in about ten minutes, if you both will stick to the subject. Let's have your theory."

"Yes, your honor. First, I want you to take a look at those two young and innocent lads and see for yourself that they could not be up to anything criminal." Castor and Pollux made a mighty effort to look the description; they were not notably successful.

Judge Warburton looked at them and scratched his chin. "That's a conclusion, ma'am. I can't see any wings sprouting from here."

"Forget it, then. They're a couple of little hellions, both of them. They've given me plenty of grief. But this time they didn't do anything wrong and they deserve a vote of thanks from your chamber of commerce —and from the citizens of Mars Commonwealth."

"The first part sounds plausible. The latter part is outside the jurisdiction of this court."

"You'll see. The key to this case is whether or not a bicycle is a production item, or a luxury. Right?"

"Correct. And the distinction depends on the end use of the imported article. Our tariff schedule is flexible in that respect. Shall I cite the pertinent cases?"

"Oh, don't bother!"

"I believe it was stipulated that the bicycles were sold for the end use of sightseeing, that the defendants knew that, that they even suggested that end use and made it part of their sales argument, and that they neglected to inform the buyer of the customs status of the articles in question. Correct?"

"Right to nine decimals, Judge."

"I've not yet gotten a glimpse of your theory. Surely you are not contending that sightseeing is anything but a luxury?"

"Oh, it's a luxury all right!"

"Madam, it seems to me that you are doing your grandsons no good. If you will withdraw, I will appoint counsel."

"Better ask them, Judge."

"I intended to." He looked inquiringly at the twins. "Are you satisfied with your representation?"

Castor caught Pollux's eye, then answered promptly, "We're as much in the dark as you are, sir—but we'll string along with Grandmother."

"I admire your courage at least. Proceed, ma'am."

"We agreed that sightseeing is a luxury. But 'luxury' is a relative term. Luxury for *whom?* Roast suckling pig is a luxury for you and me—"

"It certainly is. I haven't tasted one on this planet."

"—but it's an early death for the pig. Will the court take judicial notice of an activity known as 'Mars' Invisible Export'?"

"The tourist trade? Certainly, if it's necessary to your theory."

"Objection!"

"Just hang on to that objection, Herbert; she may not establish a connection. Proceed."

"Let's find out who eats that pig. Your tariff rules, so it has been explained, are to keep citizens of the Commonwealth from wasting valuable foreign exchange on unnecessary frills. You've got a credit gap—"

"Regrettably, we have. We don't propose to increase it."

"That's my point. Who pays the bill? Do *you* go sightseeing? Does *he?*" She pointed again at the prosecutor. "Shucks, no! It's old stuff to both of you. But *I* do—I'm a tourist. I rented one of those bicycles not a week ago—and helped close your credit gap. Your honor, we contend that the renting of bicycles to tourists, albeit a luxury to the tourist, is a productive activity for export to the unmixed benefit of every citizen of the Commonwealth and that therefore those bicycles are 'articles of production' within the meaning and intent of your tariff laws!"

"Finished?" She nodded. "Herbert?"

"Your honor, this is ridiculous! The prosecution has clearly established its case and the defense does not even dare to dispute it. I have never heard a more outlandish mixture of special pleading and distortion of the facts. But I am sure the facts are clear to the court. The end use is sightseeing, which the defense agrees is a luxury. Now a luxury is a luxury—"

"Not to the pig, son."

" 'The pig?' What pig? There are no pigs in this case? there isn't a pig on Mars. If we—"

"Herbert! Have you anything to add?"

"I—" The young prosecutor slumped. "Sorry, Dad, I got excited. We rest."

The judge turned to Hazel. "He's a good boy, but he's impetuous—like yours. I'll make a lawyer out of him yet." He straightened up. "And the court rests—ten minutes out for a pipe. Don't go away." He ducked out.

The twins whispered and fidgeted; Hazel caught the eyes of her son and daughter-in-law and gave them a solemn wink. Judge Warburton returned in less than ten minutes and the bailiff shouted for order. The judge stared at the prisoners. "The court rules," he said solemnly, "that the bicycles in question are 'articles of production' within the meaning of the tariff code. The prisoners are acquitted and discharged. The clerk will release the delivery bond."

There was very scattered applause, led by Hazel. "No demonstrations!" the judge said sharply. He looked again at the twins. "You're extremely lucky—you know that, don't you?"

"Yessir!"

"Then get out of my sight and try to stay out of trouble."

Dinner was a happy family reunion despite the slight cloud that still hung over the twins. It was also quite good, Dr. Stone having quietly taken over the cooking. Captain Vandenbergh, down on the same shuttle, joined them for dinner. By disconnecting the TV receiver and placing it temporarily on Meade's bunk and by leaving open the door to the twins' cubicle so that Captain Vandenbergh's chair could be backed into the door frame, it was just possible for all of them to sit down at once. Fuzzy Britches sat in Lowell's lap; up till now the flat cat had had its own chair.

Roger Stone tried to push back his chair to make more room for his knees, found himself chock-a-block against the wall. "Edith, we will just have to get a larger place."

"Yes, dear. Hazel and I spoke to the landlord this afternoon."

"What did he say?"

Hazel took over. "I'm going to cut his gizzard out. I reminded him that he had promised to take care of us when you two got down. He looked saintly and pointed out that he had given us two more cots. Lowell, quit feeding that mop with your own spoon!"

"Yes, Grandma Hazel. May I borrow yours?"

"No. But he did say that we could have the flat the

Burkhardts are in, come Venus departure. It has one more cubicle."

"Better," agreed Roger Stone, "but hardly a ballroom—and Venus departure is still three weeks away. Edith, we should have kept our nice room in the *War God*. How about it, Van? Want some house guests? Until you blast for Venus, that is?"

"Certainly."

"Daddy! You wouldn't go away *again?*"

"I'm joking, snub nose."

"I wasn't," answered the liner's captain. "Until Venus departure—or all the way to Venus and then back to Luna, if you choose. I got official approval of my recommendation this afternoon; you two can drag free in the *War God* until death or decommission do you part. How about it? Come on to Venus with me?"

"We've been to Venus," announced Meade. "Gloomy place."

"Whether they take you up or not," Hazel commented, "that's quite a concession to get out of Four-Planets. Ordinarily that bunch of highbinders wouldn't give away a bucketful of space."

"They were afraid of the award an admiralty court might hand out," Vandenbergh said drily. "Speaking of courts, I understand you put on a brilliant defense today, Hazel. Are you a lawyer, along with your other accomplishments?"

"No," answered her son, "but she's a fast talker."

"Who's not a lawyer?"

"You aren't."

"Of course I am!"

"When and where? Be specific."

"Years and years ago, back in Idaho—before you were born. I just never got around to mentioning it."

Her son looked her over. "Hazel, it occurs to me that the records in Idaho are conveniently far away."

"None of your sass, boy. Anyway, the courthouse burned down."

"I thought as much."

"In any case," Vandenbergh put in soothingly, "Hazel got the boys off. When I heard about it, I expected that they would have to pay the duty at least. You young fellows must have made quite a tidy profit."

"We did all right," Castor admitted.

"Nothing spectacular," Pollux hedged.

"Figure it up," Hazel said happily, "because I am going to collect a fee from you of exactly two-thirds your net profit for getting your necks out of a bight."

The twins stared at her. "Hazel, you wouldn't?" Castor said uncertainly.

"Wouldn't I!"

"Don't tease them, Mother," Dr. Stone suggested.

"I'm not teasing. I want this to be a lesson to them. Boys, anybody who sits in a game without knowing the house rules is a sucker. Time you knew it."

Vandenbergh put in smoothly, "It doesn't matter too much these days when the government—" He stopped suddenly. "What in the world!"

"What's the matter, Van?" demanded Roger.

Vandenbergh's face cleared and he grinned sheepishly. "Nothing. Just your flat cat, crawling up my leg. For a moment I thought I had wandered into your television show."

Roger Stone shook his head. "Not mine, Hazel's. And it wouldn't have been a flat cat; it would have been human gore."

Captain Vandenbergh picked up Fuzzy Britches, stroked it, then returned it to Lowell. "It's a Martian," announced Lowell.

"Yes?"

Hazel caught his attention. "The situation has multifarious ramifications not immediately apparent to the unassisted optic. This immature zygote holds it as the ultimate desideratum to consort with the dominate aborigine of the trifurcate variety. Through a judicious use of benign mendacity, Exhibit 'A' performs as a surrogate in spirit if not in letter. Do you dig me, boy?"

Vandenbergh blinked. "I think so. Perhaps it's just as well. They are certainly engaging little pets—though I wouldn't have one in any ship of mine. They—"

"She means," Lowell explained, "that I want to see a Martian with legs. I still do. Do you know one?"

Hazel said, "Coach, I tried, but they were too big for me."

Captain Vandenbergh stared at Lowell. "He's quite serious about it, isn't he?"

"I'm afraid he is."

He turned to Dr. Stone. "Ma'am, I've fair connections around here and these things can always be arranged, in spite of treaties. Of course, there would be a certain element of danger—not much in my opinion."

Dr. Stone answered, "Captain, I have never considered danger to be an evaluating factor.

"Um, no, you wouldn't, ma'am. Shall I try it?"

"If you would be so kind."

"It will pay interest on my debt. I'll let you know." He dismissed the matter and turned again to the twins. "What profit-tax classification does your enterprise come under?"

"Profit tax?"

"Haven't you figured it yet?"

"We didn't know there was one."

"I can see you haven't done much importing and exporting, not on Mars anyhow. If you are a Commonwealth citizen, it all goes into income tax, of course. But if you come from out planet, you pay a single-shot tax on each transaction. Better find yourself a tax expert; the formula is somewhat complicated."

"We won't pay it!" said Pollux.

His father answered quietly, "Haven't you two been in jail enough lately?"

Pollux shut up. For the next few minutes they exchanged glances, whispers, and shrugs. Presently Castor stood up. "Dad, Mother—may we be excused?"

"Certainly. If you can manage to squeeze out."

"No dessert, boys?"

"We aren't very hungry."

They went into town, to return an hour later not with a tax expert but with a tax guide they had picked up at the Chamber of Commerce. The adults were still seated in the general room, chatting; the table had been folded up to the ceiling. They threaded through the passageway of knees into their cubicle; they could be heard whispering in there from time to time

Presently they came out. "Excuse us, folks. Uh, Hazel?"

"What is it, Cas?"

"You said your fee was two-thirds of our net."

"Huh? Did your leg come away in my hand, chum? I wouldn't—"

"Oh, no, we'd rather pay it." He reached out, dropped half a dozen small coins in her hand. "There it is."

She looked at it. "*This* is two-thirds of all you made on the deal?"

"After taxes."

"Of course," added Pollux, "it wasn't a total loss. We had the use of the bicycles for a couple of hundred million miles."

XIV   FLAT CATS FACTORIAL

VANDENBERGH MADE GOOD his offer. Lowell and he went by stratorocket to the treaty town of Richardson, were gone about three days. When Lowell came back he had seen a Martian, he had talked with one. But he had been cautioned not to talk about it and his family could get no coherent account out of him.

But the simple matter of housing was more difficult than the presumably impossible problem of meeting a Martian. Roger Stone had had no luck in finding larger and more comforatble quarters, even after he had resigned himself to fantastic rentals. The town was bursting with tourists and would be until Venus departure, at which time those taking the triangular trip would leave—a majority, in fact. In the meantime they crowded the restaurants, took pictures of everything including each other, and ran their bicycles over the toes of pedestrians. Further packing a city already supersaturated were sand rats in from the desert and trying to arrange some way, any way, to get out to the Hallelujah Node in the Asteroid Belt.

Dr. Stone said one night at dinner, "Roger, tomorrow is rent day. Shall I pay it for a full month? Mr. d'Avril says that the Burkhardts are talking about staying on."

"Pay it for six days only," Hazel advised. "We can do better than this after Venus departure—I hope."

Roger Stone looked up and scowled. "Look here, why pay the rent at all?"

"What are you saying, dear?"

"Edith, I've been chewing this over in my mind. When we first came here our plans, such as they were,

180

called for living here through one wait." He referred to the fifteen months elapsed time from arrival Mars to Earth departure from Mars, using the economical orbits. "Then we planned to shape orbit home. Fair enough, if this overrated tourist trap had decent housing. But I haven't been able to start writing my book. When Buster isn't climbing into my lap, his pet is slithering down the back of my neck."

"What do you suggest, dear?"

"Go to Phobos tomorrow, get the old *Rock* ready to go, and blast for Venus when the others do."

"Loud cheers!" agreed Meade. "Let's go!"

Dr. Stone said, "Meade, I thought you didn't like Venus?"

"I don't. But I don't like it here and I'm tired all the time. I'd like to get back into free fall."

"You shouldn't be tired. Perhaps I had better check you over."

"Oh, Mother, I'm perfectly well! I don't want to be poked at."

Lowell grinned. "I know why she wants to go to Venus. Mr. Magill."

"Don't be a snoop, Snoop!" Meade went on with quiet dignity, "In case anyone is interested, I am not interested in Second Officer Magill—and I wouldn't be going in the *Caravan* in any case. Besides, I found out he already has a wife in Colorado."

Hazel said, "Well, that's legal. He's still eligible off Earth."

"Perhaps it is, but I don't like it."

"Neither do I," Roger Stone cut in. "Meade, you weren't really getting interested in this wolf in ship's clothing, were you?"

"Of course not, Daddy!" She added, "But I suppose I'll get married one of these days."

"That's the trouble with girls," Castor commented.

"Give them educations—*boom!* They get married. Wasted."

Hazel glared at them. "Oh, so? Where would you be if I hadn't married?"

"It didn't happen that way," Roger Stone cut in, "so there is no use talking about other possibilities. They probably aren't really possibilities at all, if only we understood it."

Pollux: "Predestination."

Castor: "Very shaky theory."

Roger grinned. "I'm not a determinist and you can't get my goat. I believe in free will."

Pollux: "Another very shaky theory."

"Make up your minds," their father told them. "You can't have it both ways."

"Why not?" asked Hazel. "Free will is a golden thread running through the frozen matrix of fixed events."

"Not mathematical," objected Pollux.

Castor nodded. "Just poetry."

"And not very good poetry."

"*Shut up!*" ordered their father. "Boys, it's quite evident that you have gone to considerable trouble to change the subject. Why?"

The twins swapped glances; Castor got the go-ahead. "Uh, Dad, the way we see it, this Venus proposition hasn't been thought out."

"Go on. I suppose you have an alternative suggestion?"

"Well, yes. But we didn't mean to bring it up until after Venus departure."

"I begin to whiff something. What you mean is that you intended to wait until the planetary aspects were wrong—too late to shape orbit for Venus."

"Well, there was no use in letting the matter get cluttered up with a side issue."

"What matter? Speak up."

Castor said worriedly, "Look, Dad, we aren't unreasonable. We can compromise. How about this: you and Mother and Buster and Meade go to Venus in the *War God*. Captain Van would love to have you do it—you know that. And—"

"Slow up. And what would you be doing? And Hazel? Mother, are you in on this?"

"Not that I know of. But I'm getting interested."

"Castor, what's on your mind? Speak up."

"Well, I will if you'll just let me, sir. You and the rest of the family could have a pleasant trip back home—in a luxury liner. Hazel and Pol and I—well, I suppose you know that Mars will be in a favorable position for the Hallelujah Node in about six weeks?"

"For a cometary-type orbit, that is," Pollux added.

"So it's the Asteroids again," their father said slowly. "We settled that about a year ago."

"But we're a year older now."

"More experienced."

"You're still not old enough for unlimited licenses. I suppose that is why you included your grandmother."

"Oh, no! Hazel is an asset."

"Thank you, boys."

"Hazel, you had no inkling of this latest wild scheme?"

"No. But I don't think it's so wild. I'm caught up and then some on my episodes—and I'm tired of this place. I've seen the Martian ruins; they're in a poor state of repair. I've seen a canal; it has water in it. I understand that the rest of the planet is much the same, right through to chapter eighty-eight. And I've seen Venus. I've never seen the Asteroids."

"Right!" agreed Castor. "We don't like Mars. The place is one big clip joint."

"Sharp operators," added Pollux.

"Sharper than you are, you mean," said Hazel.

"Never mind, Mother. Boys, it is out of the question. I brought my ship out from Luna; I intend to take her back." He stood up. "You can give Mr. d'Avril notice, dear."

"Dad!"

"Yes, Castor?"

"That was just a compromise offer. What we really hoped you would do—what we *wanted* you to do—was for *all* of us to go out to the Hallelujah."

"Eh? Why, that's silly! I'm no meteor miner."

"You could learn to be. Or you could just go for the ride. And make a profit on it, too."

"Yes? How?"

Castor wet his lips. "The sand rats are offering fabulous prices just for cold-sleep space. We could carry about twenty of them, at least. And we could put them down on Ceres on the way, let them outfit there."

"Cas! I suppose you are aware that only seven out of ten cold-sleep passengers arrive alive in a long orbit?"

"Well . . . they know that. That's the risk they are taking."

Roger Stone shook his head. "We aren't going, so I won't have to find out if you are as cold-blooded as you sound. Have you ever seen a burial in space?"

"No, sir."

"I have. Let's hear no more about cold-sleep freight."

Castor passed it to Pollux, who took over: "Dad, if you won't listen to us all going, do you have any objections to Cas and me going?"

"Eh? How do you mean?"

"As Asteroid miners, of course. We're not afraid of cold-sleep. If we haven't got a ship, that's how we would have to go."

"Bravo!" said Hazel. "I'm going with you, boys."

"Please, Mother!" He turned to his wife. "Edith, I

sometimes wonder if we brought the right twins back from the hospital."

"They may not be yours," said Hazel, "but they are my grandsons, I'm sure of that. Hallelujah, here I come! Anybody coming with me?"

Dr. Stone said quietly, "You know, dear, I don't much care for Venus, either. And it *would* give you leisure for your book."

The *Rolling Stone* shaped orbit from Phobos outward bound for the Asteroids six weeks later. This was no easy lift like the one from Luna to Mars; in choosing to take a "cometary" or fast orbit to the Hallelujah the Stones had perforce to accept an expensive change-of-motion of twelve and a half miles per second for the departure maneuver. A fast orbit differs from a maximum-economy orbit in that it cuts the orbit being abandoned at an angle instead of being smoothly tangent to it . . . *much* more expensive in reaction mass. The far end of the cometary orbit would be tangent to the orbit of the Hallelujah; matching at that point would be about the same for either orbit; it was the departure from Phobos-circum-Mars that would be rugged.

The choice of a cometary orbit was not a frivolous one. In the first place, it would have been necessary to wait more than one Earth year for Mars to be in the proper relation, orbit-wise, with the Hallelujah Node for the economical orbit; secondly, the travel time itself would be more than doubled—five hundred and eighty days for the economical orbit versus two hundred and sixty-one days for the cometary orbit (a mere three days longer than the Luna-Mars trip).

Auxiliary tanks for single-H were fitted around the *Stone*'s middle, giving her a fat and sloppy appearance, but greatly improving her mass-ratio for the ordeal. Port Pilot Jason Thomas supervised the refitting;

the twins helped. Castor got up his nerve to ask Thomas how he had managed to conn the *Stone* in to a landing on their arrival. "Did you figure a ballistic before you came aboard, sir?"

Thomas put down his welding torch. "A ballistic? Shucks, no, son, I've been doing it so long that I know every little bit of space hereabouts by its freckles."

Which was all the satisfaction Cas could get out of him. The twins talked it over and concluded that piloting must be something more than a mathematical science.

In addition to more space for single-H certain modifications were made inside the ship. The weather outside the orbit of Mars is a steady "clear but cold"; no longer would they need reflecting foil against the Sun's rays. Instead one side of the ship was painted with carbon black and the capacity of the air-heating system was increased by two coils. In the control room a time-delay variable-baseline stereoscopic radar was installed by means of which they would be able to see the actual shape of the Hallelujah when they reached it.

All of which was extremely expensive and the Galactic Overlord had to work overtime to pay for it. Hazel did not help with the refitting. She stayed in her room and ground out, with Lowell's critical help, more episodes in the gory but virtuous career of Captain John Sterling—alternating this activity with sending insulting messages and threats of blackmail and/ or sit-down strike to her producers back in New York; she wanted an unreasonably large advance and she wanted it right now. She got it, by sending on episodes equal to the advance. She had to write the episodes in advance anyhow; this time the *Rolling Stone* would be alone, no liners comfortably near by. Once out of radio range of Mars, they would not be able to contact Earth again until Ceres was in range of the *Stone's* modest equipment. They were not going to Ceres but would be not far away; the Hallelujah was riding almost the same orbit somewhat ahead of that tiny planet.

The boost to a cometary orbit left little margin for cargo but what there was the twins wanted to use, undeterred by their father's blunt disapproval of the passengers-in-cold-sleep idea. Their next notion was to carry full outfits for themselves for meteor mining—rocket scooter, special suits, emergency shelter, keyed radioactive claiming stakes, centrifuge speegee tester, black lights, Geiger counters, prospecting radar, portable spark spectroscope, and everything else needed to go quietly rock-happy.

Their father said simply, "Your money?"

"Of course. And we pay for the boost."

"Go ahead. Go right ahead. Don't let me discourage you. Any objections from me would simply confirm your preconceptions."

Castor was baffled by the lack of opposition. "What's the matter with it, Dad? You worried about the danger involved?"

"Danger? Heavens, no! It's your privilege to get yourselves killed in your own way. Anyhow, I don't think you will. You're young and you're both smart, even if you don't show it sometimes, and you're both in tiptop physical condition, and I'm sure you'll know your equipment."

"Then what is it?"

"Nothing. For myself, I long since came to the firm conclusion that a man can do more productive work, and make more money if that is his object, by sitting down with his hands in his pockets than by any form of physical activity. Do you happen to know the average yearly income of a meteor miner?"

"Well, no, but—"

"Less than six hundred a year."

"But some of them get rich!"

"Sure they do. And some make much less than six hundred a year; that's an average, including the rich strikes. Just as a matter of curiosity, bearing in mind that most of those miners are experienced and able, what is it that you two expect to bring to this trade that will enable you to raise the yearly average? Speak up; don't be shy."

"Doggone it, Dad, what would *you* ship?"

"Me? Nothing. I have no talent for trade. I'm going out for the ride—and to take a look at the bones of Lucifer. I'm beginning to get interested in planetology. I may do a book about it."

"What happened to your other book?"

"I hope that isn't sarcasm, Cas. I expect to have it finished before we get there." He adjourned the discussion by leaving.

The twins turned to leave, found Hazel grinning at them. Castor scowled at her. "What are you smirking at, Hazel?"

"You two."

"Well . . . why shouldn't we have a whirl at meteor mining?"

"No reason. Go ahead; you can afford the luxury. But see here, boys, do you really want to know what to ship to make some money?"

"Sure!"

"What's your offer?"

"Percentage cut? Or flat fee? But we don't pay if we don't take your advice."

"Oh, rats! I'll give it to you free. If you get advice free, you won't take it and I'll be able to say, 'I told you so!'"

"You would, too."

"Of course I would. There's no warmer pleasure than being able to tell a smart aleck, 'I told you so, but you wouldn't listen.' Okay, here it is, in the form of a question, just like an oracle: Who made money in all the other big mining rushes of history?"

"Why, the chaps who struck it rich, I suppose."

"That's a laugh. There are so few cases of prospectors who actually hung on to what they had found and died rich that they stand out like supernovae. Let's take a famous rush, the California Gold Rush back in 1861—no, 1861 was something else; I forget. 1849, that was it—the 'Forty-niners. Read about 'em in history?"

"Some."

"There was a citizen named Sutter; they found gold on his place. Did it make him rich? It *ruined* him. But who did get rich?"

"Tell us, Hazel. Don't bother to dramatize it."

"Why not? I may put it in the show—serial numbers rubbed off, of course. I'll tell you: everybody who had something the miners had to buy. Grocers, mostly. Boy, did *they* get rich! Hardware dealers. Men with stamping mills. Everybody but the poor miner. Even laundries in Honolulu."

"Honolulu? But that's way out in the Pacific, off China somewhere."

"It was in Hawaii the last time I looked. But they used to ship dirty laundry from California clear to Honolulu to have it washed—both ways by sailing ship. That's about like having your dirty shirts shipped from Marsport to Luna. Boys, if you want to make money, set up a laundry in the Hallelujah. But it doesn't have to be a laundry—just anything, so long as the miners want it and you've got it. If your father wasn't a Puritan at heart, I'd set up a well-run, perfectly honest gambling hall! That's like having a rich uncle."

The twins considered their grandmother's advice and

went into the grocery business, with a few general store sidelines. They decided to stock only luxury foods, things that the miners would not be likely to have and which would bring highest prices per pound. They stocked antibiotics and surgical drugs and vitamins as well, and some light-weight song-and-story projectors and a considerable quantity of spools to go with them. Pollux found a supply of pretty-girl pictures, printed on thin stock in Japan and intended for calendars on Mars, and decided to take a flyer on them, since they didn't weigh much. He pointed out to Castor that they could not lose entirely, since they could look at them themselves.

Dr. Stone found them, ran through them, and required him to send some of them back. The rest passed her censorship; they took them along.

The last episode was speeding toward Earth; the last weld had been approved; the last pound of food and supplies was at last aboard. The *Stone* lifted gently from Phobos and dropped toward Mars. A short gravity-well maneuver around Mars at the *Stone*'s best throat temperature—which produced a spine-grinding five gravities—and she was headed out and fast to the lonely reaches of space inhabited only by the wreckage of the Ruined Planet.

They fell easily and happily back into free fall routine. More advanced mathematical texts had been obtained for the boys on Mars; they did not have to be urged to study, having grown really interested—and this time they had no bicycles to divert their minds. Fuzzy Britches took to free fall as if the creature had been born in space; if it was not being held and stroked by someone (which it usually was) it slithered over wall and bulkhead, or floated gently around the compartments, undulating happily.

Castor maintained that it could swim through the air; Pollux insisted that it could not and that its maneuvers arose entirely from the air currents of the ventilation system. They wasted considerable time, thought, and energy in trying to devise scientific tests to prove the matter, one way or the other. They were unsuccessful.

The flat cat did not care; it was warm, it was well fed, it was happy. It had numerous friends all willing to take time off to reward its tremendous and undiscriminating capacity for affection. Only one incident marred its voyage.

Roger Stone was strapped to his pilot's chair, blocking out—so he said—a chapter in his book. If so, the snores may have helped. Fuzzy Britches was cruising along about its lawful occasions, all three eyes open and merry. It saw one of its friends; good maneuvering or a random air current enabled it to make a perfect landing—on Captain Stone's face.

Roger came out of the chair with a yell, clutching at his face. He bounced against the safety belt, recovered, and pitched the flat cat away from him. Fuzzy Britches, offended but not hurt, flipped itself flat to its progress, air-checked and made another landing on the far wall.

Roger Stone used several other words, then shouted, "Who put that animated toupee on my face?"

But the room was otherwise empty. Dr. Stone appeared at the hatch and said, "What is it, dear?"

"Oh, nothing—nothing important. Look, dear, would you return this tail-end offspring of a dying planet to Buster? I'm trying to think."

"Of course, dear." She took it aft and gave it to Lowell, who promptly forgot it, being busy working out a complicated gambit against Hazel. The flat cat was not one to hold a grudge; there was not a mean bone in its body, had it had bones, which it did not. The only emotion it could feel wholeheartedly was love. It got back to Roger just as he had again fallen asleep.

It again settled on his face, purring happily.

Captain Stone proved himself a mature man. Knowing this time what it was, he detached it gently and himself returned it to Lowell. "Keep it," he said. "Don't let go of it." He was careful to close the door behind him.

He was equally careful that night to close the door of the stateroom he shared with his wife. The *Rolling Stone,* being a small private ship, did not have screens guarding her ventilation ducts; they of course had to be left open at all times. The flat cat found them a broad highway. Roger Stone had a nightmare in which he was suffocating, before his wife woke him and removed Fuzzy Britches from his face. He used some more words.

"It's all right, dear," she answered soothingly. "Go back to sleep." She cuddled it in her arms and Fuzzy Britches settled for that.

The ship's normal routine was disturbed the next day while everyone who could handle a wrench or a spot welder installed screens in the ducts.

Thirty-seven days out Fuzzy-Britches had eight golden little kittens, exactly like their parent but only a couple of inches across when flat, marble-sized when contracted. Everyone including Captain Stone thought they were cute; everyone enjoying petting them, stroking them with a gentle forefinger and listening carefully for the tiny purr, so high as to be almost beyond human ear range. Everyone enjoyed feeding them and they seemed to be hungry all the time.

Sixty-four days later the kittens had kittens, eight each. Sixty-four days after that, the one hundred and forty-sixth day after Phobos departure, the kittens' kittens had kittens; that made five hundred and thirteen.

"This," said Captain Stone, "has *got* to stop!"

"Yes, dear."

"I mean it. At this rate we'll run out of food before we get there, including the stuff the twins hope to sell. Besides that we'll be suffocated under a mass of buzzing fur mats. What's eight times five hundred and twelve? Then what's eight times *that?*"

"Too many, I'm sure."

"My dear, that's the most masterly understatement since the death of Mercutio. And I don't think I've figured it properly anyway; it's an exponential expansion, not a geometric—provided we don't all starve first."

"Roger."

"I think we should— Eh? What?"

"I believe there is a simple solution. These are Martian creatures; they hibernate in cold weather."

"Yes?"

"We'll put them in the hold—fortunately there is room."

"I agree with all but the 'fortunately.' "

"And we'll keep it cold."

"I wouldn't want to kill the little things. I can't manage to hate them. Drat it, they're too cute."

"We'll hold it about a hundred below, about like a normal Martian winter night. Or perhaps warmer will do."

"We certainly will. Get a shovel. Get a net. Get a barrel." He began snagging flat cats out of the air.

"You aren't going to freeze Fuzzy Britches!" Lowell was floating in the stateroom door behind them, clutching an adult flat cat to his small chest. It may or may not have been Fuzzy Britches; none of the others could tell the adults apart and naming had been dropped after the first litter. But Lowell was quite sure and it did not seem to matter whether or not he was right. The twins had discussed slipping in a ringer on him, while he was asleep, but they had been overheard and the project forbidden. Lowell was content and his mother did not wish him disturbed in his belief.

"Dear, we aren't going to hurt your pet."

"You better not! You do and I'll—I'll *space* you!"

"Oh, dear, he's been helping Hazel with her serial!" Dr. Stone got face to face with her son. "Lowell, Mother has never lied to you, has she?"

"Uh, I guess not."

"We aren't going to hurt Fuzzy Britches. We aren't going to hurt any of the flat kitties. But we haven't got room for all of them. You can keep Fuzzy Britches, but the other kittens are going for a long nap. They'll be perfectly safe; I promise."

"By the code of the Galaxy?"

"By the code of the Galaxy."

Lowell left, still guarding his pet. Roger said, "Edith, we've got to put a stop to that collaboration."

"Don't worry, dear; it won't harm him." She frowned. "But I'm afraid I will have to disappoint him on another score."

"Such as?"

"Roger, I didn't have much time to study the fauna of Mars—and I certainly didn't study flat cats, beyond making sure that they were harmless."

"Harmless!" He batted a couple of them out of the way. "Woman, I'm drowning."

"But Martian fauna have certain definite patterns, survival adaptations. Except for the water-seekers, which probably aren't Martian in origin anyhow, their methods are both passive and persistent. Take the flat cat—"

"You take it!" He removed one gently from his chest.

"It is defenseless. It can't even seek its own food

194

very well. I understand that in its native state it is a benign parasite, attaching itself to some more mobile animal—"

"If only they would quit attaching to me! And you look as if you were wearing a fur coat. Let's put 'em in freeze!"

"Patience, dear. Probably it has somewhat the same pleasing effect on the host that it has on us; consequently the host tolerates it and lets it pick up the crumbs. But its other characteristic it shares with almost anything Martian. It can last long periods in hibernation, or if that isn't necessary, in a state of lowered vitality and activity—say when there is no food available. But with any increase in the food supply, then at once—almost like throwing a switch—it expands, multiplies to the full extent of the food supply."

"I'll say it does!"

"Cut off the food supply and it simply waits for more good times. Pure theory, of course, since I am reasoning by analogy from other Martian life forms—but that's why I'm going to have to disappoint Lowell. Fuzzy Britches will have to go on very short rations."

Her husband frowned. "That won't be easy; he feeds it all the time. We'll just have to watch him—or there will be more little visitors from heaven. Honey, let's get busy. Right now."

"Yes, dear. I just had to get my thoughts straight."

Roger called them all to general quarters; Operation Roundup began. They shooed them aft and into the hold; they slithered back, purring and seeking companionship. Pollux got into the hold and tried to keep them herded together while the others scavenged through the ship. His father stuck his head in; tried to make out his son in a cloud of flat cats. "How many have you got so far?"

"I can't count them—they keep moving around. Close the door!"

"How can I keep the door closed and still send them in to you?"

"How can I keep them in here if you keep opening the door?"

Finally they all got into space suits—Lowell insisted on taking Fuzzy Britches inside with him, apparently not trusting even "the code of the Galaxy" too far. Captain Stone reduced the temperature of the entire ship down to a chilly twenty below; the flat cats, frustrated by the space suits and left on their own resources, gave up and began forming themselves into balls, like fur-covered grapefruit. They were then easy to gather in, easy to count, easy to store in the hold.

Nevertheless the Stones kept finding and incarcerating fugitives for the next several days.

XV "INTER JOVEM
ET MARTEM PLANETAM INTERPOSUI"

THE GREAT ASTRONOMER KEPLER WROTE: "Between Mars and Jupiter I put a planet." His successors devised a rule for planetary distances, called "Bode's Law," which seemed to require a planet at precisely two and eight/tenths the distance from Sun to Earth, 2.8 astro units.

On the first night of the new nineteenth century the Monk Giuseppe Piazzi discovered a new heavenly body. It was the Asteroid Ceres—just where a planet should have been. It was large for an Asteroid, the largest in fact—diameter 485 miles. In the ensuing two centuries hundreds and thousands more were discovered, down to size of rocks. "The Asteroids" proved a poor name; they were not little stars, nor were they precisely planetoids. It was early suggested that they were the remains of a once sizable planet and by the middle of the twentieth century mathematical investigation of their orbits seemed to prove it.

But it was not until the first men in the early days of the exploration of space actually went out to the lonely reaches between the orbits of Mars and Jupiter and *looked* that we learned for certain that the Asteroids were indeed fragments of a greater planet—destroyed Lucifer, long dead brother of Earth.

As the *Rolling Stone* rose higher and ever higher above the Sun, she slowed, curved her path in, and approached the point where she would start to fall back toward the Sun. She was then at the orbit of Ceres and not far in front of that lady. The *Stone* had been in the region of the Asteroids for the past fifty million miles. The ruins of Lucifer are scattered over a wide belt of space; the Hallelujah node was near the middle of that belt.

The loose group of rocks, sand, random molecules, and microplanetoids known as the Hallelujah node was traveling in company around the Sun at a speed of eleven miles per second. The *Stone*'s vector was eight miles per second and in the same direction. Captain Stone speeded up his ship to match in by a series of blasts during the last two days, conning by a radar beacon deep in the swarm and thereby sneaking up on the collection of floating masses at a low relative speed. The final blast that positioned them dead with the swarm was a mere love tap; the *Stone* did but clear her throat—and she was one with the other rolling stones of space.

Captain Stone took a last look into the double eyepiece of the stereo radar, swung the sweep control fore and aft and all around; the masses of the Hallelujah, indistinguishable from the background of stars by naked eye, hung in greatly exaggerated perspective in the false "space" of the stereo tank while the true stars showed not at all. None of them displayed the crawling trail of relative motion.

A point brighter than the rest glowed in a fluctuating pattern fairly close by and a few degrees out-orbit; it was the radar beacon on which he had homed. It, too, seemed steady by stereo; he turned to Castor and said, "Take a doppler on City Hall."

"Just getting it, Captain." In a moment he added, "Uh, relative about ten miles an hour—nine point seven and a whisper. And just under seven hundred miles away."

"Vector?"

"Closing almost for it. We ought to slide past maybe ten, fifteen miles south and in-orbit."

Roger Stone relaxed and grinned. "How's that for shooting? Your old man can still figure them, eh?"

"Pretty good, Dad—considering."

"Considering what?"

"Considering you used Pol's figures."

"When I figure out which one of us you are insulting, I'll answer that." He spoke to the mike: "All hands, secure from maneuvers. Power room, report when secure. Edith, how soon can we have dinner?"

"It's wrapped up, son," Hazel reported.

"About thirty minutes, dear," his wife answered.

"A fine thing! A man slaves over a hot control board and then has to wait thirty minutes for his dinner. What kind of a hotel is this?"

"Yes, dear. By the way, I'm cutting your calorie ration again."

"Mutiny! What would John Sterling do?"

"Daddy's getting fat! Daddy's getting fat!" Lowell chanted.

"And strangle your child. Anybody want to come out with me while I set jato units?"

"I will, Daddy!"

"Meade, you're just trying to get out of helping with dinner."

"I can spare her, dear."

"Spare the child and spoil the fodder. Come with your fodder, baby."

"Not very funny, Daddy."

"And I'm not getting paid for it, either." Captain Stone went aft, whistling. The twins as well as Meade went out with him; they made quick work of setting jato units, the young people locking them in place and the Captain seeing to the wiring personally. They set a belt of them around the waist of the ship and matched pairs on the bow and quarter. Wired for triggering to the piloting radar, set at minimum range, they would give the ship a sharp nudge in the unlikely event that any object came toward them on a collision course at a relative speed high enough to be dangerous.

Coming through the Asteroid Belt to their present location deep in it, they had simply taken their chances. Although one is inclined to think of the Belt as thick with sky junk, the statistical truth is that there is so enormously more space than rock that the chance of being hit is negligible. Inside a node the situation was somewhat different, the concentration of mass being several hundred times as great as in the ordinary reaches of the Belt. But most of the miners took no precautions even there, preferring to bet that this unending game of Russian roulette would always work out in their favor rather than go to the expense and trouble of setting up a meteor guard. This used up a few miners, but not often; the accident rate in Hallelujah node was about the same as that of Mexico City.

They went inside and found dinner ready. "Call for you, Captain," announced Hazel.

"Already?"

"City Hall. Told 'em you were out but would call back. Nine point six centimeters."

"Come eat your dinner, dear, while it's hot."

"You all go ahead. I won't be long."

Nor was he. Dr. Stone looked inquiringly at him as he joined them. "The Mayor," he told her and the others. "Welcome to Rock City and all that sort of thing. Advised me that the Citizens' Committee has set a speed limit of a hundred miles an hour for ships, five hundred miles an hour for scooters, anywhere within a thousand miles of City Hall."

Hazel bristled. "I suppose you told him what they could do with their speed limits?"

"I did not. I apologized sweetly for having unwittingly offended on my approach and said that I would be over to pay my respects tomorrow or the next day."

"I thought Mars would have some elbow room," Hazel grumbled. "It turned out to be nothing but scissorbills and pantywaists and tax collectors. So we come on out to the wide open spaces and what do we find? Traffic cops! And my only son without the spunk to talk back to them. I think I'll go to Saturn."

"I hear that Titan Base is awfully chilly," her son answered without rancor. "Why not Jupiter? Pol, flip the salt over this way, please."

"Jupiter? The position isn't favorable. Besides I hear that Ganymede has more regulations than a girls' school."

"Mother, you are the only juvenile delinquent old enough for a geriatrics clinic whom I have ever known. You know perfectly well that an artificial colony has to have regulations."

"An excuse for miniature Napoleons! This whole system has taken to wearing corsets."

"What's a corset?" inquired Lowell.

"Uh . . . a predecessor to the spacesuit, sort of."

Lowell still looked puzzled; his mother said, "Never mind, dear. When we get back, Mother will show you one, in the museum."

Captain Stone proposed that they all turn in right after supper; they had all run short on sleep during the maneuvering approach. "I keep seeing spots before my eyes," he said, rubbing them, "from staring into the tank. I think I'll sleep the clock around."

Hazel started to answer when an alarm shrilled; he passed instantly from sleepy to alert. "Object on collision course! Grab something, everybody." He clutched at a stanchion with one hand, gathered in Lowell with the other.

But no shove from a firing jato followed. "Green," Hazel announced quietly. "Whatever it is, it isn't moving fast enough to hurt us. Chances favor a near miss, anyway."

Captain Stone took a deep breath. "I hope you're right, but I've been on the short end of too many long shots to place much faith in statistics. I've been jumpy ever since we entered the Belt."

Meade went aft with dirty dishes. She returned in a hurry, round eyed. "Daddy—somebody's at the *door.*"

"*What?* Meade, you're imagining things."

"No, I'm not. I *heard* him. Listen."

"Quiet, everyone." In the silence they could hear the steady hiss of an air injector; the lock was cycling. Roger Stone lunged toward the airlock; he was stopped by a sharp warning from his mother. "Son! Hold it a second."

"What?"

"Keep back from that door." She had her gun out and at the ready.

"Huh? Don't be silly. And put that thing away; it isn't charged anyhow."

"*He* won't know that. Whoever is coming in that lock."

Dr. Stone said quietly, "Mother Hazel, what are you nervous about?"

"Can't you see? We've got a ship here with food in it. And oxy. And a certain amount of single-H. This isn't Luna City; there are men out here who would be tempted."

Dr. Stone did not answer but turned to her husband. He hesitated only momentarily, then snapped, "Go forward, dear. Take Lowell. Meade, you go along and lock the access hatch. Leave the ship's phones open. If you hear anything wrong, radio City Hall and tell them we are being hijacked. Move!" He was already ducking into his stateroom, came out with his own gun.

By the time the hatch to the control room had clanged shut the airlock finished cycling. The four remaining waiting, surrounding the airlock inner door. "Shall we jump him, Dad?" Castor whispered.

"No. Just stay out of my line of fire."

Slowly the door swung open. A spacesuited figure crouched in the frame, its features indistinct in its helmet. It looked around, saw the guns trained on it, and spread both its hands open in front of it. "What's the matter?" a muffled voice said plaintively. "I haven't done anything."

Captain Stone could see that the man, besides being empty-handed, carried no gun at his belt. He put his own away. "Sorry. Let me give you a hand with that helmet."

The helmet revealed a middle-aged, sandy-haired man with mild eyes. "What was the matter?" he repeated.

"Nothing. Nothing at all. We didn't know who was boarding us and we were a bit nervous. My name's Stone, by the way. I'm master."

"Glad to know you, Captain Stone. I'm Shorty Devine."

"I'm glad to know you, Mr. Devine. Welcome aboard."

"Just Shorty." He looked around. "Uh, excuse me for busting in on you and scaring you but I heard you had a doctor aboard. A real doctor, I mean—not one of those science johnnies."

"We have."

"Gee, that's wonderful! The town hasn't had a real doctor since old Doc Schultz died. And I need one, bad."

"Sorry! Pol, get your mother."

"I heard, dear," the speaker horn answered. "Coming." The hatch opened and Dr. Stone came in. "I'm the doctor, Mr. Devine. Dear, I'll use this room, I think. If you will all go somewhere else, please?"

The visitor said hastily. "Oh, they needn't."

"I prefer to make examinations without an audience," she said firmly.

"But I didn't explain, ma'am—Doctor. It isn't me; it's my partner."

"Oh?"

"He broke his leg. Got careless with two big pieces of core material and got his leg nipped between 'em. Broke it. I guess I didn't do too well by him for he's a powerfully sick man. Could you come right away, Doctor?"

"Certainly."

"Now, Edith!"

"Castor, get my surgical kit—the black one. Will you help me suit up, dear?"

"But Edith, you—"

"It's all right, Captain; I've got my scooter right outside. We're only eight-five, ninety miles away; we won't be gone long."

Captain Stone sighed. "I'm going with you. Will your scooter take three?"

"Sure, sure! It's got Reynolds saddles; set any balance you need."

"Take command, Hazel."

"Aye aye, sir!"

They were gone all night, ship's time, rather than a short while. Hazel sat at the control board, tracking them all the way out—then watched and waited until she spotted them leaving, and tracked them back. Devine, profuse with thanks, had breakfast with them. Just before he left Lowell came into the saloon carrying Fuzzy Britches. Devine stopped with a bite on the way to his mouth and stared. "A flat cat! Or am I seeing things?"

"Of course it is. Its name is Fuzzy Britches. It's a Martian."

"You bet it is! Say, do you mind if I pet her for a moment?"

Lowell looked him over suspiciously, granted the boon. The prospector held it like one who knows flat cats, cooed to it, and stroked it. "Now ain't that nice! Almost makes me wish I had never left Mars—not but what it's better here." He handed it back reluctantly, thanked them all around again, and left.

Dr. Stone flexed her fingers. "That's the first time I've done surgery in free fall since the old clinic days. I must review my techniques."

"My dear, you were magnificent. And Jock Donaher is mighty lucky that you were near by."

"Was he pretty bad, Mummy?" asked Meade.

"Quite," answered her father. "You wouldn't enjoy the details. But your mother knew what to do and did it. And I was a pretty fair scrub nose myself, if I do say so as shouldn't."

"You do say so and shouldn't," agreed Hazel.

"Roger," asked Dr. Stone, "that thing they were living in—could it be operated as a ship?"

"I doubt it, not the way they've got it rigged now. I wouldn't call it a ship; I'd call it a raft."

"What do they do when they want to leave?"

"They probably don't want to leave. They'll probably die within hailing distance of Rock City—as Jock nearly did. I suppose they sell their high grade at Ceres, by scooter—circum Ceres, that is. Or maybe they sell it here."

"But the whole town is migratory. They have to move sometime."

"Oh, I imagine you could move that hulk with a few jato units, if you were gentle about it and weren't in any hurry. I think I'd decompress it before I tried it, though."

XVI ROCK CITY

THE ASTEROID BELT IS A FLATTENED torus ring or dough-nut in space encompassing thirteen thousand five hundred thousand million trillion cubic miles. This very conservative figure is arrived at by casting out of the family the vagrant blacksheep who wander in down to Mars and farther—even down close to Sun itself—and by ignoring those which strayed too far out and became slaves to mighty Jove, such as the Trojan Asteroids which made him a guard of honor sixty degrees ahead and behind him in orbit. Even those that swing too far north or south are excluded; an arbitrary limit of six degrees deviation from ecliptic has been assumed.

13,500,000,000,000,000,000,000,000 cubic miles of space.

Yet the entire human race could be tucked into one corner of a single cubic mile; the average human body is about two cubic feet in bulk.

Even Hazel's dauntless hero "Captain John Sterling" would be hard put to police such a beat. He would need to be twins, at least.

Write the figure as 1.35×10^{25} cubic miles; that makes it easier to see if no easier to grasp. At the time the *Rolling Stone* arrived among the rolling stones of Rock City the Belt had a population density of one human soul for every two billion trillion cubic miles—read 2×10^{21}. About half of these six thousand-odd lived on the larger planetoids, Ceres, Pallas, Vesta, Juno; one of the few pleasant surprises in the exploration of our system was the discovery that the largest Asteroids were unbelievably dense and thus had respectable surface gravitations. Ceres, with a diameter of only 435 miles, has an average density five times that of Earth and a surface gravity about the same as Mars. These large planetoids are believed to be mainly core material of lost Lucifer, covered with a few miles of lighter debris.

The other three thousand inhabitants constitute the Belt's "floating population" in a most literal sense; they live and work in free fall. Almost all of them are gathered into a half a dozen loose communities working the nodes or clusters of the Belt. The nodes are several hundred times as dense as the main body of the Belt—if "dense" is the proper word; a transport for Ganymede could have plowed through the Hallelujah node and Rock City and never noticed it except by radar. The chance that such a liner would hit anything is extremely small.

The miners worked the nodes for uranium, transuranics, and core material, selling their high grade at the most conveniently positioned large Asteroid and occasionally moving on to some other node. Before the strike in the Hallelujah the group calling themselves Rock City had been working Kaiser Wilhelm node behind Ceres in orbit; at the good news they moved, speeding up a trifle and passing in-orbit of Ceres, a ragtag caravan nudged through the sky by scooters, chemical rocket engines, jato units, and faith. Theirs was the only community well placed to migrate. Grogan's Boys were in the same orbit but in Heartbreak node beyond the Sun, half a billion miles away. New Joburg was not far away but was working the node known as Reynolds Number Two, which rode the Themis orbital pattern, inconveniently far out.

None of these cities in the sky was truly self-supporting, nor perhaps ever would be; but the ravenous appetite of Earth's industries for power metal and for the even more valuable planetary-core materials for such uses as jet throats and radiation shields—this insatiable demand for what the Asteroids could yield—made certain that the miners could swap what they had for what they needed. Yet in many ways they were almost self-supporting; uranium refined no further away than Ceres gave them heat and light and power; all of their vegetables and much of their protein came from their own hydroponic tanks and yeast vats. Single-H and oxygen came from Ceres or Pallas.

Wherever there is power and mass to manipulate, Man can live.

For almost three days the *Rolling Stone* coasted slowly through Rock City. To the naked eye looking out a port or even to a person standing outside on the hull Rock City looked like any other stretch of space—empty, with a backdrop of stars. A sharp-eyed person who knew the constellations well would have noticed far too many planets distorting the classic configurations, planets which did not limit their wanderings to the Zodiac. Still sharper attention would have spotted motion on the port of these "planets," causing them to open out and draw aft from the direction the *Stone* was heading.

Just before lunch on the third day Captain Stone slowed his ship still more and corrected her vector by firing a jato unit; City Hall and several other shapes could be seen ahead. Later in the afternoon he fired one more jato unit, leaving the *Stone* dead in space relative to City Hall and less than an eighth of a mile from it. He turned to the phone and called the Mayor.

"*Rolling Stone*, Luna, Captain Stone speaking."

"We've been watching you come in, Captain," came the voice of the Mayor.

"Good. Mr. Fries, I'm going to try to get a line over

to you. With luck, I'll be over to see you in a half hour or so."

"Using a line-throwing gun? I'll send someone out to pick it up."

"No gun, worse luck. With the best of intentions I forgot to stock one."

Fries hesitated. "Uh, Captain, pardon me, but are you in good practice for free-fall suit work?"

"Truthfully, no."

"Then let me send a boy across to put a line on you. No, no! I insist."

Hazel, the Captain, and the twins suited up, went outside, and waited. They could make out a small figure on the ship across from them; the ship itself looked larger now, larger than the *Stone*. City Hall was an obsolete space-to-space vessel, globular, and perhaps thirty years old. Roger Stone surmised correctly that she had made a one-way freighter trip after she was retired from a regular run.

In close company with City Hall was a stubby cylinder; it was either smaller than the spherical ship or farther away. Near it was an irregular mass impossible to make out; the sunlight on it was bright enough but the unfilled black shadows gave no clear clues. All around them were other ships or shapes close enough to be distinguished from the stars; Pollux estimated that there must be two dozen within as many miles. While he watched a scooter left a ship a mile or more away and headed toward City Hall.

The figure they had seen launched himself across the gap. He seemed to swell; in half a minute he was close by, checking himself by the line he carried. He dropped to an easy landing near the bow of the *Stone;* they went to meet him.

"Howdy, Captain. I'm Don Whitsitt, Mr. Fries' bookkeeper."

"Howdy, Don." He intoduced the others; the twins helped haul in the light messenger line and coil it; it was followed by a steel line which Don Whitsitt shackled to the ship.

"See you at the store," he said. "So long." He launched himself back the way he came, carrying the coiled messenger line and not bothering with the line he had rigged.

Pollux watched him draw away. "I think I could do that."

"Just keep on thinking it," his father said, "and loop yourself to that guide line."

One leap took them easily across the abyss, provided one did not let one's loop twist around the guide line. Castor's loop did so; it braked him to a stop. He had to unsnarl it, then gain momentum again by swarming along the line hand over hand.

Whitsitt had gone inside but he had recycled the lock and left it open for them. They went on in, to be met there by the Honorable Jonathan Fries, Mayor of Rock City. He was a small, bald, pot-bellied man with a sharp, merry look in his eye and a stylus tucked back of his ear. He shook hands with Roger Stone enthusiastically. "Welcome, welcome! We're honored to have you with us, Mister Mayor. I ought to have a key to the city, or some such, for you. Dancing girls and brass bands."

Roger shook his head. "I'm an ex-mayor and a private traveler. Never mind the brass bands."

"But you'll take the dancing girls?"

"I'm a married man. Thanks anyhow."

"If we had any dancing girls I'd keep 'em for myself. And I'm a married man, too."

"You certainly are!" A plump, plain but very jolly woman had floated up behind them.

"Yes, Martha." They completed the rest of the introductions; Mrs. Fries took Hazel in tow; the twins trailed along with the two men, into the forward half of the globe. It was a storeroom and a shop; racks had been fitted to the struts and thrust members; goods and provisions of every sort were lashed or netted to them. Don Whitsitt clung with his knees to a saddle in the middle of the room with a desk folded into his lap. In his reach were ledgers on lazy tongs and a rack of clip holding several hundred small account books. A miner floated in front of him. Several more were burrowing through the racks of merchandise.

Seeing the display of everything a meteor miner could conceivably need, Pollux was glad that they had concentrated on luxury goods—then remembered with regret that they had precious little left to sell; the flat cats, before they were placed in freeze, had eaten so much that the family had been delving into their trade goods, from caviar to Chicago sausage. He whispered to Castor, "I had no idea the competition would be so stiff."

"Neither did I."

A miner slithered up to Mr. Fries. "One-Price, about that centrifuge"

"Later, Sandy. I'm busy."

Captain Stone protested, "Don't let me keep you from your customers."

"Oh, Sandy hasn't got anything to do but wait. Right, Sandy? Shake hands with Captain Stone—it was his wife who fixed up old Jocko."

"It was? Say, I'm mighty proud to know you, Captain! You're the best news we've had in quite a while." Sandy turned to Fries. "You better put him right on the Committee."

"I shall. I'm going to call a phone meeting this evening."

"Just a moment!" objected Roger Stone. "I'm just a visitor. I don't belong on your Citizens' Committee."

Fries shook his head. "You don't know what it means to our people to have a medical doctor with us again. The Committee ain't any work, really. It's just to let you know we're glad you've joined us. And we'll make Mrs. Stone—I mean Doctor Stone—a member if she wants it. She won't have time for it, though."

Captain Stone was beginning to feel hemmed in. "Slow down! We expect to be leaving here come next Earth departure—and my wife is not now engaged in regular practice, anyhow. We're on a pleasure trip."

Fries looked worried. "You mean she won't attend the sick? But she operated on Jock Donaher."

Stone was about to say that she positively would not under any circumstances take over a regular practice when he realized that he had very little voice in the matter. "She'll attend the sick. She's a doctor."

"Good!"

"But, confound it, man! We didn't come here for that. She's on vacation."

Fries nodded. "We'll see what we can work out to make it easy on her. We won't expect the lady to go hopping rocks the way Doc Schultz did. Get that, Sandy? We can't have every rock-happy rat in the swarm hollering for the doctor every time he gets a sore finger. We want to get the word around that if a man gets sick or gets hurt it's up to him and his neighbors to drag him in to City Hall if he can possibly wear a suit. Tell Don to draft me a proclamation."

The miner nodded solemnly. "That's right, One-Price."

Sandy moved away; Fries went on, "Let's go back into the restaurant and see if Martha has some fresh coffee. I'd like to get your opinion on several civic matters."

"Frankly, I couldn't possibly have opinions on your public affairs here. Things are so different."

"Oh, why don't I be truthful and admit I want to gossip about politics with another pro—I don't meet one every day. First, though, did you have any shopping in mind today? Anything you need? Tools? Oxy? Catalysts? Planning on doing any prospecting and if so, do you have your gear?"

"Nothing especial today—except one thing: we need to buy, or by preference rent, a scooter. We'd like to explore a bit."

Fries shook his head. "Friend, I wish you hadn't asked me that. That's the one thing I haven't got. All these sand rats booming in here from Mars, and even from Luna, half of 'em with no equipment. They lease a scooter and a patent igloo and away they go, red hot to make their fortunes. Tell you what I can do, though—I've got more rocket motors and tanks coming in from Ceres two months from now. Don and I can weld you up one and have it ready to slap the motor in when the *Firefly* gets here."

Roger Stone frowned. "With Earth departure only five months away that's a long time to wait."

"Well, we'll just have to see what we can scare up. Certainly the new doctor is entitled to the best—and the doctor's family. Say—"

A miner tapped him on the shoulder. "Say, storekeeper, I—"

Fries' face darkened. "You can address me as 'Mr. Mayor!' "

"Huh?"

"And beat it! Can't you see I'm busy?" The man backed away; Fries fumed, " 'One-Price' I'm known as, to my friends and to my enemies, from here to the Trojans. If he doesn't know that, he can call me by my title—or take his trade elsewhere. Where was I? Oh, yes! You might try old Charlie."

"Eh?"

"Did you notice that big tank moored to City Hall? That's Charlie's hole. He's a crazy old coot, rock-happy as they come, and he's a hermit by intention. Used to hang around the edge of the community, never mixing—but with this boom and ten strangers swarming in for every familiar face Charlie got timid and asked could he please tie in at civic center? I guess he was afraid that somebody would slit his throat and steal his hoorah's nest. Some of the boomers are a rough lot at that."

"He sounds like some of the old-timers on Luna. What about him?"

"Oh! Too much on my mind these days; it wanders. Charlie runs sort of a fourth-hand shop, and I say that advisedly. He has stuff I won't handle. Every time a rock jumper dies, or goes Sunside, his useless plunder winds up in Charlie's hole. Now I don't say he's got a scooter —though you just might lease his own now that he's moored in-city. But he might have parts that could be jury-rigged. Are you handy with tools?"

"Moderately. But I've got just the team for such a job." He looked around for the twins, finally spotted them pawing through merchandise. "Cas! Pol! Come here."

The storekeeper explained what he had in mind. Castor nodded. "If it worked once, we'll fix it."

"That's the spirit. Now let's go test that coffee."

Castor hung back. "Dad? Why don't Pol and I go over there and see what he's got? It'll save you time."

"Well—"

"It's just a short jump," said Fries.

"Okay, but don't jump. Use your lines and follow the mooring line over."

The twins left. Once in the airlock Pollux started fuming. "Stow it," said Cas. "Dad just wants us to be careful."

"Yes, but why does he have to say it where everybody can hear?"

Charlie's hole, they decided, had once been a tow tank to deliver oxygen to a colony. They let themselves into the lock, started it cycling. When pressure was up, they tried the inner door; it wouldn't budge. Pollux started pounding on it with his belt wrench while Castor searched for a switch or other signal. The lock was miserably lighted by a scant three inches of glow tube.

"Cut the racket," Castor told Pollux. "If he's alive, he's heard you by now." Pollux complied and tried the door again—still locked.

They heard a muffled voice; "Who's there?"

Castor looked around for the source of the voice, could not spot it. "Castor and Pollux Stone," he answered, "from the *Rolling Stone*, out of Luna."

Somebody chuckled. "You don't fool me. And you can't arrest me without a warrant. Anyhow I won't let you in."

Castor started to explode; Pollux patted his arm. "We aren't cops. Shucks, we aren't old enough to be cops."

"Take your helmets off."

"Don't do it," Castor cautioned. "He could recycle while we're unsealed."

Pollux went ahead and took his off; Castor hesitated, then followed. "Let us in," Pollux said mildly.

"Why should I?"

"We're customers. We want to buy things."

"What you got to trade?"

"We'll pay cash."

"Cash!" said the voice. "Banks! Governments! What you got to *trade?* Any chocolate?"

"Cas," Pollux whispered, "have we got *any* chocolate left?"

"Maybe six or seven pounds. Not more."

"Sure we got chocolate."

"Le'me see it."

Castor interrupted. "What sort of nonsense is this? Pol, let's go back and see Mr. Fries again. He's a businessman."

The voice moaned, "Oh, don't do that! He'll cheat you."

"Then open up!"

After a few seconds of silence the voice said wheedlingly, "You look like nice boys. You wouldn't hurt Charlie? Not old Charlie?"

"Of course not. We want to trade with you."

The door opened at last. In the gloom a face, etched by age and darkened by raw sunlight, peered out at them. "Come in easy. Don't try any tricks—I know you."

Wondering if it were the sensible thing to do the boys pulled themselves in. When their eyes adjusted to the feeble circle of glow tube in the middle of the space they looked around while their host looked at them. The tank, large outside, seemed smaller by the way it was stuffed. As in Fries' shop, every inch, every strut, every nook was crammed, but where the City Hall was neat, this was rank disorder, where Fries' shop was rational, this was nightmare confusion. The air was rich enough but ripe with ancient and nameless odors.

Their host was a skinny monkey of a man, covered with a single dark garment, save for head, hands, and bare feet. It had once been, Pollux decided, heated underwear for spacesuit use far out starside, or in caves.

Old Charlie stared at them, then grinned, reached

up and scratched his neck with his big toe. "Nice boys," he said. "I knew you wouldn't hurt Charlie. I was just foolin'."

"We wouldn't hurt anybody. We just wanted to get acquainted and do a little business."

"We want a—" Pollux started; Castor's elbow cut off the rest; Castor went on,

"Nice place you've got here."

"Comfortable. Practical. Just right for a man with no nonsense about him. Good place for a man who likes to be quiet and think. Good place to read a book. You boys like to read?"

"Sure. Love to."

"You want to see my books?" Without waiting for an answer he darted like a bat into the gloom, came back in a few moments with books in both hands and a half dozen held by his feet. He bumped to a stop with his elbows and offered them.

There were old-style bound books, most of them, the twins saw, ships' manuals of ships long dead. Castor's eyes widened when he saw the dates on some of them, and wondered what the Astrogation Institute would pay for them. Among them was a dog-eared copy of Mark Twain's *Life on the Mississippi*.

"Look 'em over, boys. Make yourselves comfortable. Bet you didn't expect to find a literary man out here among these yokels. You boys can read, can't you?"

"Sure we can."

"Didn't know. They teach such funny things nowadays. Quote a bit of Latin to 'em and they look like you're crazy in the head. You boys hungry? You want something to eat?" He looked anxious.

They both assured him that they had fed well and recently; he looked relieved. "Old Charlie ain't one to let a man go hungry, even if he hasn't got enough himself." Castor had noted a net of sealed rations; there must have been a thousand of them by conservative estimate. But the old man continued, "Seen the time, right here in this node—no, it was the Emmy Lou—when a man didn't dare make breakfast without he barred his lock first and turned off his beacon. It was about that time that Lafe Dumont ate High-Grade Henderson. He was dead first, naturally—but it brought on a crisis in our community affairs. They formed up the vigilantes, what they call the Committee nowadays."

"Why did he eat him?"

"Why, he was *dead*. I told you that. Just the same, I don't think a man ought to eat his own partner, do you?"

The boys agreed that it was a breech of etiquette.

"I think he ought to limit it to members of his own family, unless the two of them have got a signed and sealed contract. Seen any ghosts yet?"

The acceleration was so sharp that it left both the twins a bit confused. "Ghosts?"

"You will. Many's the time I've talked to High-Grade Henderson. Said he didn't blame Lafe a bit, would 'a' done the same thing in his place. Ghosts all around here. All the rockmen that have died out here, they can't get back to Earth. They're in a permanent orbit—see? And it stands to reason that you can't accelerate anything that doesn't have mass." He leaned toward them confidentially. "Sometimes you see 'em, but mostly they whisper in your earphones. And when they do, *listen*—because that's the only way you'll ever find any of the big strikes that got found and then got lost again. I'm telling you this because I like you, see? So listen. If it's too faint, just close your chin valve and hold your breath; then it comes clearer."

They agreed and thanked him. "Now tell me about yourselves, boys." To their surprise he appeared to mean it; when they slowed down he taxed them for details, filling in only occasionally with his own disjointed anecdotes. At last Castor described the fiasco of the flat cats. "So that's why we don't have much food to trade with. But we do have some chocolate left and lots of other things."

Charlie rocked back and forth from his perch in the air. "Flat cats, eh? I ain't had my hands on a flat cat in a power of years. Nice to hold, they are. Nice to have around. Philosophical, if we just understand 'em." He suddenly fixed Castor with his eye. "What you planning to do with all those flat cats?"

"Why, nothing, I guess."

"That's just what I thought. You wouldn't mind giving a poor old man who hasn't kith or kin nor wife nor chick one of those harmless flat cats? An old man who would always give you a bite to eat and a charge for your suit bottle?"

Castor glanced at Pollux and agreed cautiously that any dicker they reached would certainly include a flat cat as a mark of faith in dealing. "Then what do you want? You talked about scooters. You know old Charlie hasn't got a scooter—except the one I have to have myself to stay alive."

Castor broached the notion about repairing old parts, fitting together a scooter. Charlie scratched an inch-long stubble. "Seems to me I did have a rocket motor—you wouldn't mind if it lacked a valve or two? Or did I trade that to Swede Gonzalez? No, that was another one. I think—just a second while I take a look." He was gone more nearly six hundred seconds, buried in the mass; he came out dragging a piece of junk behind. "There you are! Practically new. Nothing a couple of bright boys couldn't fix."

Pollux looked at Castor. "What do you think it's worth?"

Castor's lips moved silently: "He ought to pay us to take it away." It took them another twenty minutes but they got it for three pounds of chocolate and one flat cat.

XVII FLAT CATS FINANCIAL

IT TOOK THE BETTER PART of two weeks to make the ancient oxy-alcohol engine work; another week to build a scooter rack to receive it, using tubing from Fries' second-hand supply. It was not a pretty thing, but, with the *Stone*'s stereo gear mounted on it, it was an efficient way to get around the node. Captain Stone shook his head over it and subjected it to endless tests before he conceded that it was safe even though ugly.

In the meantime the Committee had decreed a taxi service for the doctor lady; every miner working within fifty miles of City Hall was required to take his turn at standby watch with his scooter, with a fixed payment in high grade for any run he might have to make. The Stones saw very little of Edith Stone during this time; it seemed as if every citizen of Rock City had been saving up ailments.

But they were not forced to fall back on Hazel's uninspired cooking. Fries had the *Stone* warped into contact with City Hall and a passenger tube sealed from the *Stone*'s lock to an unused hatch of the bigger ship; when Dr. Stone was away they ate in his restaurant. Mrs. Fries was an excellent cook and she raised a great variety in her hydroponics garden.

While they were rigging the scooter the twins had time to mull over the matter of the flat cats. It had dawned on them that here in Rock City was a potential, unexploited market for flat cats. The question was: how best to milk it for all the traffic would bear?

Pol suggested that they peddle them in the scooter; he pointed out that a man's sales resistance was lowest, practically zero, when he actually had a flat cat in his hands. His brother shook his head. "No good, Junior."

"Why not?"

"One, the Captain won't let us monopolize the scooter; you know he regards it as ship's equipment, built by the crew, namely us. Two, we would burn up our profits in scooter fuel. Three, it's too slow; before we could move a third of them, some idiot would have fed our first sale too much, it has kittens—and there you are, with the market flooded with flat cats. The idea is to sell them as nearly as possible all at one time."

"We could stick up a sign in the store—One-Price would let us—and sell them right out of the *Stone*."

"Better but not good enough. Most of these rats shop only every three or four months. No, sir, we've got to build that better mouse trap and make the world beat a path to our door."

"I've never been able to figure out why anybody would want to trap a mouse. Decompress a compartment and you kill all of them, every time."

"Just a figure of speech, no doubt. Junior, what can we do to make Rock City flat-cat conscious?"

They found a way. The Belt, for all its lonely reaches —or because of them—was as neighborly as a village. They gossiped among themselves, by suit radio. Out in the shining blackness it was good to know that, if something went wrong, there was a man listening not five hundred miles away who would come and investigate if you broke off and did not answer.

They gossiped from node to node by their more powerful ship's radios. A rumor of death, of a big strike, or of accident would bounce around the entire belt, relayed from rockman to rockman, at just short of the speed of light. Heartbreak node was sixty-six light-minutes away, following orbit; big news often reached it in less than two hours, including numerous manual relays.

Rock City even had its own broadcast. Twice a day One-Price picked up the news from Earthside, then rebroadcast it with his own salty comments. The twins decided to follow it with one of their own, on the same wave length—a music & chatter show, with commercials. Oh, decidedly with commercials. They had hundreds of spools in stock which they could use, then sell, along with the portable projectors they had bought on Mars.

They started in; the show never was very good, but, on the other hand, it had no competition and it was free. Immediately following Fries' sign-off Castor would say, "Don't go away, neighbors! Here we are again with two hours of fun and music—and a few tips on bargains. But first, our theme—the war-r-rm and friendly purr of a Martian flat cat." Pollux would hold Fuzzy Britches up to the microphone and stroke it; the good-natured little creature would always respond with a loud buzz. "Wouldn't that be nice to come home to? And now for some music: Harry Weinstein's Sunbeam Six in 'High Gravity.' Let me remind you that this tape, like all other music on this program, may be purchased at an amazing saving in Flat Cat Alley, right off the City Hall—as well as Ajax three-way projectors in the Giant, Jr., model, for sound, sight, and stereo. The Sunbeam Six—hit it, Harry!"

Sometimes they would do interviews:

Castor: "A few words with one of our leading citizens, Rocks-in-his-head Rudolf. Mr. Rudolf, all Rock City is waiting to hear from you. Tell me, do you like it out here?"

Pollux: "Naw!"

Castor: "But you're making lots of money, Mr. Rudolf?"

Pollux: "Naw!"

Castor: "At least you bring in enough high grade to eat well?"

"Naw!"

"No? Tell me, why did you come out here in the first place?"

Pollux, "Bub, was *you* ever married?"

Sound effect of blow with blunt instrument, groan, and the unmistakable cycling of an airlock—Castor: "Sorry, folks. My assistant has just spaced Mr. Rudolf. To the purchaser of the flat cat we had been saving for Mr. Rudolf we will give away—absolutely free!—a beautiful pin-up picture printed in gorgeous living colors on fireproof paper. I hate to tell you what these pictures ordinarily sell for on Ceres; it hurts me to say how little we are letting them go for now, until our limited stock is exhausted. To the very first customer who comes in that door wanting to purchase a flat cat we will— Lock that door! Lock that door! All right, all right—all three of you will receive pin-up pictures; we don't want anyone fighting here. But you'll have to wait until we finish this broadcast. Sorry, neighbors—a slight interruption but we settled it without bloodshed. But I find myself in a dilemma. I made you a promise and I did not know what would happen, but the truth is, too many customers were already here, pounding on the door of Flat Cat Alley. But to make good our promise I am enlarging it: not to the first customer, not to the second, nor to the third—but to the next *twenty* persons purchasing flat cats will go, absolutely free, one of these gorgeous pictures. Bring no money—we accept high grade or core material at the standard rates."

Sometimes they varied it by having Meade sing. She was not of concert standards, but she had a warm, intimate contralto. After hearing her, a man possessing not even a flat cat felt lonely indeed. She pulled even better than the slick professional recordings; the twins found it necessary to cut her in for a percentage.

But in the main they depended on the flat cats themselves. The boomers from Mars, almost to a man, bought flat cats as soon as they heard that they were available, and each became an unpaid traveling salesman for the enterprise. Hardrock men from Luna, or directly from Earth, who had never seen a flat cat, now had opportunities to see them, pet them, listen to their hypnotic purr—and were lost. The little things not only stirred to aching suppressed loneliness, but, having stimulated it, gave it an outlet.

Castor would hold Fuzzy Britches to the mike and coo, "Here is a little darling—Molly Malone. Sing for the boys, honey pet." While he stroked Fuzzy Britches Pollux would step up the power. "No, we can't let Molly go—she's a member of the family. But here is Bright Eyes. We'd like to keep Bright Eyes, too, but we mustn't be selfish. Say hello to the folks, Bright Eyes." Again he would stroke Fuzzy Britches. "Mr. P., now hand me Velvet."

The stock of flat cats in deep freeze steadily melted. Their stock of high grade grew.

Roger Stone received their suggestion that they save out a few for breeding stock with one of his more emphatic refusals; once, he declaimed, was enough to be swamped in flat cats. Fuzzy Britches could stay, safely on short rations—but one was enough.

They had reached the last few at the back of the hold and were thinking about going out of business when a tired-looking, gray-haired man showed up after their broadcast. There were several other customers; he hung back and let the twins sell flat cats to the others. He had with him a girl child, little older than Lowell. Castor had not seen him before but he guessed that he might be Mr. Erska; bachelors far outnumbered families in the node and families with children were very rare. The Erskas picked up a precarious living down orbit and north; they were seldom seen at City Hall. Mr. Erska spoke Basic with some difficulty; Mrs. Erska spoke it not at all. The family used some one of the little lingos—Icelandic, it might have been.

When the other customers had left the *Stone* Castor put on his professional grin and introduced himself. Yes, it was Mr. Erska. "And what can I do for you today, sir? A flat cat?"

"I'm afraid not."

"How about a projector? With a dozen tapes thrown in? Just the thing for a family evening."

Mr. Erska seemed nervous. "Uh, very nice, I'm sure. No." He tugged at the little girl's hand. "We better go now, babykin."

"Don't rush off. My baby brother is around somewhere—or was. He'd like to meet your kid. Maybe he's wandered over into the store. I'll look for him."

"We better go."

"What's the rush? He can't be far."

Mr. Erska swallowed in embarrassment. "My little girl. She heard your program and she wanted to see a flat cat. Now she's seen one, so we go."

"Oh." Castor brought himself face to face with the child. "Would you like to hold one, honey?" She did not answer, but nodded solemnly. "Mr. P., bring up the Duchess."

"Right, Mr. C." Pollux went aft and fetched the Duchess—the first flat cat that came to hand, of course. He came back, warming it against his belly to revive it quickly.

Castor took it and massaged it until it flattened out and opened its eyes. "Here, honeybunch. Don't be afraid."

Still silent, the child took it, cuddled it. The small furry bundle sighed and began to purr. Castor turned to her father. "Don't you want to get it for her?"

The man turned red. "No, no!"

"Why not? They're no trouble. She'll love it. So will you."

"No!" He reached out and tried to take the flat cat from his daughter, speaking to her in another language.

She clung to it, replying in what was clearly the negative. Castor looked at them thoughtfully. "You would like to buy it for her, wouldn't you?"

The man looked away. "I *can't* buy it."

"But you want to." Castor glanced at Pollux. "Do you know what you are, Mr. Erska. You are the *five hundredth* customer of Flat Cat Alley."

"Uh?"

"Didn't you hear our grand offer? You must have missed some of our programs. The five hundredth flat cat is *absolutely free*."

The little girl looked puzzled but clung to the flat cat. Her father looked doubtful. "You're fooling?"

Castor laughed. "Ask Mr. P."

Pollux nodded solemnly. "The bare truth, Mr. Erska. It's a celebration of a successful season. One flat cat, absolutely free with the compliments of the management. And with it goes either one pin-up, or two candy bars—your choice."

Mr. Erska seemed only half convinced, but they left with the child clinging to "Duchess" and the candy bars. When the door was closed behind them Castor said fretfully, "You didn't need to chuck in the candy bars. They were the last; I didn't mean us to sell them."

"Well, we didn't sell them; we gave 'em away."

Castor grinned and shrugged. "Okay, I hope they don't make her sick. What was her name?"

"I didn't get it."

"No matter. Or Mrs. Fries will know." He turned around, saw Hazel behind them in the hatch. "What are *you* grinning about?"

"Nothing, nothing. I just enjoy seeing a couple of cold-cash businessmen at work."

"Money isn't everything!"

"Besides," added Pollux, "it's good advertising."

"Advertising? With your stock practically gone?" She snickered. "There wasn't any 'grand offer'—and I'll give you six to one it wasn't your five hundredth sale."

Castor looked embarrassed. "Aw, she wanted it! What would you have done?"

Hazel moved up to them, put an arm around the neck of each. "My boys! I'm beginning to think you may grow up yet. In thirty, forty, fifty more years you may be ready to join the human race."

"Aw, lay off it!"

XVIII   THE WORM IN THE MUD

Cost-accounting on the flat-cat deal turned out to be complicated. The creatures were all descendants of Fuzzy Britches, chattel of Lowell. But the increase was directly attributable to food fed to them by everyone—which in turn had forced them to eat most of the luxury foods stocked by the twins for trade. But it had been the twins' imaginative initiative which had turned a liability into an asset. On the other hand they had used freely the capital goods (ship and electronic equipment) belonging to the entire family. But how to figure the probable worth of the consumed luxury foods? Whatever the figure was, it was not just original cost plus lift fuel.

Roger Stone handed down a Solomon's decision. From the gross proceeds would be subtracted Meade's percentage for singing; the twins would be reimbursed for the trade goods that had been commandeered; the balance would be split three ways among the twins and Lowell—all to be settled after they had traded high grade for refined metal at Ceres, then sold their load at Luna.

In the meantime he agreed to advance the twins' money to operate further, Fries having promised to honor his sight draft on Luna City National.

But for once the twins found no immediate way to invest money. They toyed with the idea of using their time to prospect on their own, but a few trips out in the scooter convinced them that it was a game for experts and one in which even the experts usually made only a bare living. It was the fixed illusion that the next mass would be "the glory rock"—the one that would pay for years of toil—that kept the old rockmen going. The twins knew too much about statistics now, and they believed in their ability rather than their luck. Finding a glory rock was sheer gamble.

They made one fairly long trip into the thickest part of the node, fifteen hundred miles out and back, taking all one day and the following night to do it. They got the scooter up to a dawdling hundred and fifty miles per hour and let it coast, planning to stop and investigate if they found promising masses, having borrowed a stake-out beacon from Fries with the promise that they would pay for it if they kept it.

They did not need it. Time after time they would spot a major blip in the stereo radar, only to have someone's else beacon wink on when they got within thirty miles of the mass. At the far end they did find a considerable collection of rock traveling loosely in company; they matched, shackled on their longest lines (their father had emphatically forbidden free jumping) and investigated. Having neither experience nor a centrifuge, their only way of checking on specific gravity was by grasping a mass and clutching it to them vigorously, thus getting a rough notion of its inertia by its resistance to being shoved around. A Geiger counter (borrowed) had shown no radioactivity; they were searching for the more valuable core material.

Two hours of this exercise left them tired but no richer. "Grandpa," announced Pollux, "this is a lot of left-over country rock."

"Not even that. Most of it's pumice, I'd say."

"Git for home?"

"Check."

They turned the scooter around by flywheel and homed on the City Hall beacon, boosting it up to four hundred miles per hour before letting it coast, that being the top maneuver they could figure on for the juice they had left in their tanks. They would have preferred to break the speed limit, being uneasily aware that they were late—and being anxious to get home; the best designed suit is not comfortable for too long periods. They knew that their parents would not be especially worried; while they were out of range for their suit radios, they had reported in by the gossip grapevine earlier.

Their father was not worried. But the twins spent the next week under hatches, confined to the ship for failing to get back on time.

For a longer period nothing more notable took place than the incident in which Roger Stone lost his breathing mask while taking a shower and almost drowned (so he claimed) before he could find the water cutoff valve. There are very few tasks easier to do in a gravity field than in free fall, but bathing is one of them.

Dr. Stone continued her practice, now somewhat reduced. Sometimes she was chauffeured by the miner assigned to that duty; sometimes the twins took her around. One morning following her office hours in City Hall she came back into the *Stone* looking for the twins. "Where are the boys?"

"Haven't seen them since breakfast," answered Hazel. "Why?"

Dr. Stone frowned slightly. "Nothing, really. I'll ask Mr. Fries to call a scooter for me."

"Got to make a call? I'll take you—unless those lunks have taken our scooter."

"You needn't, Mother Hazel."

"I'd enjoy it. I've been promising Lowell a ride for weeks. Or will it take too long?"

"Shouldn't. It's only eight hundred miles or so out."

The doctor was not held down to the local speed limit in her errands of mercy.

"Do it in two hours, with juice to spare." Off they went, with Buster much excited. Hazel allotted one-fourth her fuel as safety margin, allotted the working balance for maximum accelerations, figuring the projected mass-ratios in her head. Quite aside from the doctor's privilege to disregard the law, high speed was not dangerous in the sector they would be in, it being a "thin" volume of the node.

Their destination was an antiquated winged rocker, the wings of which had been torched off and welded into a tent-shaped annex to give more living room. Hazel thought that it had a shanty-town air—but so did many of the ships in Rock City. She was pleased enough to go inside and have a sack of tea and let Lowell out of his spacesuit for a time. The patient, Mr. Eakers, was in a traction splint; his wife could not pilot their scooter, which was why Dr. Stone granted the house call.

Dr. Stone received a call by radio while they were there; she came back into the general room looking troubled. " 'Smatter?" inquired Hazel.

"Mrs. Silva. I'm not really surprised; it's her first child."

"Did you get the coordinates and beacon pattern? I'll run you right over."

"Lowell?"

"Oh. Oh, yes." It would be a long time in a suit for a youngster.

Mrs. Eakers suggested that they leave the child with her. Before Lowell could cloud up at the suggestion Dr. Stone said, "Thanks, but it isn't necessary. Mr. Silva is on his way here. What I was trying to say, Mother Hazel, is that I probably had better go with him and let you and Lowell go back alone. Do you mind?"

"Of course not. Pipe down, Lowell! I'll have us

home in three-quarters of an hour and Lowell can have his nap or his spanking on time, as the case may be."

She gave Dr. Stone one of two spare oxygen bottles before she left; Dr. Stone refused to take both of them. Hazel worked the new mass figures over: with Edith, her suit, and the spare bottle subtracted she had spare fuel. Better hit it up pretty fast and get home before the brat got cranky—

She lined up on City Hall by flywheel and stereo, spun on that axis to get the sun out of her eyes, clutched her gyros, and gave it the gun.

The next thing she knew she was tumbling like a liner in free fall. She remembered from long habit to cut the throttle but only after a period of aimless acceleration, for she had been chucked around in her saddle, thrown against her belts, and could not at first find the throttle.

When they were in free fall again she remembered to laugh. "Some ride, eh, Lowell?"

"Do it again, Grandma!"

"I hope not." Quickly she checked things over. There was not much that could go wrong with the little craft, it being only a rocket motor, an open rack with saddles and safety harness, and a minimum of instruments and controls. It was the gyros, of course; the motor had been sweet and hot. They were hunting the least bit, she found, that being the only evidence that they had just tumbled violently. Delicately she adjusted them by hand, putting her helmet against the case so that she could hear what she was doing.

Only then did she try to find where they were and where they were going. Let's see—the Sun is over there— and that's Betelgeuse over yonder—so City Hall must be out that way. She ducked her helmet into the hemispherical "eye shade" of the stereo. Yup! there she be!

The Eakers place was the obvious close-by point on

which to measure her vector. She looked around for it, was startled to discover how far away it was. They must have coasted quite a distance while she was fiddling with the gyros. She measured the vector in amount and direction, then whistled. There were, she thought, few grocery shops out that way—darn few neighbors of any sort. She decided that it might be smart to call Mrs. Eakers and tell her what had happened and ask her to call City Hall—just in case.

She could not raise Mrs. Eakers. The sloven, she thought bitterly, has probably switched off her alarm so she could sleep. Lazy baggage! Her house looked it—and smelled it, too.

But she kept trying to call Mrs. Eakers, or anyone else in range of her suit radio while she again lined up the ship for City, with offset to compensate for the new vector. She was cautious and most alert this time—in consequence she wasted only a few seconds of fuel when the gyros again tumbled.

She unclutched the gyros and put them out of her mind, then took careful measure of the situation. The Eakers' dump was now a planetary light in the sky, shrinking almost noticeably, but it was still the proper local reference point. She did not like the vector she got. As always, they seemed to be standing still in the exact center of a starry globe—but her instruments showed them speeding for empty space, headed clear outside the node.

"What's the matter, Grandma Hazel?"

"Nothing, son, nothing. Grandma has to stop and look at some road signs, that's all." She was thinking that she would gladly swap her chance of eternal bliss for an automatic distress signal and a beacon. She reached over, switched off the child's receiver, then repeatedly called for help.

No answer. She switched Lowell's receiver back on. "Why did you do that, Grandma Hazel?"

"Nothing. Just checking it."

"You can't fool me! You're scared! Why?"

"Not scared, pet. Worried a little, maybe. Now shut up; Grandma's got work to do."

Carefully she lined up the craft by flywheel; carefully she checked it when it tried to swing past. She aimed both to offset the new and disastrous vector and to create a vector for City Hall. She intentionally left the gyros unclutched. Then she restrapped Lowell in his saddle, checked its position. "Hold still," she warned. "Move your little finger and Grandma will scalp you."

Just as carefully she positioned herself, considering lever arms, masses, and angular moments in her head. Without gyros the craft must be balanced just so. "Now," she said to herself, "Hazel, we find out whether you are a pilot—or just a Sunday pilot." She ducked her helmet into the eyeshade, picked a distant blip on which to center her crosshairs, and gunned the craft.

The blip wavered; she tried to rebalance by shifting her body. When the blip suddenly slipped off to one side she cut the throttle quickly. Again she checked her vector. Their situation was somewhat improved. Again she called for help, not stopping to cut the child out of hearing. He said nothing and looked grave.

She went through the same routine, cutting power again when the craft "fell off its tail." She measured the vector, called for help—and did it all again. A dozen times she tried it. On the last try the thrust stopped with the throttle still wide open.

With all fuel gone there was no need to be in a hurry. She measured her vector most carefully on the Eakers' ship, now far away, then checked the results against the City Hall blip, all the while calling for help.

She ran through the figures again; in a fashion she had been successful. They were now unquestionably headed for City Hall, could not miss it by more than a few miles at most—almost jumping distance. But, while the vector was correct in direction, it was annoyingly small in quantity—six hundred and fifty miles at about forty miles an hour; they would be closest in about sixteen hours.

She wondered whether Edith really had needed that other spare oxygen bottle. Her own gauge showed about half full.

She called for help again, then decided to go through the problem once more; maybe she had dropped a decimal in her head. While she was lining up on City Hall, the tiny light in the stereo tank faded and died. Her language caused Lowell to inquire, "What's the matter now, Grandma?"

"Nothing more than I should have expected, I guess. Some days, hon, it just isn't worth while to wake up in the morning." The trouble, she soon found, was so simple as to be beyond repair. The stereo radar would no longer work because all three cartridges in the power pack were dead. She was forced to admit that she had been using it rather continuously—and it took a lot of power.

"Grandma Hazel! I want to go home!" She pulled out of her troubled thoughts to answer the child.

"We're going home, dear. But it's going to take quite a while."

"I want to go home *right now!*"

"I'm sorry but you can't."

"But—"

"Shut it up—or when I get you out of that sack, I'll give you something to yelp for. I mean it." She again called for help.

Lowell made one of his lightning changes to serenity.

"That's better," approved Hazel. "Want to play a game of chess?"

"No."

"Sissy. You're afraid I'll beat you. I'll bet you three spanks and a knuckle rub."

Lowell considered this. "I get the white men?"

"Take 'em. I'll beat you anyhow."

To her surprise she did. It was a long drawn-out game; Lowell was not as practiced as she was in visualizing a board and they had had to recount the moves on several occasions before he would concede the arrangement of men . . . and between each pair of moves she had again called for help. About the middle of the game she had found it necessary to remove her oxygen bottle and replace it with the one spare. She and the child had started out even but Lowell's small mass demanded much less oxygen.

"How about another one? Want to get your revenge?"

"*No!* I want to go *home*."

"We're going home, dear."

"How soon?"

"Well . . . it'll be a while yet. I'll tell you a story."

"What story?"

"Well, how about the one about the worm that crawled up out of the mud?"

"Oh, I know that one! I'm tired of it."

"There are parts I've never told you. And you can't get tired of it, not really, because there is never any end to it. Always something new." So she told him again about the worm that crawled up out of the slime, not because it didn't have enough to eat, not because it wasn't nice and warm and comfortable down there under the water—but because the worm was restless. How it crawled up on dry land and grew legs. How part of it got to be the Elephant's Child and part of it got to be a monkey, grew hands, and fiddled with things.

How, still insatiably restless, it grew wings and reached up for the stars. She spun it out a long, long time, pausing occasionally to call for aid.

The child was either bored and ignored her, or liked it and kept quiet on that account. But when she stopped he said, "Tell me another one."

"Not just now, dear." His oxygen gauge showed empty.

"Go on! Tell me a new one—a better one."

"Not now, dear. That's the best story Hazel knows. The very best. I told it to you again because I want you to remember it." She watched his anoxia warning signal turn red, then quietly disconnected the partly filled bottle on her own suit, closing the now useless suit valves, and replaced his empty bottle with hers. For a moment she considered cross-connecting the bottle to both suits, then shrugged and let it stand. "Lowell—"

"What, Grandma?"

"Listen to me, dear. You've heard me calling for help. You've got to do it now. Every few minutes, all the time."

"Why?"

"Because Hazel is tired, dear. Hazel has to sleep. Promise me you'll do it."

"Well . . . all right."

She tried to hold perfectly still, to breathe as little of the air left in her suit as possible. It wasn't so bad, she thought. She *had* wanted to see the Rings—but there wasn't much else she had missed. She supposed everyone had his Carcassonne; she had no regrets.

"Grandma! Grandma Hazel!" She did not answer. He waited, then began to cry, endlessly and without hope.

Dr. Stone arrived back at the *Rolling Stone* to find only her husband there. She greeted him and added, "Where's Hazel, dear? And Lowell?"

"Eh? Didn't they come back with you? I supposed they had stopped in the store."

"No, of course not."

"Why 'of course not'?"

She explained the arrangement; he looked at her in stunned astonishment. "They left the same time you did?"

"They intended to. Hazel said she would be home in forty-five minutes."

"There's a bare possibility that they are still with the Eakers. We'll find out." He lunged toward the door.

The twins returned to find their home and City Hall as well in turmoil. They had been spending an interesting and instructive several hours with old Charlie.

Their father turned away from the *Stone*'s radio and demanded, "Where have you two been?"

"Just over in Charlie's hole. What's the trouble?"

Roger Stone explained. The twins looked at each other. "Dad," Castor said painfully, "you mean Hazel took Mother out in *our* scooter?"

"Certainly." The twins questioned each other wordlessly again. "Why shouldn't she? Speak up."

"Well, you see . . . well, it was like this—"

"Speak up!"

"There was a bearing wobble, or something, in one of the gyros," Pollux admitted miserably. "We were working on it."

"You were? In Charlie's place!"

"Well, we went over there to see what he had in the way of spare parts and, well, we got detained, sort of."

Their father looked at them for several seconds with no expression of any sort. He then said in a flat voice, "You left a piece of ship's equipment out of commission. You failed to log it. You failed to report it to the Captain." He paused. "Go to your room."

"But Dad! We want to help!"

"Stay in your room; you are under arrest."

The twins did as they were ordered. While they waited, the whole of Rock City was alerted. The word went out: the doctor's little boy is missing; the boy's grandmother is missing. Fuel up your scooters; stand by to help. Stay on this wave length.

"Pol, quit jittering!"

Pollux turned to his brother. "How can I help it?"

"They can't be lost, not really lost. Why, the stereo itself would stand out on a screen like a searchlight."

Pollux thought about it. "I don't know. You remember I said I thought we might have a high-potential puncture in the power pack?"

"I thought you fixed that?"

"I planned to, just as soon as we got the bugs smoothed out in the gyros."

Castor thought about it. "That's bad. That could be really bad." He added suddenly, "But quit jittering, just the same. Start thinking instead. What happened? We've got to reconstruct it."

" 'What happened?' Are you kidding? Look, the pesky thing tumbles, then anything can happen. No control."

"Use your head, I said. What would *Hazel* do in this situation?"

They both kept quiet for some moments, then Pollux said, "Cas, that derned thing always tumbled to the left, didn't it? Always."

"What good does that do us? Left can be any direction."

"No! You asked what Hazel would do. She'd be along her homing line, of course—and Hazel *always* oriented around her drive line so as to get the Sun on the back of her neck, if possible. Her eyes aren't too good."

Castor screwed up his face, trying to visualize it. "Say Eakers' is off that way and City Hall over here;

if the Sun is over on this side, then, when it tumbles, she'd vector off *that* way." He acted it with his hands.

"Sure, sure! When you put in the right coordinates, that is. But what else would she do? What would *you* do? You'd vector back—I mean vector home."

"Huh? How could she? With no gyros?"

"Think about it. Would you quit? Hazel is a *pilot*. She'd ride that thing like a broomstick." He shaped the air with his hands. "So she'd be coming back, or trying to, along *here*—and everybody will be looking for her 'way over *here*."

Castor scowled. "Could be."

"It had better be. They'll be looking for her in a cone with its vertex at Eakers'—and they ought to be looking in a cone with its vertex right *here*, and along one side of it at that."

Castor said, "Come along!"

"Dad said we were under arrest."

"*Come along!*"

City Hall was empty, save for Mrs. Fries who was standing watch, red-eyed and tense, at the radio. She shook her head. "Nothing yet."

"Where can we find a scooter?"

"You can't. Everybody is out searching."

Castor tugged at Pollux's sleeve. "Old Charlie."

"Huh? Say, Mrs. Fries, is old Charlie out searching?"

"I doubt if he knows about it."

They rushed into their suits, cycled by spilling and wasting air, did not bother with safety lines. Old Charlie let them in. "What's all the fuss about, boys?"

Castor explained. Charlie shook his head. "That's too bad, that really is. I'm right sorry."

"Charlie, we've got to have your scooter."

"Right now!" added Pollux.

Charlie looked astonished. "Are you fooling? I'm the only one can gun that rig."

"Charlie, this is serious! We've *got* to have it."

"You couldn't gun it."

"We're both pilots."

Charlie scratched meditatively while Castor considered slugging him for his keys—but his keys probably weren't on him—and how would one find anything in that trash pile? Charlie finally said, "If you've just got to, I suppose I better gun it for you."

"Okay, okay! Hurry up! Get your suit on!"

"Don't be in such a rush. It just slows you down."

Charlie disappeared into the underbrush, came out fairly promptly with a suit that seemed to consist mostly of vulcanized patches. "Dog take it," he complained as he began to struggle with it, "if your mother would stay home and mind her own business, these things wouldn't happen."

"Shut up and hurry!"

"I am hurrying. She made me take a bath. I don't need no doctors. All the bugs that ever bit me, died."

When Charlie had dug his scooter out of the floating junkyard moored to his home they soon saw why he had refused to lend it. It seemed probable that no one else could possibly pilot it. Not only was it of vintage type, repaired with parts from many other sorts, but also the controls were arranged for a man with four hands. Charlie had been in free fall so long that he used his feet almost as readily for grasping and handling as does an ape; his space suit had had the feet thereof modified so that he could grasp things between the big toe and the second, as with Japanese stockings.

"Hang on. Where we going?"

"Do you know where the Eakers live?"

"Sure. Used to live out past that way myself. Lonely stretch." He pointed. "Right out there, 'bout half a degree right of that leetle second-magnitude star—say eight hundred, eight hundred ten miles."

"Cas, maybe we'd better check the drift reports in the store?"

Charlie seemed annoyed. "I know Rock City. I keep up with the drifts. I have to."

"Then let's go."

"To Eakers'?"

"No, no—uh, just about . . ." He strained his neck, figured the position of the Sun, tried to imagine himself in Hazel's suit, heading back. "About there—would you say, Pol?"

"As near as we can guess it."

The crate was old but Charlie had exceptionally large tanks on it; it could maintain a thrust for plenty of change-of-motion. Its jet felt as sweet as any. But it had no radar of any sort. "Charlie, how do you tell where you are in this thing?"

"That."

"That" proved to be an antiquated radio compass loop. The twins had never seen one, knew how it worked only by theory. They were radar pilots, not used to conning by the seats of their suits. Seeing their faces Charlie added, "Shucks, if you've got any eye for angle, you don't need fancy gear. Anywhere within twenty miles of the City Hall, I don't even turn on my suit jet—I just jump."

They cruised out the line that the twins had picked. Once in free fall Charlie taught them how to handle the compass loop. "Just plug it into your suit in place of your regular receiver. If you pick up a signal, swing the loop until it's least loud. That's the direction of the signal—an arrow right through the middle of the loop."

"But which way? The loop faces both ways."

"You have to know that. Or guess wrong and go back and try again."

Castor took the first watch. He got plenty of signals;

the node was buzzing with talk—all bad news. He found, too, that the loop, while not as directional as a "salad bowl" antenna, usually did not pick up but one signal at a time. As they scooted along, endlessly he swung the loop, staying with each signal just long enough to be sure that the sound could not be Hazel.

Pollux tapped his arm and put his helmet in contact with Castor's. "Anything?"

"Just chatter."

"Keep trying. We'll stay out until we find them. Want me to spell you?"

"No. If we don't find them, I'm not going back."

"Quit being a cheap hero and listen. Or give me that loop."

City Hall dropped astern until it was no longer a shape. Castor at last reluctantly gave over the watch to Pollux. His twin had been at it for perhaps ten minutes when he suddenly made motions waving them to silence even though he could not have heard them in any case. Castor spoke to him helmet to helmet. "What is it?"

"Sounded like a kid crying. Might have been Buster."

"Where?"

"I've lost it. I tried to get a minimum. Now I can't raise it."

Charlie, anticipating what would be needed, had swung ship as soon as he had quit accelerating. Now he blasted back as much as he had accelerated, bringing them dead in space relative to City Hall and the node. He gave it a gentle extra bump to send them cruising slowly back the way they had come. Pollux listened, slowly swinging his loop. Castor strained his eyes, trying to see something, anything, other than the cold stars.

"Got it again!" Pollux pounded his brother.

Old Charlie killed the relative motion; waited. Pollux cautiously tried for a minimum, then swung the loop, and tried again. He pointed, indicating that it had to be one of two directions, a hundred and eighty degrees apart.

"Which way?" Castor asked Charlie.

"Over that way."

"I can't see anything."

"Me neither. I got a hunch."

Castor did not argue. Either direction was equally likely. Charlie gunned it hard in the direction he had picked, roughly toward Vega. He had hardly cut the gun and let it coast in free fall when Pollux was nodding vigorously. They coasted for some minutes, with Pollux reporting the signal stronger and the minimum sharper . . . but still nothing in sight. Castor longed for radar. By now he could hear crying in his own phones. It could be Buster—it *must* be Buster.

"There she is!"

It was Charlie's shout. Castor could not see anything, even though old Charlie pointed it out to him. At last he got it—a point of light, buried in stars. Pollux unplugged from the compass when it was clear that what they saw was a mass, not a star, and in the proper direction. Old Charlie handled his craft as casually as a bicycle, bringing them up to it fast and killing his headway so that they were dead with it. He insisted on making the jump himself.

Lowell was too hysterical to be coherent. Seeing that he was alive and not hurt, they turned at once to Hazel. She was still strapped in her seat, eyes open, a characteristic half-smile on her face. But she neither greeted them nor answered.

Charlie looked at her and shook his head. "Not a chance, boys. She ain't even wearing an oxy bottle."

Nevertheless they hooked a bottle to her suit—Castor's bottle; no one had thought to bring a spare. The twins went back cross-connected on what was left in Pollux's bottle, temporarily Siamese twins. The family scooter they left in orbit, to be picked up and towed in by someone else. Charlie used almost all his fuel on the way back, gunning to as high a speed as he dared while still saving boost to brake them at City Hall.

They shouted the news all the way back. Somewhere along the line someone picked up their signal; passed it along.

They took her into Fries' store, there being more room there. Mrs. Fries pushed the twins aside and applied artificial respiration herself, to be displaced ten minutes later by Dr. Stone. She used the free-fall method without strapping down, placing herself behind Hazel and rhythmically squeezing her ribs with both arms.

It seemed that all of Rock City wanted to come inside. Fries chased them out, and, for the first time in history, barred the door to his store. After a while Dr. Stone swapped off with her husband, then took back the task after only a few minutes' rest.

Meade was weeping silently; old Charlie was wringing his hands and looking out of place and unhappy. Dr. Stone worked with set face, her features hardened to masculine, professional lines. Lowell, his hand in Meade's, was dry-eyed but distressed, not understanding, not yet knowing death. Castor's mouth was twisted, crying heavily as a man cries, the sobs wrung from him; Pollux, emotion already exhausted, was silent.

When Edith Stone relieved him, Roger Stone backed away, turned toward the others. His face was without anger but without hope. Pollux whispered, "Dad? Is she?"

Roger Stone then noticed them, came over and put

an arm around Castor's heaving shoulders. "You must remember, boys, that she is very old. They don't have much comeback at her age."

Hazel's eyes opened. "*Who* doesn't, boy?"

XIX THE ENDLESS TRAIL

HAZEL HAD USED the ancient fakir's trick, brought to the west, so it is said, by an entertainer called Houdini, of breathing as shallowly as possible and going as quickly as may be into a coma. To hear her tell it, there never had been any real danger. Die? Shucks, you couldn't suffocate in a coffin in that length of time. Sure, she had had to depend on Lowell to keep up the cry for help; he used less oxygen. But deliberate suicide to save the boy? Ridiculous! There hadn't been any need to.

It was not until the next day that Roger Stone called the boys in. He told them, "You did a good job on the rescue. We'll forget the technical breach of confinement to the ship."

Castor answered, "It wasn't anything. Hazel did it, really. I mean, it was an idea that we got out of her serial, the skew orbit episode."

"I must not have read that one."

"Well, it was a business about how to sort out one piece of space from another when you don't have too much data to go on. You see, Captain Sterling had to—"

"Never mind. That's not what I wanted to talk with you about. You did a good job, granted, no matter what suggested it to you. If only conventional search methods had been used, your grandmother would unquestionably now be dead. You are two very intelligent men—when you take the trouble. But you didn't take the trouble soon enough. Not about the gyros."

"But Dad, we never dreamed—"

"Enough." He reached for his waist; the twins noticed

that he was wearing an old-fashioned piece of apparel —a leather belt. He took it off. "This belonged to your great grandfather. He left it to your grandfather—who in turn left it to me. I don't know how far back it goes—but you might say that the Stone family was founded on it." He doubled it and tried it on the palm of his hand. "All of us, all the way back, have very tender memories of it. Very tender. Except you two." He again whacked his palm with it.

Castor said, "You mean you're going to beat us with that?"

"Have you any reason to offer why I shouldn't?"

Castor looked at Pollux, sighed and moved forward. "I'll go first, I'm the older."

Roger moved to a drawer, put the belt inside. "I should have used it ten years ago." He closed the drawer. "It's too late, now."

"Aren't you going to do it?"

"I never said I was going to. No."

The twins swapped glances. Castor went on, "Dad—Captain. We'd rather you did."

Pollux added quickly, "Much rather."

"I know you would. That way you'd be through with it. But instead you're going to have to live with it. That's the way adults have to do it."

"But Dad—"

"Go to your quarters, sir."

When it was time for the *Rolling Stone* to leave for Ceres a good proportion of the community crowded into City Hall to bid the doctor and her family good-by; all the rest were hooked in by radio, a full town meeting. Mayor Fries made a speech and presented them with a scroll which made them all honorary citizens of Rock City, now and forever; Roger Stone tried to answer and choked up. Old Charlie, freshly bathed, cried openly. Meade sang one more time into the microphone, her soft contralto unmixed this time with commercialism. Ten minutes later the *Stone* drifted out-orbit and back.

As at Mars, Roger Stone left her circum Ceres, not at a station or satellite—there was none—but in orbit. Hazel, the Captain, and Meade went down by shuttle to Ceres City, Meade to see the sights, Roger to arrange the disposal of their high grade and core material and for a cargo of refined metal to take back to Luna, Hazel to take care of business or pleasure of her own. Doctor Stone chose not to go—on Lowell's account; the shuttle was no more than an over-sized scooter with bumper landing gear.

The twins were still under hatches, not allowed to go.

Meade assured them, on return, that they had not missed anything. "It's just like Luna City, only little and crowded and no fun."

Their father added, "She's telling the truth, boys, so don't take it too hard. You'll be seeing Luna itself next stop anyway."

"Oh, we weren't kicking!" Castor said stiffly.

"Not a bit," insisted Pollux. "We're willing to wait for Luna."

Roger Stone grinned. "You're not fooling anyone. But we will be shaping orbit home in a couple of weeks. In a way I'm sorry. All in all, it's been two good years."

Meade said suddenly, "Did you say 'home,' Daddy? It seems to me we *are* home. We're going back to Luna, but we're taking home with us."

"Eh? Yes, I suppose you're right; the good old *Rolling Stone* is home, looked at that way. She's taken us through a lot." He patted a bulkhead affectionately. "Right, Mother?"

Hazel had been unusually silent. Now she looked at her son and said, "Oh, sure, sure. Of course."

Dr. Stone said, "What did you do downside, Mother Hazel?"

"Me? Oh, not much. Swapped lies with a couple of old-timers. And sent off that slough of episodes. By the way, Roger, better start thinking about story lines."

"Eh? What was that, Mother?"

"That's my last. I'm giving the show back to you."

"Well, all right—but why?"

"Uh, I'm not going to find it so convenient now." She seemed embarrassed. "You see—well, would any of you mind very much if I checked out now?"

"What do you mean?"

"The *Helen of Troy* is shaping for the Trojans and the *Wellington* is matching there for single-H and a passenger. Me. I'm going on out to Titan."

Before they could object she went on, "Now don't look at me that way. I've always wanted to see the Rings, close up—close enough to file my nails on 'em. They must be the gaudiest sight in the System. I got to thinking right seriously about it when the air was getting a little stuffy back—well, back you-know-when. I said to myself: Hazel, you aren't getting any younger; you catch the next chance that comes your way. I missed one once, Roger, when you were three. A good chance, but they wouldn't take a child and well, never mind. So now I'm going."

She paused, then snapped, "Don't look so much like a funeral! You don't need me now. What I mean is, Lowell is bigger now and not such a problem."

"I'll always need you, Mother Hazel," her daughter-in-law said quietly.

"Thanks. But not true. I've taught Meade all the astrogation I know. She could get a job with Four-Planets tomorrow if they weren't so stuffy about hiring female pilots. The twins—well, they've soaked up all the meanness I can pass on to them; they'll put up a good fight, whatever comes up. And you, Son, I finished with you when you were in short pants. You've been bringing me up ever since."

"Mother!"

"Yes, Son?"

"What's your real reason? Why do you want to go?"

"Why? Why does anybody want to go anywhere? Why did the bear go round the mountain? To see what he could see! I've never seen the Rings. That's reason enough to go anywhere. The race has been doing it for all time. The dull ones stay home—and the bright ones stir around and try to see what trouble they can dig up. It's the human pattern. It doesn't need a reason, any more than a flat cat needs a reason to buzz. Why anything?"

"When are you coming back?"

"I may never come back. I *like* free fall. Doesn't take any muscle. Take a look at old Charlie. You know how old he is? I did some checking. He's at least a hundred and sixty. That's encouraging at my age—makes me feel like a young girl. I may see quite a few things yet."

Dr. Stone said, "Of course you will, Mother Hazel."

Roger Stone turned to his wife. "Edith?"

"Yes, dear?"

"What's your opinion?"

"Well . . . there's actually no reason why we should go back to Luna, not just now."

"So I was thinking. But what about Meade?"

"Me?" said Meade.

Hazel put in drily, "They're thinking you are about husband-high, hon."

Dr. Stone looked at her daughter and nodded slightly. Meade looked surprised, then said, "Pooh! I'm in no hurry. Besides—there's a Patrol base on Titan. There ought to be lots of young officers."

Hazel answered, "It's a Patrol *research* base, hon—probably nothing but dedicated scientists."

"Well, perhaps when I get through with them they won't be so dedicated!"

Roger Stone turned to the twins. "Boys?"

Castor answered for the team. "Do we get a vote? Sure!"

Roger Stone grasped a stanchion, pulled himself forward. "Then it's settled. All of you—Hazel, boys, Meade—set up trial orbits. I'll start the mass computations."

"Easy, son—count me out on that."

"Eh?"

"Son, did you check the price they're getting for single-H here? If we are going to do a cometary for Saturn instead of a tangential for Earth, it's back to the salt mines for me. I'll radio New York for an advance, then I'll go wake Lowell and we'll start shoveling gore."

"Well . . . okay. The rest of you—mind your decimals!"

All stations were manned and ready; from an instruction couch rigged back of the pilot and co-pilot Meade was already running down the count-off. Roger Stone glanced across at his mother and whispered, "What are you smiling about?"

"And *five!* And *four!*" chanted Meade.

"Nothing much. After we get to Titan we might—"

The blast cut off her words; the *Stone* trembled and threw herself outward bound, toward Saturn. In her train followed hundreds and thousands and hundreds of thousands of thousands of restless rolling Stones . . . to Saturn . . . to Uranus, to Pluto . . . rolling on out to the stars . . . outward bound to the ends of the Universe.

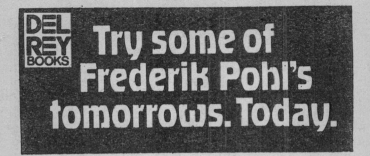